M
Brown

Brown, Rita Mae.

Hiss of death.

DATE			

Hiss of Death

Hiss of Death

A MRS. MURPHY MYSTERY

RITA MAE BROWN
& SNEAKY PIE BROWN

ILLUSTRATIONS BY MICHAEL GELLATLY

BANTAM BOOKS•NEW YORK

Copyright © 2011 by American Artists, Inc.

Illustrations copyright © 2011 by Michael Gellatly

Published in the United States by Bantam Books,
an imprint of The Random House Publishing Group,
a division of Random House, Inc., New York.

BANTAM BOOKS and the rooster colophon are registered
trademarks of Random House, Inc.

Library of Congress Cataloging-in-Publication Data
Brown, Rita Mae.
Hiss of death : a Mrs. Murphy mystery / by Rita Mae Brown & Sneaky Pie Brown;
illustrations by Michael Gellatly.
p. cm.
ISBN 978-0-553-80708-0
eBook ISBN 978-0-553-90808-4
1. Haristeen, Harry (Fictitious character)—Fiction. 2. Murphy, Mrs.(Fictitious character)—Fiction.
3. Women detectives—Virginia—Fiction. 4. Cats—Fiction. 5. Virginia—Fiction. I. Title.
PS3552.R698H57 2011
813'.54—dc22   2010047836

Printed in the United States of America on acid-free paper

www.bantamdell.com

2 4 6 8 9 7 5 3 1

FIRST EDITION

Dedicated with admiration
to
Lima
the Texas cat who saved her human from a pit bull attack

Cast of Characters

Mary Minor Haristeen, "Harry"—Hardworking, frugal, forty, and good-looking, although she doesn't think so. Her curiosity might kill her as well as her cats.

Pharamond Haristeen, D.V.M., "Fair"—He loves his work, his wife, and his farm. At forty-two, he's known Harry all of his life. He accepts her for herself, despite the fact that she all too often courts danger.

Susan Tucker—Harry's best friend since cradle days, she tries to act as the brake on Harry's speed. It rarely works. Her two children are in college and graduate school; her husband was elected to the statehouse a year ago.

Cory Schaeffer, M.D.—A surgeon acquiring a big reputation, he thinks he's smarter than most everybody else. He does care about medicine, and he wants to improve people's lives.

Annalise Vernonese, M.D.—As a pathologist, she sees the ravages diseases and addictions can do to the body. She is passionate about health and fitness.

Paula Benton—A much-respected operating-room nurse, she is very detail-oriented as well as occasionally direct. Then again, she's not from the South, so she sees this as a virtue.

Toni Enright—Another respected operating-room nurse, she works out at Heavy Metal Gym with Annalise. She figures if you're fit, you can fight much of what life throws at you.

Thadia Martin—Once a gifted athlete and a pretty girl, she blew up her life on drugs. After serving a prison sentence and recovering from her problem, she now counsels others who are battling addictions.

Noddy Cespedes—Now in her forties, Noddy had a wonderful career as a bodybuilder. She owns Heavy Metal Gym, is completely committed to pushing iron as a way to avoid many conditions, not the least being osteoporosis. She's a formidable presence.

Big Al and Nita Vitebsk—In their fifties, they own Pinnacle Records as well as a mutt named JoJo. Both are active in the community and stalwarts at the Reformed Temple.

Franny Howard—She is a member of a cancer support group, has a good sense of humor, and owns a tire store. She believes regardless of what you paid for your vehicle, it's only as good as the tires on it. She has a point.

BoomBoom Craycroft—A real bombshell, she is another one of Harry's childhood friends. Their relationship has been on again and off again. Now it's on. She owns her late husband's concrete business but has turned over day-to-day handling to a manager.

Alicia Palmer—One of the most beautiful women of her generation, she is a former movie star in her fifties and finally truly happy. It was a long, hard road to get there.

The Reverend Herbert Jones—As Pastor of St. Luke's Lutheran Church, he guides his flock with humor, insight, and quiet encouragement. He's not much evident in this particular volume, but he's always there when his parishioners or anyone else needs him.

The Really Important Characters

Mrs. Murphy—She's a sleek tiger cat in her prime who has less curiosity and more sense than her human.

Pewter—A sometimes-petulant gray cannonball of a cat who can't believe how limited humans are. She does not suffer in silence.

Tee Tucker—Alert and sagacious, she's like every other corgi—pound for pound, quite a dog. She loves her humans, horses, and even the cats.

Tomahawk—A seventeen-year-old Thoroughbred, he's what horsemen call typy, looking exactly like a TB should. He's usually turned out with Shortro, a young horse whom he guides.

Shortro—A five-year-old Saddlebred being trained for hunt seat. He can jump the moon and is very people-oriented.

Simon—This possum lives in Harry's hayloft and has a sweet tooth.

Flatface—The great horned owl lives in the cupola of the barn.

Matilda—The blacksnake also lives in the barn, and she's grown to nearly four feet. She's made a cozy nest in the hayloft in the back, and has been there for years, emerging after hibernation. As the spring nights are still cold, she returns to her nest at sundown.

Hiss of Death

1

*M*oldy money." Susan Tucker jabbed her best friend, Harry Haristeen, with her elbow.

"Come on, you all, I'm cautious with money. That doesn't mean I'm
cheap," Harry said, defending herself.

"Cautious? How about paralyzed?" BoomBoom Craycroft, another
friend from childhood, said, laughing.

"My concern is I want to make as much money as possible for our
five-K run this Saturday. I just think a thousand pink rubber bracelets is
five hundred too many."

Paula Benton, an ER nurse at Central Virginia Hospital and one of the
prime organizers of the 5K Run for Breast Cancer Awareness, said,
"Harry, they're already here. What's the point of complaining?"

Toni Enright, another operating-room nurse, agreed. "They'll sell
like hotcakes. Think positive, Harry."

"I know. I know. I'm sorry. I just get nervous. Hey, we all have our
quirks. I know a nurse who can't give herself a shot."

Paula reached over to pinch Harry. "No fair."

"'Fess up," Harry teased her. "If you all are going to pick on me, I'll
pick back."

"Paula, are you really afraid to give yourself a shot?" Susan queried.
"I thought you were allergic to bees, wasps, and hornets. Don't you
have to carry a little kit around? Shoot yourself up with the antidote?"

Paula rolled her eyes. "Luckily, I've never had to use it as an adult. Mom shot me up once. I suppose I could do it, but it just creeps me right out." She playfully lunged for Harry. "I could hit you up, though."

As they all laughed, Nita Vitebsk, the treasurer of the group, older than the others, in her mid-fifties, pushed her polka-dot reading specs up on the bridge of her nose, bringing them back to business. "The runners' entry fees have paid for all our expenses. Those are the pre-entry fees, to be exact. You know we're going to pick up more entries, and Harry, since you're the check-in girl, you have the happy task of toting up the sums."

The group of women, this Wednesday evening, April 14, sat cross-legged in a circle on the floor, bracelets in the middle, along with most of the numbers to be worn on runners' backs. They had been working on this project since last year's run.

Every year, the oncology department of Central Virginia Hospital offered staff support, and individual physicians wrote personal checks, too. The nominal head of the 5K run was Dr. Cory Schaeffer, a surgeon specializing in cancer as well as new therapies for healing. As he was developing a large reputation, his name on the fund-raising letterhead was a plus. He didn't do the scut work, nor did most of the other doctors, understandably enough. Dr. Jennifer Potter, the new kid on the block, actually came to some meetings, as did Dr. Annalise Veronese, a pathologist. Annalise said that as she personally witnessed the ravages of cancer in a way others did not, she especially wanted a cure. Many doctors would be at the run, as would the media. The group could thank Alicia Palmer for that. The former movie star wheedled the media into cooperation. Then again, she could pretty much wheedle anyone into cooperation as she remained a dazzler, even in her mid-fifties.

The run would go off the first Saturday after April 15, a date picked because spring would be in its initial blush. Also, it would take people's minds off the financial horrors of April 15. The other factor was that it usually was quite cool in the morning—mid-forties to low fifties, often warming to the mid-sixties—perfect weather for a run.

All the high school cross-country teams participated. The University of Virginia made a showing, too, unless there was an ACC track meet. Charlottesville nurtured a dedicated running club, and the members turned out in full force. Nadine "Noddy" Cespedes urged all her members at Heavy Metal Gym to run. Every year, the race had a big turnout. As it was one of the first celebrations of the spring, the public especially enjoyed it. The streets of the town were closed for three hours, and people lined the sidewalks, many offering drinks or towels. Volunteers dutifully grabbed the empty bottles and towels when runners stretched out their arms. Everyone felt as if they were part of the event. The police liked the run, as did the sheriff's department.

The city of Charlottesville funded its own police department. The county, Albemarle, kept a sheriff's department. The city and county were separate political entities. They cooperated with each other, but in many ways the two law enforcement groups faced different problems. The city police confronted endless fender benders as traffic increased each year. Certain "businessmen" from other countries moved in to sell hard drugs. In a wealthy city of 42,000, this was hardly surprising. The city did have its poor sections, along with the problems universally associated with poverty. The police department never had enough money, no surprise there.

This problem was shared by the county sheriff. Money was ever in short supply, yet people needed more services. However, country folks are less demanding, most times, than city folks. Sheriff Rick Shaw and his officers also faced traffic problems, but often enough they involved as many deer as humans. And all too often the county's twisty narrow roads sent many a drunken speeder to his or her death. Unfortunately, these drunks often took other innocents with them.

Another distinctive problem for the county was meth. More of this drug circulated here than in the city. The labs could be set up in the back of a van if the "cooker" knew what she or he was doing. Didn't matter that drugstores limited the sale of Sudafed and the like, which contained the pseudoephedrine used in making meth. The people making it never seemed to run out of supplies. Then, too, illegal distilleries abounded because of the pure water running off the Blue Ridge Mountains. While Albemarle County boasted of some folks who could turn out what is called "country waters," Nelson County felt their county produced premier products.

When the sheriff's people weren't chasing the "white dog," another name for country waters, they faced the usual quota of domestic abuse, suicide, and thefts. To call country waters moonshine marked one as an outsider. Meant you'd never be able to buy it.

This amused both the police department and the sheriff's department. Sooner or later the sterling reputation for the local product's quality reached a newcomer's ears. They wanted a sip but couldn't find it. After determining that they weren't law enforcement or a plant, a bighearted local usually found a drop for them. A regular customer was born.

Perhaps all these things made the wholesome 5K something both law enforcement agencies liked. Closing the streets was preferable to their normal duties. The other reason they liked it? Many officers ran in the race.

This year, Deputy Cynthia Cooper—"Coop" to her buddies—Harry's next-door neighbor, suggested that each participant from the sheriff's department wear an armband with an outline of his or her badge.

Truth was, all those men and women in law enforcement—like everyone else—knew what cancer could do. The horrible disease seemed to miss no family, or any profession, leaving behind loved ones who had watched the painful struggle. A law enforcement officer fixes things, but you can't fix cancer.

Of the group of women who'd worked to pull this together for the last five months, cancer had savaged their lives as well. Each of them had lost someone—a parent, a sibling, a co-worker, or, worst of all, a child—to the disease. A few had battled the disease themselves and won.

Harry decided not to fuss about the bracelets but to make a huge pink sign advertising them. Every participant received a bracelet, but Paula had wanted extras so people could buy them as a sign of support. Harry—who agonized over every expenditure, thereby driving her friends and her husband to distraction—couldn't quite grasp that a non-runner would purchase a pink rubber bracelet.

Committee work finished, Alicia and BoomBoom brought out the food and drinks. Their strict rule was no gossip, eating, or imbibing until the official work was done. This removed extraneous chat. All was accomplished in a timely manner, a small miracle, given the human propensity for useless chatter.

Alicia's dog, Max, tried to keep awake as they worked but had fallen asleep on the floor next to Alicia. When she rose, Max raised his head, bounced up, and followed the person he loved into the kitchen.

Each committee meeting was held at a different member's house. This spread out the cost of entertaining, but it also drew the group closer. When you see someone's furniture, pictures, the colors they chose for fabrics and the walls, you gain insight into them. Granted, most of these people had known one another from grade school. Others, like Alicia, had lived in the area off and on for thirty years. Nita Vitebsk was a sixteen-year resident. Toni Enright was originally from Harrisonburg, so she fit right in. Paula Benton, there for two years, was such a sunny personality that the ladies in the group had a hard time remembering when she had first come into their lives. Somehow it seemed she was always there.

Alicia's subdued and elegant home reflected her tastes and her income. Any woman who has a Munnings on the wall can't be poor. Sir Alfred Munnings's canvases, the larger ones, routinely sold for two million and some for more. However, you never felt overpowered or smothered by Alicia's money. Her home warmly enveloped you.

Susan Tucker's home contained a mixture of Georgian furniture and some startlingly modern pieces, and Nita Vitebsk's home was Art Deco. This just about sent the old Virginians into a tizzy. They hadn't reached the 1930s in design terms just yet. As for Harry's Virginia farmhouse, it boasted a huge library with many old, valuable books from preceding generations. She'd read most of them. Their monetary worth was a mystery to her. It never occurred to her to hire Jerry Showalter, a well-known antiquarian book dealer, to create an inventory of value. Sandy McAdams, owner of Daedalus Bookshop, encouraged her, too, but his sage advice went in one of Harry's ears and out the other. The furniture—again inherited, some pieces quite good, especially a Sheraton sideboard—did not scream "new money." They whispered "slender means but loving care." The freshly painted walls pointed to some aesthetic consideration, but that was her husband's. Pharamond Haristeen, D.V.M., had reached the point where he couldn't stand it anymore, so he had painted the entire house himself.

When you walked into Harry's barn, you saw perfection. When you

trod into the equipment sheds, you saw old equipment fanatically main-
tained, everything in order, down to the jars of screws, marked with
sizes and head types. When you cast your eyes over the vines, the sunflowers, the corn rows, the acres filled with hay just now popping up in
force, you saw what mattered to this woman. She never stinted on her
horses, who gleamed, or her land.

Harry good-naturedly endured the jibes of her friends. She even submitted to Susan and BoomBoom once dragging her to Nordstrom in
Short Pump, outside of Richmond, where they forced her to try on
clothes. She had resisted the prices, so they each bought her one outfit,
which shamed her into buying the rest. Her husband proved far more
grateful for this fashion intervention than Harry.

When the 5K group met at her house, it was invariably clean and
tidy. She served fried chicken, the ubiquitous ham biscuits, corn bread,
and a wonderful salad with mandarin oranges. She would spend money
on food for her friends and for her animals, as well as the wild animals
she had befriended. Harry just had a hard time spending it on other
things. The credit card debt the average American carried, about fifteen
thousand dollars' worth, sometimes made her wonder if she was as
American as she should be.

As they caught up on gossip, politics, taxes, and the effects the severe
winter had had on Virginia, each woman was, in her own way, happy to
be part of the group. Their work gave them a purpose outside of their
own lives, and that seems to make people content.

As they sat at the graceful table—Alicia could never bear to eat with
her plate on her knees; she always set the table—they discussed the
school budget cuts. They passed on to postal service cuts. Harry was
once the postmistress of Crozet. Then on to other things, and Alicia
pulled from her blouse a little newspaper clipping.

She rapped her crystal glass with her knife. "Ladies."

"Is this a pronouncement from Mount Olympus?" BoomBoom, the
person Alicia loved most in the world, rolled her eyes.

"No. This is a clipping from *The London Sunday Times*. I'm not going to
read all of it, but you've got to hear it. Ready? The *Times* has converted
Australian dollars into pounds, so when I get to that part, bear with me.
I'm not converting it back."

"Can't wait." Harry smiled as the others agreed.

"In Adelaide, Australia, a restaurant, Thai Spice, was ordered to pay compensation to a blind man. Ian Jolly, the blind man, wanted to take his dog into the restaurant. Obvious enough. But the waiter, who we shall assume does not speak English as a first language, turned him away because he thought the dog was gay."

"What!" Nita exploded with laughter.

"Are you making this up?" Paula, too, was disbelieving.

"I couldn't possibly make this up. No one could. I'll pass this around. But let me finish. Okay. Thai Spice must pay nine hundred pounds' compensation. The waiter thought the dog—whose name is Nudge, by the way—was gay. He misunderstood Mr. Jolly, who said this was a 'guide dog.' Thought the blind man said 'gay dog.' It gets worse. At what must have been a very unusual hearing before the judge, the staff at Thai Spice reported that they thought Nudge was a pet dog who had been de-sexed to become gay!"

How they laughed. That absurd story brought up others. They laughed until they cried.

Later, each woman would look back and recall that at that meeting they were all together and so very happy.

2

S lut," Thadia Martin spit.

"Look who's talking," Paula Benton fired right back. "And just what the hell are you doing in my driveway at six at night?"

"I couldn't stand it anymore. I'm sick and tired of your lying."

"Thadia, you're back on drugs."

"How convenient. My past. I haven't taken a drink or a toot in eleven years. I'm as sober as a judge, and you know it." Thadia pulled the soft cashmere scarf tighter around her neck, exposing a graceful scarab bracelet on her left wrist. She jammed her hands back into her pockets as the air turned sharp, cold, this Thursday early evening.

"So what are you talking about?" Paula crossed her arms over her chest.

"Cory Schaeffer."

"What has Dr. Schaeffer got to do with this? I assist him in the operating room."

"You're in love with him."

Paula involuntarily smacked her forehead with her gloved hand. "You're certifiable. Get out of my driveway."

"You've been sleeping with him for the last year, I know it. I see how you look at him. How you make unnecessary trips to his office, and if he isn't there you leave disappointed."

Realizing that insulting Thadia wasn't going to drive her away, Paula settled down as best she could under the volatile circumstances. "One, I am not sleeping with Cory Schaeffer. Two, he's not my type. Three, he's not my type emotionally. He asks for me whenever he operates, so, naturally, I see him in his office as well as in the operating room. If you're this crazed about Cory, it must be you that's in love with him. Not me."

Good-looking Cory had boxed as an undergraduate at Iowa State. He continued as an amateur throughout medical school, still doing bag work, rope jumping, and speed bag work at Heavy Metal Gym. He participated in boxing matches if he felt he was in good condition. Certainly, he looked good to Thadia, or to any woman who admired a well-muscled man.

Thadia's baby face mottled. "There's more to it. You're a liar."

"People have been shot for calling someone that in Virginia. That's what the natives tell me."

"Well, I'm a native, and I'm telling you you're a liar and a slut."

"If it isn't too much of an effort, upon what do you base your erroneous conclusion?"

"He always, always asks for you when he operates. Toni Enright is just as good an operating nurse as you are. This way the two of you can pretend to go over stuff after the operation and before the operation. I'm not fooled. Like I said, he could use Toni Enright at least some of the time."

"Look. You're not a doctor, and you're not a nurse. You're a drug rehab counselor. You don't know as much as you think you know about procedure and protocol. A family practitioner sees or feels a lump. An X ray, mammogram, or MRI is administered. The patient does, in fact, have cancer. The family practitioner sends that person to Cory or another surgeon who might order a second set of diagnostics. Cory's very good at pinpointing anything murky in the first set or looking for more in the tests he's ordered. He sees things others don't. If he operates, I go over those tests with him before the operation. I don't always see what he sees. He doesn't have to do that. He feels we'll be a better team if I have seen the test results."

"Bullshit."

Paula threw up her hands. "Why am I wasting my time talking to a crazy woman? I'm going inside, and you can go back down the driveway."

As Paula turned around, Thadia reached for her shoulder and clamped her bare hand on it. She spun Paula around. Paula threw up her arm, expecting a blow. Thadia reached up to pull her arm down. She hadn't intended to hit Paula, but her scarab bracelet snagged Paula's old coat and a stone flew out. Thadia, enraged, didn't notice. Neither did Paula.

"Don't you turn your back on me."

Paula, one hand in her coat, felt for her cellphone. If she had to, she'd call the sheriff's department—whatever it took to get away from this nutcase.

"Thadia, if you do not take your hand off me, if you do not get in that sorry old heap of yours and haul ass down my driveway, I am calling the sheriff."

As furious as Thadia was, she immediately dropped her hand, pulling herself together. She'd been in prison. She'd endured three years of parole. She now had a good job working with people who had been what she once was. She understood her clients. Most drug counselors who were not former addicts did not. No matter how shaky she felt at this moment, she had enough self-possession to know that if the sheriff's department came and wrote a complaint or, worse, took her away, she'd lose her job. It would be a long, long time before she'd find another. Her family had already disowned her. Rich though they were, she'd never inherit a penny. Her old friends had no time for her anymore, either.

"I'm sorry." Tears came.

"You should be. You're in love with someone who will never love you back."

"Why?"

"Because he loves himself too much."

"I thought you liked him. I thought you loved him." Thadia blinked, confused.

"I wouldn't love Cory Schaeffer if he was the last man on earth, but I'll work with him until one of us dies."

Thadia was more upset than ever, but no longer angry at Paula, she walked toward her car. "He's a brilliant man. He's a good man. He's not afraid to try new methods."

"No, he's not. I wish he'd be a little *less* experimental, but that's me. He has a wife and three children. Thadia, he cheats on his wife a lot. Forget him."

"I can't."

"In fact, forget any man who works in the hospital but most especially a doctor. Hospitals are like petri dishes: Infidelity flourishes." With that, Paula strolled back into her modest but attractive farmhouse.

Thadia got in her car and left. She worried that she was probably a nicer person when she was on drugs. She'd been happier inside until she had reached the point where she couldn't afford her habit. She also knew that if you become addicted, you stop maturing when you start drinking or drugging. Emotionally, she was about twenty-five. Intellectually, she knew that, but that didn't mean she could control her emotions in a mature manner. The irresponsibility that attends immaturity and all addictions was so much easier than growing up. However, it was hell on everyone else.

Most of all, Thadia felt wretched because she was in love with Cory Schaeffer. She wanted the attention and respect he gave Paula.

Thadia wanted a lot of things that she would probably never get.

• • •

Taking off her coat in the front hall, Paula wanted a glass of wine. Already fatigued, and now more tired out from Thadia's outburst, she wanted only to relax. Tomorrow she wasn't working, and she'd happily spend the day fooling around in her potting shed—an area she'd fixed up in the old barn. That gave her something to look forward to.

She smiled at last, grateful she wasn't Thadia Martin.

3

Still tight, colored deep magenta, the redbuds bent slightly west-ward as a stiff breeze charged down the eastern face of the Blue Ridge Mountains. Wild white dogwoods threatened to open, and the forsythias—already huge splashes of yellow—were peaking.

The old 1978 Ford F-150 truck, big engine growling, carried Harry, and her two cats and dog, just west of the nondescript Virginia town of Crozet. Born there, suffering no inclination to live anywhere else, she smiled at the riches of early spring. Any winter was worth enduring for the luxury, the new life, that inevitably followed.

She recited a line from Shelley, hoping she got it right: "Blow, blow thou winter winds, can spring be far behind."

"What's she babbling about?" wondered Pewter, the often-peevish gray cat.

The sleek tiger cat, Mrs. Murphy, paws on the dash, hind feet on the bench seat, replied, *"She's quoting poetry."*

"Bother," the gray cat grumbled as she joined Mrs. Murphy to gaze through the brand-new windshield.

So many windshields in this part of the world cracked, although they didn't shatter. Even though the local gravel trucks now covered their loads with heavy canvas, motorists hereabouts were forced to acknowl-edge that sooner or later a stone would fly off, or a preceding vehicle would kick up stones from one of the many dirt roads.

Harry would rather buy a new windshield than see the tertiary roads paved. Paved roads meant development. Development cannibalized farmland. It also meant an influx of "comeheres"—as locals dubbed new residents.

Suspicious but always friendly, Harry belonged to every preservation and environmental group she could find. Her husband proved less xenophobic. Much as Harry wanted to be open, deep down she hotly resented what she considered the flaunted superiority of the new people. The fact that they all had a lot of money fanned the flames.

At this moment she was driving to the home of a comehere. A flash of guilt filled her, because Paula Benton, an operating-room nurse, was one of the most helpful, lovely people she'd ever met.

Then she told herself, Paula was the exception that proved the rule. Harry had learned just how organized Paula was by working with her on the 5K. Like all of us, Paula had her quirks. Although a very competent nurse, one of her peculiarities was that she couldn't give herself a shot. Once a week, Annalise Veronese gave Paula her B_{12} shot.

How the group teased Paula, who took it all with good humor. She also feared spiders, as do many people. The girls gave her a big fuzzy stuffed toy spider to overcome her phobia. It didn't work, but she kept the toy anyway.

Pulling into the long dirt drive down to Paula's farm, Harry marveled at the work the divorced, quite pretty nurse had done in two years' time. Lined with glossy green Nellie Stevens hollies, the drive funneled down to the restored frame farmhouse.

Even in her crabby moments, Harry was grateful for the number of old farms and larger estates the new-monied people had not only saved but improved. Then there were those who built the McMansions on five acres, but all of America was jam-packed full of those. Couldn't blame the comeheres for that environmentally disastrous fad.

As she approached Paula's farmhouse, Harry noticed that the hollies encircling the drive now reached five feet. The effect was pretty. In a few years' time it would be dramatic, for Nellie Stevenses could top out at thirty feet.

Due to the odd hours she kept, Paula had no pets. This disappointed

Tucker, the corgi, who evidenced a social streak. Nothing better than catching up with another canine. Living with two cats could pluck one's last nerve.

Paula's brand-new Dodge half-ton, sparkling silver, was parked off to the side of the house.

Harry cut the engine and let her animals out in the crisp spring air, then walked onto the porch and knocked on the door. No answer.

"She knows I'm coming," Harry said aloud to her animals. "She's got the extra runner numbers for me. They came in late. Sure glad they made it, or I'd be sitting up cutting out paper."

"Paula!" Harry called.

Harry would happily ride a horse anywhere, but she avoided running since she did quite enough walking, trotting, and lifting on the farm. By the end of the day her thighs often ached—hence her willingness to do the "bench work" at the 5K.

The door was unlocked; Harry peeked in. "Paula?"

She walked around the house to the old barn in the back, to Paula's potting-shed refuge, a pleasant place to force bulbs.

Pewter, feeling she already had enough exercise this morning, turned to go back to the truck.

Tucker paused to watch, then waited for Mrs. Murphy to join her. "No wonder she's fat."

"I heard that," the gray cat called over her shoulder.

"You heard me, yet you're doing nothing about it," Tucker persisted.

"Bubble butt." Pewter raised her head, her tail upright, as she marched toward the truck.

Mrs. Murphy and Tucker fell in behind Harry. As the temperature hung in the low fifties and probably would stay there all day, the barn doors were closed, but a light shone in the area Paula had closed off.

"Knew it. She lost track of time." Harry smiled as she pushed open the barn doors.

She opened the door to the potting room, lit by both skylights in the roof and some infrared lights casting their odd color. The smile froze on her face.

"Paula!" Harry rushed to the woman slumped at her potting table, head on the table. Next to Paula, a dead hornet lay on the table, too.

Harry touched her. Cool. She took her pulse. None.

"*She smells funny. I've smelled that odor before, but I can't place it,*" the corgi commented, her powers of smell surpassing anything a human could imagine.

"*Yes, I know what you mean,*" said Mrs. Murphy, no slouch in the nose department, either.

Not one to panic, Harry gently placed Paula's hand back on the table, then left the room, animals with her.

Now she ran. Sprinting for the truck, she nearly stepped on Pewter's tail, for the cat was under the truck, playing with something she'd found.

Opening the glove compartment, Harry pulled out her cell. She kept it in there so she wouldn't be tempted to call while driving. This strategy forced her to pull over to make calls. Taking your eyes off country roads could wipe you out in a skinny minute.

She dialed 911, gave information and directions, and waited. Then her mind started spinning. Paula Benton, in her late thirties, was a runner. She didn't smoke and drank alcohol in moderation. She regularly endured mammograms and her annual checkup, passing with flying colors. Her death appeared peaceful.

She picked up Tucker, since Mrs. Murphy had jumped up onto the truck. Then she got down on her knees. "Pewter, come on."

"*No.*" The gray batted something to and fro.

"Dammit, I'm in no mood to fool with you!" Harry grabbed her tail and pulled out the protesting cat, who had the sense to put whatever she was playing with in her mouth.

Once Pewter was in the truck, Harry closed the door. She climbed in on the driver's side.

Mrs. Murphy and Tucker wanted to know what Pewter had. Finally, the gray dropped it; a tiger stone, brown with a golden stripe, fell from her mouth. The size of an oblong nickel, it had been carved into a scarab beetle.

"*I thought it was a mole.*" Mrs. Murphy was disappointed.

"*It glitters in the sun. It's a good size to play with.*" Pewter didn't protest as Harry picked it up.

She wiped it on her jeans, then held the stone scarab in the palm of her hand. "Is this an Egyptian symbol for death?"

Then she thought, How morbid. She so liked Paula. Harry wasn't the weepy type, but her heart raced and she felt a sinking sensation in her stomach.

The sirens of Crozet's rescue squad howled in the near distance. Hearing their shrill call, she slipped the scarab into her pocket.

Within two minutes, she saw the flashing lights at the turn of the farm driveway. She would have to see Paula's body again, for Harry would need to lead them to it. Her one comfort was that Paula had died doing something she loved. Then she wondered what comfort that was. A good woman had died much too young.

4

*T*he large carton with one thousand pink rubber bracelets covered a fourth of Harry's kitchen table. Mrs. Murphy and Pewter had inspected the carton when it was first placed on the old wooden farm table. Now their faces were in the crunchie bowl on the counter, out of reach of Tucker.

Cynthia Cooper, an officer in the Albemarle County sheriff's department and Harry's closest neighbor, sat at the table. Harry gave her a Coca-Cola, grabbing one herself as she sat down.

"How long before Fair gets home?" Coop asked.

"No telling. Now's when all the crossbreds, quarter horses, and Warmbloods are foaling. The Thoroughbreds are done, of course. He says he'll get here as soon as he can. I'm okay. I mean, it was a shock to find her. I liked Paula so much."

"Glad they let you take the carton and the additional numbers. Otherwise you'd have a scramble. I'd help."

"I know you would." Harry rattled the ice cubes in her glass. "Guess I'll find out if Paula was right."

"About what?" Coop wondered.

"Huh, oh, I forgot you aren't on that committee."

"I'm on the wetlands committee with you, not the five-K. You're on more committees than I can remember. I don't know how you do it."

Coop paused, then kindly suggested, "Maybe the shock was greater than you realize."

"Because I'm not normally forgetful?"

Coop nodded. "Sort of."

"She was in the prime of life."

Coop nodded. "Right. What was Paula right about?"

"Oh, that. Well, I do know, but we had a fulsome discussion about how many bracelets to order. I wanted to save money and only get five hundred. Paula said we needed more because we could sell them. Paula said widen the circle. I'm afraid I was stubborn. The whole committee leaned on me, so Paula ordered the extra five hundred."

"She was right, I think."

"Well, she said charge five dollars for anyone not running. The runners also get their nice chain with the ID tag, plus their number. Not that they'll wear their number after the race."

"BoomBoom will."

They both laughed, for BoomBoom Craycroft never showed much interest in running. She did Pilates and that sort of exercise.

"She just might. Poor Boom. She'll have to wear one of those horrible compression bras or she'll black her eyes," Harry mused.

"She is a well-built woman."

"You know a man isn't overly bright about women if he's talking to you and his eyes never move above your breasts." Harry shook her head.

"I lift his chin until his eyes meet mine," Coop said, smiling.

Harry thought a moment. "You remember Fair and I were given those three wonderful Thoroughbred mares?"

"Do."

"Anyway, I did my homework, and we bred them. I love bloodline research, as you know. Three gorgeous foals. You see the two yearlings out there now. They're at that goofy stage. But the big bay colt, six months old, was following me when I walked out to check my vines. He whinnied. I turned just as he collapsed. That fast." She snapped her fingers. "Fair opened him up. His aorta burst. Fair said it rarely happens, but the wall of the aorta was very thin in a spot. Boom. He was such a good guy. I miss him. Actually, I miss a lot of people and animals who have gone on."

"Me, too." Coop sighed.

"I keep going back to the sight of Paula slumped over her table. I feel like I'm missing something. There was the hornet. She didn't have her kit. Odd, she was afraid to give herself a shot." She paused. "I just have a funny feeling, a little tinge of fear myself."

"People are afraid enough as it is." Cooper finished her Coca-Cola.

"The media sells fear daily. Terrorists. Your cholesterol. Pollution. Every syndrome they can think of, make up, or find initials for. Buy this potion or that bottle of prescription pills. It's all commercially motivated."

"I think so, too." Coop studied the carton. "Want me to help you bag these with the numbers and ID tags?"

"Coop, that would be great. I always feel better if I'm busy. But this is your day off. I don't want to keep you from anything."

"Mulching the garden. That can wait."

As the two gathered the tote bags with *5K Breast Cancer Awareness* printed on them, the bracelets, and the ID tags, they worked in harmony, as those close to each other do.

"Whose idea was it to tie the ID tags on the outside of the bags so you don't waste time writing at the check-in table?" Coop inquired. "I mean, for those who have preregistered."

"Mine. If someone shows up who has preregistered, we can quickly write their name on the ID tag. Doesn't look as nice as the printed ones, but that's okay. Anything to simplify the process."

"Good idea. Is Susan running?" She mentioned Harry's friend since cradle days.

"Whole family."

"That's great. Poor Susan and Ned, though. One kid in undergraduate school, one in graduate. My God, it must cost a fortune."

"Brooks helps by going in-state. Danny," Harry said, now mentioning Susan's son, the older child and only son, "is at the Wharton School of Business at the University of Pennsylvania, and he worked to pay his tuition. They help with his rent. Danny is incredibly motivated."

"He has to be. The University of Pennsylvania isn't cheap."

"No, it isn't. It's a great school. Susan teases him that when he's rich he can keep her in the style to which she is unaccustomed."

Coop laughed. "He'll go out in the world and be one of the fifty-three percent of Americans who pay for the forty-seven percent who pay no taxes—like you and I, who work our asses off."

"That fact isn't lost on me." Harry clipped a shiny ID tag to the out-side of a tote bag. "Paula used to talk about what healthcare is going to cost. She used to bemoan it and wonder why doctors and nurses had let control of medicine slip out of their hands."

"Who knows?" Coop shrugged. "It's not healthcare reform, it's in-surance reassignment."

"Whatever it is, all this spending scares me."

Coop stifled a guffaw. "Harry, you don't like spending money. It pains you."

"My parents taught me to save for a rainy day." She thought for a sec-ond. "But I'm not ungenerous."

"No, you're not. You feed your friends, you make us wonderful pots of flowers, and you'll help anyone with their outdoor chores, plus you do all your own. I remember how shocked I was last winter when you bought Fair that beautiful cashmere sweater. Made me glad every now and then you could have a weak moment like the rest of us."

"He looks so good in it."

"He looks good in everything."

"Does. Poor guy, foaling season wears him out. He's no different than an OB/GYN. Babies always arrive at the most inconvenient times, and you have to be there. He's more upset about not being here right this minute than I am. It was upsetting to find Paula. She hadn't been dead for long. Cool but not waxy-looking. No rigor mortis. She looked as though she fell asleep. She died too young, but I hope she didn't suf-fer. I remember Paula talking about her patients at our meetings. There's so much cancer. So much suffering. I don't just mean breast cancer. I mean cancer. It seems every time I turn around, someone is diagnosed with some form of it."

"Yeah, I know. I don't understand it."

"Oh, hey." Harry reached into her jeans pocket to pull out the tiger's-eye scarab, which she put on the table. "Found this in Paula's driveway. Pewter was playing with it."

"*I found it.*"

"*Pewter, she gave you credit,*" Mrs. Murphy said.

"*Yeah, well, you can never be too careful. They take credit for our work. You'd think they invented life. Ever listen to the way they teach history? It's all about them,*" Pewter complained.

"*They are self-centered,*" Mrs. Murphy agreed, "*but Mom isn't.*"

"*She's okay,*" Pewter grudgingly agreed. "*That doesn't mean I shouldn't be vigilant.*"

No point in arguing with Pewter when she slipped into one of her moods. Plus, Mrs. Murphy knew Pewter was right. Harry really was good, but even with Harry, half the time you had to think for her. Humans missed so much. However, Harry always put out breakfast right on time. That alone was worth overlooking flawed senses and cockeyed interpretations of events.

"Remember in high school when scarab bracelets were the thing?" Cooper admired the neatly carved stone bug.

"I've never understood why the ancient Egyptians made so many representations of them. After all, they are dung beetles."

"Who knows? That will give me something to look up on the Internet."

"Aren't they part of the death cult? Can't remember."

"I'll look that up, too."

Harry put a pink bracelet in a bag. "Odd, isn't it, I mean, if I'm right about the death stuff, that I found this in Paula's drive?"

"*I found it!*" Pewter hollered, a crunchie falling out of her mouth.

5

*B*y eleven Saturday morning, at the race registration table Harry had run out of pink bracelets. Five hundred and forty-two graced competitors' wrists. The rest were sold. She sat there wishing Paula could have known she was right. Next year, Harry would know to order more, to overcome her natural reticence to be optimistic, especially when a check was to be written.

Many people stopped by and expressed sorrow. If nothing else, Harry consoled herself with the fact that Paula Benton had lived a good life, touched many people, helped many. Harry had not chosen a helping profession. Her husband, Paula, and Coop had. Every single day they gave and gave and gave. They endured long training for this, particularly Fair. A physician or nurse need learn only one muscular and skeletal system; a veterinarian had to learn many. Then there was the matter of blood chemistry. It made her head spin.

Cory Schaeffer, as titular head of the 5K race, was the first one to begin running when the gun sounded. A split second later, he was engulfed by others.

As the participants ran through the streets of Charlottesville, numbers clearly visible on their backs, Harry and Alicia toted up the sums. The registration fees netted $10,840. The sale of bracelets to noncompetitors brought another $2,290. Spontaneous donations added up to $3,556. The BMW dealership had donated a new 3 Series, and raffle tickets to win it sold for $100. The drawing would be at a dinner weeks later to give the organizers time to sell all the tickets. So far that had already garnered more than $75,000. The raffle tickets numbered up to one thousand. They had two hundred and fifty left to sell.

Dr. Isadore Wineberg, whom everyone called Izzy, one of Paula's favorite doctors in the operating room, had approached the dealership. His pitch to the manager was, given the number of BMWs you sell to those of us in the medical profession, how about donating one for this good cause? The manager agreed.

Alicia checked the time. "Someone ought to be crossing the finish line soon." She nudged Harry. "Wake up."

"Sorry."

"Want to bet five dollars that the first one to cross the finish line will be a member of the running club?"

"No. You'd win. I say we bet on the age of that person."

"Now, there's a thought." Alicia touched her lips for a moment with her forefinger.

Both Harry and Alicia looked healthy and fit. Alicia looked ten years younger than her age.

"I say the fastest person will be thirty-two." Harry pulled out five dollars.

"Five dollars?" Alicia matched the bill.

"Right."

"Twenty-five," Alicia said.

"What happens if we're both wrong?"

"We put that sum into the kitty." Alicia leaned back in her rickety chair.

"Fair enough."

Within three minutes, they discovered they'd both lost the bet as a roar went up at the finish line. The winner, Mac Dennison, was forty-eight and a workout buddy of Annalise's. Right on his heels was a cross-country runner from the high school, Tara Poletsky, all of sixteen.

As people crossed the finish line, they were handed bottles of water and could stand under the hose if they wished. Coop did very well, coming in twenty-first.

Noddy Cespedes finished in front of Coop. One of Noddy's gym rats, sixty-three years old, Jim O'Hanran, finished behind Coop.

Each participant received a rousing cheer. Each cheer reminded both Harry and Alicia why they lived in Crozet. They never found a place they loved as much as central Virginia. Each woman hoped other people loved where they lived, too.

Happiness is pretty simple: someone to love, something to do, something to look forward to. That's what Alicia's grandmother used to say, and to that the two friends added, "Animals to love and a place to love."

When Susan crossed the line, her family had preceded her. Both Alicia and Harry waited there to cheer her on. They'd put the little strongbox of cash in Alicia's hard-used Range Rover, locking it up.

Once Susan caught her breath, she put her hands on her hips, bent over, took another big gulp, and stood up. "Harry, Alicia, let's all make a date for our mammograms."

"Oh, God, Susan!" Harry laughed.

"She's right," Alicia commented. "It's an easy thing to put off."

"It isn't the most pleasant thing." Harry grimaced.

"Better than a colonoscopy." Susan laughed. "I ran for a while next to Dr. Izzy. He said that every hospital employee that could ran today, but that everyone will buy a BMW ticket in honor of Paula. That means we've just finished off selling all the tickets to the BMW."

"Wonderful." Alicia beamed.

Harry walked back to the table in case anyone needed anything. Garvey Watson, the owner of a men's clothing store, had taken her place so she could watch her friends finish. Susan looked for her family, and Alicia waited for BoomBoom, who soon heaved into sight.

She gladly took the water bottle from Alicia when she finished. BoomBoom took a swig, received a congratulatory kiss, and whispered, "Damned hard on the knees!"

• • •

Meanwhile, at the Central Virginia Hospital, Dr. Jerome Neff stood by the head of pathology as she performed an autopsy on Paula Benton. Dr.

Neff, like all of the surgeons, had greatly respected and liked Paula. He often requested her for his surgeries, as well as Toni Enright. He thought those two nurses were the best he'd worked with in the operating room during his long career. After gaining permission from her mother, Dr. Neff arranged the autopsy. Given Paula's excellent health and her continual positive outlook, Dr. Neff remained very curious to know what had snatched her away.

Dr. Annalise Veronese, young, pretty, highly competent and motivated, finished the procedure. Sewed back up, Paula's remains were respectfully placed in a body bag, then in the cooler, to be called for by the local mortuary. Her mother had requested that Paula be cremated.

After washing up, Annalise walked out with Dr. Neff. "Anaphylactic shock."

He sighed. "The tissues were pale. The fluids don't stay in vessels. No pressure in the pipe. Classic shock."

She put her hand on his forearm. "If only she'd had a kit out there. People who are allergic to anything that causes this type of shock should have kits in cars, in the bedroom, in the kitchen, wherever they spend a lot of time."

His jaw tightened, then relaxed. "Annalise, ever notice how medical people, and I include myself, never take our own advice?"

"Yes, I do. It's one of the puzzling things about our profession. I'd give Paula her B-twelve shots. She'd have to turn her head away. She wouldn't do it herself. But I believe if she'd had a kit within reach she would have jammed that needle in her arm." Annalise sighed. "I'm going to miss her."

"Me, too," Jerome sadly agreed.

Once alone, Annalise called Cory Schaeffer, who had finished his run.

"Anything?" Cory got right to the point.

"Yes, anaphylactic shock. The hornet's sting killed her."

After a brief silence, Cory said, "It's not a good way to die, but it doesn't take long. Poor Paula." Then he said, "All of us who worked in surgery with Paula will pay you for your time. I know this is a day off, and—"

Annalise cut him off. "Cory, no. It was important to do this. She meant a lot to a lot of people. Don't even mention money." She changed the subject. "How'd the five-K go?"

"Successful. Big turnout. Some of your buddies from Heavy Metal Gym ran. Mac Dennison hit the tape first. A good day." He then returned to Paula. "Isn't it amazing, if you stop to think about it, that a small insect could kill so quickly?"

A note of irritation crept into Annalise's voice. "I suppose, but think how small a virus is. And the wrong kind of virus, one that can spread and replicate rapidly, can destroy millions of lives."

"Of course," he said and sighed.

Annalise added with feeling, "Her organs were like those of a twenty-five-year-old woman." She took a breath. "Most people find autopsies gruesome, but if I could show films to high school kids of, say, Paula's arteries, liver, lungs, heart, et cetera, with another woman, say, ten years younger, who drank, smoked, drugged, it just might drive the point home for those teenagers to practice good health habits."

"Once they finished puking," Cory sarcastically replied.

She responded, "I know, but I find it fascinating. Beautiful, even. The human body is put together like a great machine. Some are Chevys, some are trucks, some are Ferraris. Paula was a Ferrari."

"Thanks, sugar. As always, you done good." He used the colloquial expression. "Paula was a good hand in the operating room."

"No more," Annalise flatly said.

"Gotta go. Brody has a soccer game." He named his oldest child, eleven.

"I'll see you Monday," she replied.

"Right. Be good to see you, as always." He pushed the off button on his cellphone.

·   ·   ·

Dr. Jerome Neff, a thoughtful man, called Harry that night. They knew each other, a nodding acquaintance, but as she had found Paula, he wanted to let her know.

"Thank you, Dr. Neff." Harry hung up the phone and told Fair.

·   ·   ·

Later that evening, the long twilight casting a silver-blue light bright enough to see everything, Harry and Fair, hand in hand, walked along the rows of corn, little tips just breaking through the soil. The sunflowers had also just broken ground; the broccoli in the garden was already four inches out of the ground. The petite manseng vines flashed early green leaves.

The two cats and the dog trailed them.

"Gotcha." Mrs. Murphy leapt straight up to catch a moth, but it eluded her with a flutter.

"They aren't fast. They just go higher," Pewter noted.

Harry and Fair stopped to lean against the back pasture fence.

"Never get tired of looking at the mountains." Harry smiled.

"Me neither, but I'm creaky tonight."

"After delivering four foals, I expect your back aches. Take a hot shower when we get back, and I'll massage your back and shoulders."

"I need it. Hey, how about Coop coming in twenty-first?"

"I know. It really was a perfect day for a race. They were hot when they finished, but the temperature hung in the mid-sixties all day."

"It was a perfect day." He put his arm around her waist. "So, next week, are you and the girls going to your mammogram party?"

She wrinkled her nose. "I guess."

He squeezed her slightly. "I know you don't like the boob squisher."

"Well, honey, imagine if you flopped your part on a tray and a big flattish camera pressed down on it for a second or two."

"I'd rather not."

6

*H*arry, Susan, BoomBoom, Alicia, and Coop laughed as they ran across the parking lot at the hospital auxiliary on Pantops Mountain through a sudden hard spring rain, drenching them.

"Thank God for remote keys." Susan pushed the unlock icon on her overlarge fob.

Harry, already at the passenger side of Susan's Audi station wagon, jumped in the second she heard the lock release. Dripping, Harry leaned over the passenger seat to grab the towel Susan kept in the back to wipe up after her own corgi, Owen.

BoomBoom scrambled to get into Alicia's Mustang, and Coop got in her own car.

Susan slid behind the wheel. "Where did that rain come from? Wasn't on the weather report."

Harry shrugged as she wiped herself down. "Being a weatherman is the only job where you can be wrong half of the time and still pull a paycheck."

"Got that right." Susan glanced in the rearview mirror. "There goes the hair."

After handing Susan the towel, Harry ran her fingers through her hair. "Just fixed mine."

"You know, I'd whack this all off, but Ned loves my long hair. He even likes to brush it. I think when he was little he became mesmerized by his mother sitting at her makeup table." She started her fancy station wagon, a gift from Ned, who wanted his wife to ride in style.

Susan couldn't imagine living without her Audi, which she'd driven for two years.

"Funny, I haven't thought of a dressing table in years," said Harry. "My mom had one, too. You saw it. Had fabric around the two sides, hung to the ground. As I recall, it was a big rose print. She'd sit right up in the open middle, face to the mirror, lights blazing."

"Your mother, like you, was so organized," said Susan. "All her lipsticks stuck out from this little wooden box she'd made. Full of holes. Every lipstick had a place, and they'd never fall over or roll on the ground. Given her cats, I suppose that was an invention born of necessity."

"I disappointed Mom. She wanted a girly girl and got me."

"Oh, Harry, she loved you, and every Saturday the farm was full of cars, overflowing with boys. You were the most popular girl at school."

"Because I could throw a football farther than they could." Harry laughed. "BoomBoom was the most popular."

"Maybe." Susan turned toward Route 64, following Alicia and BoomBoom, as well as Coop. "Isn't it great that Alicia bought a Mustang convertible? She could have bought a Ferrari or a Porsche—"

Harry interrupted Susan, something she rarely did even to her dearest friend, since she considered it impossibly rude. "Can't believe you just named a Ferrari. I'm the gearhead, not you."

"But I listen." Susan flattered her, but it was true. "I just love that she bought an American car. Of course, she has her Range Rover for serious farm chores, but for her thrill car, she bought American. Said it makes her feel like she did in the sixties. Young."

"Hmm. I never think about Alicia being in her fifties, because she's so glamorous. Well, so is BoomBoom, but her face wasn't plastered all over America like Alicia's." Harry considered that. "It's a curse, fame. The people who seek it deserve it."

Susan laughed. "My, aren't we profound."

Harry replied, "I'd punch you, but you're driving. Anyway, Alicia never sought it. She more or less stumbled into film, and the camera did the rest. Camera loves her."

"Yes, it does. And she had the sense to get out with bundles of money when she reached middle age. Course, inheriting Mary Pat Reines's estate hardly hurt."

"Ever notice how some people are just lucky? Lucky in love. Lucky in their careers. Some are lucky with money. I don't know if you can have it all, but, boy, some people come close." Harry studied the car in front of them. "Love that she bought the five-point-zero-L engine and tricked the Mustang out in red candy metallic."

"Pretty cool. You never owned a convertible. Given how much you love cars—both you and BoomBoom—I'm surprised." Susan got in the right lane so a Honda could pass her. "How come you never bought a convertible?"

"Couldn't afford luxuries. All I could swing was the F-One-fifty, which I bought used. That 1978 isn't the smoothest ride, but I think it looks terrific, especially since my wonderful husband had it painted and the upholstery tweaked for our anniversary."

"You still haven't answered my question."

Harry blinked. "Sorry. I'm a little concerned that you all had to wait for me while they called me back for second pictures."

"That happened to me once. Sometimes the first set of mammograms isn't clear. In my case, a bit of scar tissue showed up."

"How'd you get that scar tissue in your breast?"

"I'll answer that when you answer my question."

"I can afford a convertible now, but I really am a purist. I love the line of a roof if a car is well designed, and the Mustang really is. So's the Charger. Like the Camaro, that's the Mustang's competitor, in case you don't know."

"Didn't."

"Anyway, they're all retro but forward, great designs and truly American. But to be safe, a convertible has to weigh more, sometimes as much as four hundred pounds more, and I abhor that. Hence, no convertible."

"So it's not a safety thing?"

"No. Most cars have roll bars that pop up. If they don't, they're usually built in so that if you flip, for instance, you won't land flat up, which means you'll be dead. There might be a kind of lip, which keeps you intact. I'm not being precise. Okay, I answered your question. Answer mine."

"When we played lacrosse in high school, that complete shithead from Saint Anne's whacked me right across the boob when no one was looking."

"Thadia Martin. She was a bitch. There's a great lesson in karma."

"That she is. And it wasn't a league game, either. We weren't on Saint Anne's schedule, since we're a public school and they're private. They've always been the big dog in lacrosse, and we were good. They thought they'd teach us a lesson." Susan smiled broadly. "Wiped the field up with them."

"Yeah, we really did. She's out of prison now, and I heard she's a rehab counselor. I think Paula mentioned her once with distaste."

"Actually, she runs the entire drug counseling program, and Harry, I think they were smart to hire her. Who else knows how drugs can blow up your life but someone who's served time for selling, for armed robbery?" Susan shook her head. "Crazy."

"This country is crazy." Harry looked ahead. "Turnoff. Route Three-forty."

"I know."

"I know you know. I just wanted to sound smart."

The friends ate at South River Grille in Waynesboro. Coop, on her day off, enjoyed them all enormously and was very entertaining with her stories of the dumb stuff a sheriff's officer sees, like picking up a fellow walking into the Mud House, a coffee shop, in red lace panties, brassiere to match.

• • •

That afternoon, when Susan dropped off Harry, the rain continued, though lessening in intensity.

Opening the kitchen door, Harry beheld kitty wrath.

"Wasn't me." Tucker glanced up, her big brown eyes radiating honesty.

"Brownnoser," Pewter spat.

"Who did this?" Harry surveyed the broken vase knocked off the kitchen table, her lovely pink and white tulips still fresh.

Harry picked them up, snipped off the ends, put them in another vase, and filled it, adding a little sugar to the water. Slipping her fingers into heavy work gloves, she picked up the big pieces of glass. She'd learned the hard way never to pick up glass with bare hands. The fragments were dropped in a small cardboard carton, and she swept up anything she might have missed. Next came the mop. Finally done, she sat down to stare at Pewter, who pointedly sat next to the refreshed tulips with her back turned. Mrs. Murphy, head leaning on the table, sat opposite on a chair.

"*Pewter, you could at least turn around and look at her.*"

"*She smells funny,*" Pewter said, justifying her pointed inattention.

"*Maybe it's her new perfume. I've noticed it, too.*"

Tucker, the olfactory expert, pronounced judgment. "*Not the perfume. It's a little different odor, not bad, just something different.*"

"Pewter, I'm not fooled. You did the damage."

"*Mrs. Murphy chased me. I couldn't help it.*"

"*What a fib.*" Mrs. Murphy climbed up on the table now and boxed Pewter's ears.

Harry grabbed the vase. "This is how it happened in the first place. You two."

"*It's a rainy day.*" Pewter knocked Mrs. Murphy upside the head, but she didn't unleash her claws.

"*You jumped on the table, and I followed. How was I to know you'd slipped sideways to take out the vase? You're like a Porsche, Pewter, sixty percent of your weight is in your rear.*"

"*How do you know that?*"

"*I listen to everything Mom says about cars.*"

"*I'm not fat. I'm not built like a car. I have big bones.*"

"*Oh la.*" Tucker rolled her eyes.

"*I can jump down there and bloody your nose, Bubble butt.*" Pewter leaned over the table, looking convincingly menacing.

"Calm down," said Harry. "I'd like to sit here in peace."

"*You should have taken us with you,*" Pewter sagely advised.

"*That's the truth.*" Mrs. Murphy agreed with Pewter, which meant now they were best friends.

The phone rang. Harry checked the old railroad clock. Three-thirty.

Could be the feed store. She'd ordered sweet feed. Usually they deliver. If they called, it meant they had run out.

"Hello. Crozet zoo," Harry answered.

"The question is, is it a petting zoo?" Dr. Regina MacCormack, Harry's general practitioner, laughed on the other end of the line.

"Now, there's a thought."

"Harry, come into the office tomorrow. I want to go over your mammogram with you."

Harry hesitated. "That means it isn't good."

"No point in keeping you worried. There is a peculiar small mass in the back of your right breast. Let's look at it together, and I'll tell you what I think and what comes next. Can you make it at ten?"

"I can. Thanks for not being evasive."

"I know you too well. And no one wants a call like this. Is it cancerous? I don't know. Come in tomorrow. Let's talk. There is a test that I'll recommend. You'll have to think about it."

"See you at ten." Harry hung up the phone and looked at her three friends. "Dammit to hell."

7

*D*r. MacCormack's office, along with many other physicians', was located along the outer road belt of the new enormous Central Virginia Hospital.

The old hospital, the main brick building constructed in 1930, could no longer meet the demands of a wealthy county. Like the other doctors who had worked at the old hospital, Dr. MacCormack rejoiced in the new one.

Two years ago, Central Virginia Medical Complex, west of Charlottesville, opened to great fanfare. The cost of the hospital, outbuildings, and equipment staggered the imagination and probably exceeded the gross national product of Namibia.

Flanked by Regina and Jerome Neff, as well as the hospital administrator and the county commissioners, Dr. Isadore Wineberg, sixty-one, had cut the ribbon.

The old-timers wondered what those who practiced at the old hospital and who had since passed away would make of the building, with its gleaming wings radiating off the main hub. In particular, Izzy and Regina thought of Larry Johnson, a general practitioner who often took vegetables and even chickens in payment for his services. It was a sure bet the doctors at Central Virginia Hospital would take no chickens. They were a different breed from Larry Johnson, a different breed from Izzy and Regina, too.

The new generation, in thrall to technology, forgot to study the patient as an entire organism. The focus was on scans, blood tests, numbers, numbers, numbers. The flaw in this overreliance on technology was an underreliance on common sense. This misstep was most apparent in the dispensing of drugs, the ordering of batteries of unnecessary tests. The unnecessary tests covered the physician's ass from lawsuits, mostly. Meanwhile, the bills spiraled ever upward, and if the patient wasn't horribly sick before treatment, the depletion of funds contributed to malaise afterward.

Rehabilitation also underlined the difference between older and younger doctors. How did the patient live? Was he or she a horseman? Not an idle question in central Virginia, for horsemen are stoics. They might hurt like hell, but they won't tell you. And if you don't pay attention to them, they will launch into rehabilitation in ways the young doctor never imagined. Horsemen with kidney transplants would climb up on a horse's back three weeks after surgery. A person leading a sedentary life in front of a computer would be walking and little more at three weeks.

This blindness to the total person drove Izzy, Regina, and the younger Jerome nuts. The older doctors took those with brilliance and common sense, like Jennifer Potter, a young surgeon, under their wings. Cory Schaeffer they left alone. To his credit, he was usually surrounded by athletes in his off-hours, kept himself in shape, and seemed to recognize another athlete when he saw one, even if it was on the operating table. But his arrogance ensured that the old guard would never invite him to learn the nuances—not just of medicine but of Virginia. They'd sit back and watch him make those mistakes that can be costly—if not in medical terms, then in social.

After the ribbon-cutting ceremony, Izzy and Regina repaired for a drink.

"I'm glad I'll be retiring soon," Izzy said as he reached for his second Scotch and soda.

"If only we could just practice medicine," Regina wistfully said.

"Those days are gone, Regina, gone forever."

"Well, I'll do the best I can."

And she did.

Central Virginia Hospital sat in the middle of a large, round beltway. Spokes were the various departments, the core of the new building being a large six-story square. The architects felt they had created a state-of-the-art medical center, but like so many new things, it was confusing as hell. Did one go to the core building to check in, or did one go to the wing that housed one's specialist?

One thing they did right was the emergency room, which was easy to find. It was the first spoke off the main building once one turned off the state highway onto the beltway. The overhang where ambulances pulled in had a series of lights. You couldn't miss it.

Another thing the designers accomplished was exciting landscaping and plantings. One saw lots of green spaces, too. Dr. MacCormack's office sat on one of the roads off the beltway, away from the hospital. Like the hospital, those buildings were sparkling new. Many doctors could perform minor procedures in their offices, a great convenience to patients. Harry drove along to Willow Lane, turned right, and within less than a minute arrived at the modern glass-and-steel three-story building. An expensive carved and painted sign with Apollo's caduceus identified this as Willow Lane Medical Associates. Once at the front door, another painted sign, again expensively done with incised letters in black with gilt edges, cited all the doctors within.

Harry passed through Regina's office door at ten and passed back out at ten-thirty. She felt a weight on her shoulders she'd never felt before.

As she walked through the parking lot to her truck, she said hello to Cory Schaeffer, M.D.

"How are you, Harry?" he asked.

"Fine," she lied. "And you?"

"Good, thank you." He locked the door of a small car painted a pretty light metallic misty green.

"Is that an electric car?"

"It is. The Lampo. Just bought it last week. You put the key in, there's no motor noise. That's taken me a bit to get used to, but the mileage is unbelievable. Even better, screw the Arabs. I don't need their gas."

Given Cory's aggressive views on that and other subjects, Harry demurred. "There's wisdom in that. Correct me if I'm wrong. Doesn't the battery for this thing cost twelve thousand dollars?"

"Uh, I'm not sure of the exact price, but there's no danger of me having to buy a battery. I have a cruising range of four hundred miles. Now, that's really incredible. The car will switch to a four-cylinder engine should the voltage drop too low. I've not yet heard those four cylinders. I expect I will sometime or other."

"So, if you drove, say, to the Greenbrier," Harry said, mentioning a gorgeous retreat in White Sulphur Springs, West Virginia, "you wouldn't need gas?"

"Not a drop."

"Where do you plug in the car? I mean, you'd have to put it in the parking lot. How would you recharge the battery?"

"Right now gas stations and retreats like Hot Springs or the Greenbrier don't have a facility for a recharge. But given the push for autonomy from foreign powers when it comes to transportation and energy, I'm confident that within a year or two we will pull into a gas station or a parking lot even at a motel and there will be a recharge station so more than one car can fill up, so to speak. I envision it as a low bank with big square outlets."

"I hope you're right, or you won't be going too far." Harry couldn't resist the little jab.

"Trust technology, Harry. It's gotten us this far."

She wanted to say "And yes, it's polluted our rivers, our skies; ruined our eyes in many cases as people stare into screens all day; it's helped create far too much obesity as people sit hours upon hours; but worse, it's broken the bonds between people."

She knew he wouldn't see it that way, but then again, maybe a physician couldn't. So much of what happened in their world involved nanotechnology, lasers, imaging, new ways to heal without cutting, and more tests than even a genius could remember. It overwhelmed her, and she mistrusted it. It was her nature to distrust the new.

"I'll try," she fibbed.

Cory rested his hand on the short hood of the Lampo. "You found her, didn't you?"

"Yep."

"Well, I'm sorry for that, Harry. What a good nurse she was. If you're in the operating room, you want Paula."

"Didn't mean to criticize you about trusting technology."

He reached over and touched Harry's shoulder. "We can't know everything, but we can try, and so often technology can show us the problem much faster than our own senses."

"It's good to see you, Cory. Thanks for talking to me about your car."

"Oh, I know you're a gearhead." He smiled. "One of the first conversations I had with you when I moved here from Minneapolis was why a live axle is a rougher ride but better for a truck. I thought, well, I haven't met too many women who know stuff like that, and then I met BoomBoom Craycroft. Must be something in the water in these parts."

"Hope so. Saves us money when we go for auto repair."

Cory blinked. "I hadn't thought of that."

"Men usually don't."

A puzzled look crossed his face. "What's being a man got to do with it? I figure if you know motors, you can tell the mechanic where to look first. Save some money."

"True enough. However, Cory, there are those dishonest mechanics out there who figure a woman is as dumb as a sack of hammers about motors. So they give you a laundry list of repairs, all of which are unnecessary. The woman foots the bill. That's never happened to Boom-Boom or me."

He smiled slyly. "No, but I bet a lot else has."

Harry laughed and waved him off as he walked away. She then hopped up into the high seat of her F-150 with the live axle—so good for hauling. She cranked the engine and luxuriated in the rumble of that big old gas-guzzling V-8.

"Damned if I'd buy an electric car." She rolled down the road, then pulled over.

She opened the glove compartment, fished out her cellphone, which was taped together after many little accidents, and dialed Susan Tucker.

"Hey."

"Hey back at you. Where you at?" Susan used the grammatically incorrect sentence.

"Dr. MacCormack's. Can I see you? Now."

After so many years of friendship, Susan knew Harry was in trouble.

"I'm on the golf course. Want to meet me at the Nineteenth Hole or home?"

"Home."

"Be there in about a half hour."

"Good enough."

• • •

When Susan pulled into her driveway, Harry felt a flood of relief and love. She needed Susan, and Susan never failed her. Harry prayed that she had never failed her friend, either.

Within minutes, the two sat at Susan's kitchen table, tea in front of them, as well as Harry's problem.

"You're going to have the procedure, aren't you?"

"I am, but I'm not looking forward to it. I have to lie on a table, drop my boob through it, and they go in with a tiny, tiny scalpel with a little fishhook, sort of, pull out some tissue, then test it."

"They'll put some numbing cream on. That will help."

"There isn't going to be any numbing cream at the back of my boob. It's going to hurt like hell."

Susan put both hands around her beautiful bone china cup. One's chinaware, silver, and crystal still counted in these parts. Susan had inherited delicate china from her paternal line going back to 1720.

"Harry, I'm sorry. You have to do it."

"Will you go with me?"

"Of course I will. Tell me when."

"I'll know tomorrow. Dr. MacCormack is making the appointment. She says she just won't know anything until we have tissue. A mammogram can miss a lot or sometimes just get it wrong. Obviously, she's worried, or I wouldn't have to do this."

Susan took a deep breath, stared straight into Harry's light brown eyes. "Okay. What if it is cancer? You aren't going to ignore it, which I know you can do. For one thing, I won't let you, and neither will your husband."

Tears misted over Harry's eyes. "What if it is? I mean, what if I lost my breast? How will I look to Fair?"

Susan reached over and placed her manicured hand over Harry's hand. "He loves you. Do you think he loves one of your breasts more than you?"

Harry sighed deeply. "No, but still."

"Okay. Let me ask you this. If he had to have one of his testicles removed, would you love him any less?"

"Oh, Susan, that's not a fair question. I don't go around looking at his parts and getting a buzz. But you know as well as I do, take off your blouse, take off your bra, and they go crazy."

Susan paused. "Well, you got a point there. I can't say as I find Ned's lower regions beautiful. I'm delighted everything functions properly, and I tell him how wonderful it is, but—"

"It's the difference between women and men." Harry smiled. "I should amend that. It's the difference between most women and most men. I don't want to look ugly to him."

"Harry, for God's sake. Fair will be with you every step of the way. He isn't going to stop loving you, and he isn't going to stop being sexually attracted to you. Give the man some credit."

This lifted Harry's spirits. "Well, what if the worst happens and they lop off my right boob. Does that mean I'll list to port?"

Susan laughed because it was funny but mostly because Harry was picking up again. "If you do, I'll hold your left arm and prop you up."

"Ha!"

"Look, don't jump to conclusions. One, it may not be cancerous. Two, if it is, they will probably remove the tumor but not your whole breast. Three, if the worst does happen and they remove your breast, you'll have reconstructive surgery. But I hope it doesn't come to that."

Harry, silent for a time, finally said, "You know, I'm being shortsighted. The worst would be if it is cancer and it has spread."

"Don't even say that!"

"Wouldn't you think that if it were you?"

A silence followed from Susan, who then broke it. "Yes."

Harry fingered the lilies in the violet-glass vase on the table. "Sucks. But I won't know until I get hooked, so what good does it do to worry?" She looked up at Susan, her eyes misting again. "Do you think I'll smell funny to Mrs. Murphy, Pewter, and Tucker? Do you think they'll stay away from me? Hospitals have such strange odors." She then added, "I need them with me."

Owen, sitting at her feet, piped up. "*My sister loves you, and those awful cats love you. Doesn't matter how you smell.*"

The two humans looked down into the dog's expressive brown eyes.

Susan, not really knowing what Owen said, replied, "He's telling you all will be well."

$$8$$

*P*ud Benton held up a graceful ruby wineglass. The light streamed through, creating a shaft of ruby light that fell on the wall.

Harry noticed that Paula's mother twirled the glass in her fingers, but she didn't pack it away in the carton.

"Mrs. Benton, would you like me to help with the glasses? I'm almost finished with the stuff in the kitchen closet."

The sixty-five-year-old woman—attractive, with gray hair—blinked. "I must have spaced out."

Harry closed her carton, walked over to Pud, and began wrapping ruby glasses in tissue paper, stuffing more paper in the glasses, then rolling them in Bubble Wrap. "Happens."

Mrs. Benton softly said, "I so appreciate all of Paula's friends helping John and me to pack up."

Paula's house, not huge at three bedrooms, still contained enough goods to keep people busy. Packing is always a pain, and under these circumstances it was very difficult for Paula's parents.

Fair, Cory, Ned, Rev. Jones, and Paula's father packed up her garage, not as crowded as the house. In the barn, Annalise carefully placed the potted plants and dried bulbs in a large carton. She carefully dug up the bulbs coming up on the shelves in the warm light, placing each one in a plastic cup. She wrote on the cup the flower's name—tulip, hyacinth, jonquil—for Paula had tacked small signs on the shelf's lip. Pud didn't want the plants, but she and John had decided each helper should get one.

Most of the people in the house had worked either at Central Virginia Hospital with Paula or on the 5K run.

Harry kept her news to herself except for her husband. Why blab until she had the biopsy results?

"Mrs. Benton, how did you get the nickname Pud?" Harry hoped a different kind of conversation might help Paula's mother.

She reached for a fluted champagne glass. "Well, first off, my grand-mother's name was Paulette, my mother's name was Paula, and I was named Paulette. So Grandmother and Mother called me Pud. Then, of course, I named Paula after my mother. Too many P's, but you know how families are. Or maybe you don't."

"I know." Harry smiled.

"Paula's nickname was Pooch. When she went off to Michigan State, she made her girlfriends swear not to use her nickname. They did any-way. Burned her up. So finally when she moved south, she was able to be Paula again. No one knew her as Pooch. It's all silly."

"Pretty funny, really. I can't imagine calling her Pooch."

"And I can't imagine anything else." Mrs. Benton paused, her hand dangling over the open carton. "When we had the service back home, her pastor referred to her as Pooch. I console myself with the hope that she suffered no pain, it was quick. John and I spoke to Annalise Veronese, the pathologist. She was so kind. Everyone has been so kind. Dr. Veronese assured us that Pooch was in good health. One never knows."

"No, ma'am."

Mrs. Benton finally put the glass in the carton. "I can't get used to being called ma'am. Makes me feel like an old lady."

"You look just like Paula, or I should say she looked just like you. You two could have passed for sisters."

"Aren't you sweet? Come on, now, the gray hair gives me away."

"There are rock stars that dye their hair so blond it's gray. Say, have you seen photos of the DJ in England called Mamy Rock? She's seventy-five, close-cropped gray hair. She looks fabulous."

"Haven't. I'll look her up on the Internet." Mrs. Benton saw her husband, with Ned, Fair, and Rev. Jones, pushing a riding mower up a makeshift ramp into the rented U-Haul. "John will get a hernia."

Harry studied the men. "He looks fit. Must run in the family."

"He's in pretty good shape, but I like to tease him. Pooch was a runner. John, too. That was one thing Dr. Veronese told us, how good Pooch's heart was."

Curiosity overtaking her reserve, Harry asked, "Did she have any enemies?"

"Pooch?"

"Curious. I'm not thinking about foul play, but just that I never heard a bad word about her." Harry fibbed, because such thoughts had indeed crossed her mind. Harry's probing mind could irritate her friends and scare the bejesus out of her husband. Fair never knew what his wife would get into next. Mrs. Murphy, Pewter, and Tucker had resigned themselves to extracting her from whatever mess she stumbled into. Mrs. Benton was pensive for a moment.

"She wasn't a person to arouse envy or strong emotions, one way or another. In high school she rarely fell victim to the kind of gossipy swirl girls indulge in at that time. I hated that when I was in high school. I can't think of anyone who disliked her." She paused. "Really."

"That's a wonderful tribute."

"The only thing she ever said to me, and this wasn't about a personal dislike, was she'd become so interested in alternative cancer treatments because of her work on the five-K. She felt some of them were bogus medical scams that preyed on people when they were most vulnerable. She thought others held out such promise for a cure, but the federal government prevented their use. She felt some doctors were so angry they used outlawed substances and treatments. They hid it, of course. Pooch, herself, was disgusted at how pharmaceutical companies, the insurance companies, and the government have corrupted medicine. After hearing that, I inquired as to what she'd seen at the hospital. She said she'd tell me later. Now there's no later."

Harry considered that. "Every time I pick up the newspaper there seems to be some squib about a new cancer treatment. One article says that eating almonds keeps cancer at bay—you know, that sort of thing. I never know what to believe."

"Nor I." Mrs. Benton's eyes lit up for the first time since she'd come to Virginia. "John and I are fortunate. Cancer doesn't run in either of our families. Pooch became interested in nursing when a childhood friend died of leukemia in eleventh grade. It was an interest that deepened with the years."

"She had a good mind," Harry said.

Mrs. Benton put lots of Bubble Wrap on top of the glasses, for the carton was full. "There. One more done."

"I'm beginning to understand where Paula acquired her organizational ability. In our meetings, if anyone got off track, she'd say, 'Let's cut to the chase.' I'd tell her she was being a Yankee. Southerners live for anecdotes and diversion. However, I always did just what she said."

For the first time, Mrs. Benton truly laughed. "I can just hear her."

Hearing laughter, BoomBoom, Alicia, and Susan looked in from the next room. They each smiled slightly, for they believed laughter healed. A shock such as the one the Bentons had endured would take a lot of laughter and love.

So many people had helped that the house was emptied, tidied up, and the large U-Haul was loaded by three-thirty that afternoon. Mrs. Benton handed each person a potted plant. The dried bulbs in old Ball jars she gave to Alicia as a special thank-you for the pleasure Alicia's movies had given her and her husband.

As the Bentons walked up to the truck, Dr. Cory Schaeffer stepped up to the driver's side. Both Bentons looked at him as the other workers crowded around.

"We hope your journey is safe. We know in time the grief will fade and happy memories will remain. We all would like you to know that your daughter's memory will remain with us. We have renamed the five-K in her honor. From now on it will be known as the Paula Benton Five-K Run for Breast Cancer Research."

John Benton burst into tears. Words wouldn't come. His wife reached for his hand, squeezing it.

He nodded to his wife, composed himself. "Thank you. Thank you."

• • •

Later that evening, as Harry finished up her farm chores, she returned to what Pud Benton said about Paula not having any enemies. Maybe she didn't have any personal enemies, but maybe something else had happened, something to make her a target.

She caught herself. "I watch too many crime shows on TV."

Mrs. Murphy, Pewter, and Tucker, who always helped with the chores—well, Pewter made a stab at it before sitting down—knew their human's mind was preoccupied.

"Think this has to do with her test Wednesday? The one she's calling 'the hook'?" Tucker picked up a blue rubber bone she'd left in the barn yesterday.

"Not a chance." Pewter tossed her head.

"Well, she does have that on her mind," Tucker said.

"Pewter's right. Mom's displaying that nosy look. First there was the distressed look and the weird smell, and now there's the nosy look." Mrs. Murphy batted the blue rubber bone.

Tucker sighed. "Yeah, I know. I was hoping I was wrong. That nosy look is never good for her."

"'Her'? It's never good for us," Pewter said with conviction.

9

The sun bathed the mountains, meadows, and rooftops in soft afternoon light. Harry—an art history major who had graduated from Smith—always thought of this time of day as being wrapped in spun gold. People who didn't know her well would ask how she shifted from Smith to down-and-dirty farming, and Harry answered truthfully that farming taught her to appreciate nineteenth-century painting. Her eye—good to begin with, and trained at Smith—found in nature such symmetry, change, and ravishing beauty that farming was the perfect life for an art history major.

In an hour, the sun's outer rim would dip behind the Blue Ridge Mountains. The colors depended on the pollen in the air, dust particles, and the angle of the sun to the earth. Most spring sunsets, like today's in late April, were a clear sky, which then deepened. However, if there were clouds, the colors radiated salmon, peach, and periwinkle, with streaks of flaming scarlet. This would settle into lavenders, dusty roses, and finally purple, transforming into a pulsating Prussian blue. As for the mountains, the shadows in the deep crevices and bowls turned from dove gray to gray to charcoal and finally black. The normal blue of the mountains became a cobalt blue with dark gray streaks until at last sky and mountains accepted nightfall.

She would turn forty-one in August. With the exception of college in Northampton, Massachusetts, and weekends at Yale and Dartmouth, as well as Boston, her life was in central Virginia. She loved New York City, but what art history major wouldn't? For graduation, her parents, not rich, had sent her to Europe. Susan's parents sent her, too. The friends went to different colleges, but instead of weakening their bond, it had strengthened it. Harry loved England and Ireland, especially the countryside. The biggest surprise to both of them was how small Europe was. Driving east through Austria, they realized an hour would dump them into Hungary. Even Germany, a relatively large country in Europe, seemed tiny compared to the United States. But art, well, Harry often thought of what she had seen in galleries, in cathedrals, and on the people themselves. The Viennese were stylish, the Parisians more so in an obvious manner; the Berliners and Hamburgers certainly threw themselves together; and then there was London. Somehow she expected everyone to look like the since-departed, much-loved Queen Mum. The Brits' reputation for dowdiness was undeserved. Wherever she and Susan traveled, they were dazzled by the artifacts and the people, all of whom were kind to two kids from Virginia.

Much as she learned and loved it all, looking at the mountains, seeing the peach trees in full bloom, the pastures turning an impossible emerald green, she knew she'd be a country girl forever. Given the lump in her breast, Harry wondered how long forever would be. Putting that out of her mind, as well as the nasty fact that Wednesday loomed, for it was already Sunday, she handed Cynthia Cooper a gin rickey.

"When did you learn to make one of these?" Coop admired the tall, thin glass, leaning back in the lawn chair in Harry's backyard. "My mother used to make these, and gin and tonics."

"Once the weather turned, right? That's when your mother made them?"

"Right."

"Well, I am officially welcoming spring. We're more than a month on the other side of the equinox, but damn, March twenty-first was cold. It's stayed cold. Today feels like spring, the light looks like spring."

"Yes, it does." Coop gratefully sipped the drink, her fingerprints on the frosted glass. "Did your mother show you how to make a gin rickey?"

"She did. One and one-half ounces of good gin. Momma stressed *good.* Juice of half a lime and ice-cold club soda. Fill the glass with ice, then add the gin and lime juice, and finally fill it up with club soda. But you know, I've turned into a lazy toad. If it takes preparation I don't do much, and that includes food—unless we're entertaining or if Fair's had a brutal day."

"We're all starved for time, aren't we?" Coop pondered.

"My mother always arranged fresh flowers; she handed Dad a Scotch and soda the minute he walked through the door. She made meals with fresh ingredients. Who can live like that anymore?" Harry shrugged.

"I don't know. I'm lucky if I have time to water my garden. The sheriff's department hasn't hired new people since the crash. We need help. I'm working more hours than ever," Coop noted.

Then Coop added, "Seems like a lame excuse. My mother did it all herself, and she worked as a telephone operator, long hours sometimes. I don't know as she had any more time than I do."

"Mine, too. She worked in the library both because they needed the money and she loved it. You know, she's been dead for eighteen years. Dad, too; one really couldn't live without the other, and I think about them every day. I miss them, I'd give anything to talk to them. You're lucky yours are still with you."

"I am. Say, how did it go packing up Paula's?"

"Great. So many people turned up to help the Bentons, we had it all knocked out by three-thirty. Hey, Paula's nickname was Pooch. Her mother told me."

"Funny." Coop took a long sip, then closed her eyes, leaning back on the lawn chair.

Both women wore sweaters, for the mercury stubbornly hung at fifty-four degrees all day. However, it was such a lovely time of day, just six P.M., both wanted to be outside.

The cats sat on the fence to watch the horses. Tucker flopped on her side, slept under Harry's lawn chair.

"Rick's on a diet," Coop said, referring to her boss, Sheriff Rick Shaw. "His mood is like the stock market."

"And you're in the squad car with him most of the time."

"Friday he plucked my last nerve. I told him his wife could divorce him, I can't. Take pity on me. Made him laugh. He's not really that out of shape. Ten pounds. If he loses that, he'll look good. No, he wants to go back to his weight when he played football for Davidson."

"Give him credit for a high goal."

"He was the middle linebacker. You know that, I think. He's got that linebacker brain, which is actually about perfect for law enforcement: Stop the run!"

Harry laughed. "Guess it is."

"Oh, I did a little research on the scarab beetle. It isn't a symbol of death. First, I'm sorry it took me a while."

"Don't apologize. We're both busy as cat's hair."

The cats, with their sharp hearing, turned to look at Harry, who was about fifty yards from where they sat.

"*Is that a slur?*" Pewter wondered.

"*Nah, it's one of those expressions that doesn't exactly make sense. You know, like 'the exception proves the rule.'*"

"*I don't get that one, either,*" Pewter agreed. "*She has quite a few. 'A square peg in a round hole' confuses me. She doesn't own any square pegs.*"

Back on the lawn, Cooper shared her research. "The Egyptians thought the dung beetle, the scarab beetle, kept the sun moving. That's why they were so important. If they stopped rolling the sun, we'd all die. Turns out, obviously, once I got on the Internet I couldn't stop." Coop paused. "Maybe that's why our mothers could accomplish so much. No Internet. Your mother would have been obsessed with it."

"You're probably right, but she loved holding a book in her hands, so perhaps she could moderate her impulse to know everything right this minute."

"The apple doesn't fall far from the tree." Coop took another delicious sip. "Back to the poop, literally. Turns out, Harry, that the dung beetle is the strongest beetle in the world. The male can pull one thousand one hundred and forty-one times his own body weight."

"I'll be. I'm as amazed that you've remembered all this."

"Got hooked. Plus, I'm a cop. I'm trained to remember detail." Coop said this not realizing Harry really was going to get hooked midweek. "Okay, there's more. If you and I were that strong, we'd be able to pull six double-decker London buses filled with passengers."

"Jeez." Harry began to admire the beetle.

"Furthermore, the males battle rivals. They descend into the tunnels the female digs under dung. If another male is there, they duke it out. Has to be the heavyweight contest of the world. They actually lock horns. Whoever pushes out his opponent wins."

"Actually, Coop, the female wins, which is the way of the world."

The tall, lean deputy thought about this. "True. That explains so much male dysfunction, which I see every day, whether it's violence, drunkenness, crazy risks. Most crimes are committed by men, and there are millions of unhappy men out there. For some, the unhappiness turns to anger. They have to lash out at somebody or something."

"Funny. When I was young and the feminist movement was firing up, Mother always said that it didn't matter how much political power men had. Nature had given women the most powerful weapons."

"Your mother had a lot of insight. Even the Muslim radicals can't control women one hundred percent. Instead, they kill them."

"We don't have to look to the Mideast for nutcases."

"Right. How'd we get from dung beetles to this?"

"Friendship. One of the greatest joys of my life is sitting talking to you, to someone I love, and letting our minds go wherever."

"It's a luxury, isn't it?" Coop said.

"'Tis. Thanks for the research."

"Glad to do it."

"I keep wondering whether Paula saw something amiss at the hospital. In my head, there was no crime committed, but my weakness is I want a reason."

"Your weakness is you want the truth. Millions are satisfied with a reason that has no relationship to the truth. Think about that. Every day I see people who are so irrational, so completely off the rails. Even worse, some of them are armed."

"Yes, but if we give up our guns, then only the criminals have them."

"I know. Listen, I don't know any of us who are in law enforcement who don't have our concealed-weapon permit for when we're off-duty. You see too much, and, Harry, it happens so fast."

"I don't know how you do it."

"Sometimes I wonder why I am out there, but I really believe I'm making a difference, and that makes me feel like I'm living a life of purpose."

"You are. And you're a good researcher, too."

Coop smiled. "Your beetle has led you nowhere, at least as far as unexplained natural death is concerned."

"True, but it led me closer to you."

• • •

That night, wrapped up in Fair's arms to go to sleep, Harry told him about her conversation with Coop.

"Coop's a deeper thinker than I give her credit for," he said.

Fair always loved holding Harry, but since her news, the uncertainty, he didn't want to let her go. He was trying not to let his fear show. She was taking it better than he was.

"That she is," said Harry. "Honey, apart from Paula's untimely passing, which couldn't be helped, and my needing tests, it's been awfully quiet. I could use a little excitement."

The cats—at the foot of the bed—and Tucker—on the rug by the bed—perked up.

Mrs. Murphy spoke for the other two: "Mom, be careful what you wish for."

hen you look back on things, they're clear. When you're in the middle of them, they're a mess." Susan cupped her hand under Harry's elbow to walk her out to the parking lot.

"Susan, I'm not recovering from anesthesia."

Susan dropped her hand. "Right, but that was unpleasant."

"Damn straight."

Wednesday, nine on the dot, Harry and Susan appeared at Dr. Jennifer Potter's office. While Dr. Potter used Central Virginia Hospital for large, complicated procedures, she could perform simpler procedures in her office. Most patients hated the idea of being in a hospital.

The expense of the equipment she'd purchased made the young woman worry that she'd be paying those bills into her mid-fifties. The uproar over healthcare reform amplified that worry. Like many physicians, Dr. Potter considered raising prices, but so many people labored now just to make ends meet. She didn't want to raise her rates. She figured she'd learn to live with less.

Regina MacCormack provided Harry with a list of doctors who could perform the procedure of harvesting her breast cells. In some cases, a surgeon wasn't needed. A physician specializing in oncology, such as Cory Schaeffer, could perform it. However, Dr. MacCormack believed Dr. Potter was the quickest and the best. She always figured out the quickest way to deliver any necessary discomfort. No reason to keep anyone on the table too long.

Harry submitted to the process, and Dr. Potter liked having Susan there to support Harry. Fair wanted to be there, but Harry forbade him. For one thing, Alicia's wonderful mare was about to foal, a late foaling. For another thing, she'd known her husband since childhood. He was more upset than she was. He didn't need the added stress, nor did she in worrying about him later.

She had to lie down on a padded table and drop her right breast through an opening in the table, which was then adjusted to fit and hold her breast secure.

Before this, Dr. Potter smeared the spot with lidocaine and God knows what else. It tingled. Once the numbing agent took full effect, the procedure started.

It was mercifully short, but Harry sure felt the hook and snatch. There was a puncture wound but no obvious incision. A Band-Aid took care of that.

Like most horse people, Harry was tough.

Stoic or not, the body knows it is under attack. She sweated, felt a tri-fle woozy, but recovered as she sat up. She hadn't eaten breakfast to prevent any possible nausea.

Dr. Potter told her she could leave, as she'd gotten a good sample from the growth. Harry liked Jennifer Potter. Everyone did.

Toni Enright—who came in to assist because Harry had helped so much on the 5K—walked them to the door. "Harry, whatever the result, you're in good hands. I hope it's nothing, really."

"Me, too."

"Thanks, Toni," Susan said at the office door.

Once in her Volvo station wagon, Harry exhaled.

"Why don't you let me drive?" Susan offered. "I've wanted to do that."

"Thanks, Susan. I guess I'm shakier than I think, huh?"

"I don't know if I could do it. They'd have to knock me out."

"Oh, you could. Doesn't last long, and I'll tell you what, hurt like hell. I'm not doing that again."

They switched places. Harry showed Susan how to keep her foot on the brake, push in the rectangular key, and then press a button next to that to start the engine.

"Can't carmakers use a simple key anymore?"

"Apparently not. I hate it, too, but I love the wagon."

They drove to a T intersection, and Susan turned right onto the two-lane highway, heading for Charlottesville.

"Don't want to take Sixty-four?" Harry mentioned the interstate.

"No. I want to see how this handles on twisty roads."

"You picked a good one. I like it. I never thought I'd drive a station wagon. I like your Audi, but it costs more than the Volvo. You've got everything on your wagon."

"Fair was right to buy this Volvo for you. It's a lot of car for a good price. If he'd bought you one like mine or the Mercedes wagon, you'd have had a fit. You needed a safe vehicle, a station wagon, to haul stuff but something that doesn't gulp gas like the old F-One-fifty."

"I like the Tahoe, but I'll admit it isn't good on gas. The Volvo's center of gravity is lower, too. Hey, did I tell you about Cory Schaeffer's Lampo?"

"Did. He's a bit of a pompous ass."

"What he is is a holier-than-thou liberal, and I don't like them any more than the nuts on the far right fringe."

"Remember how your mother used to call liberals the people to the left of Pluto? What'd she call the right-wingers?" Susan thought a moment, then smiled. "To the right of Genghis Khan."

They both laughed, remembering Harry's mother.

"You're not taking me home in my own car?"

"You didn't eat breakfast. I'm taking you to the club," Susan said.

As they tackled waffles drenched in Vermont maple syrup, grits swimming in butter, and a thin slice of early melon, they didn't avoid the pressing subject. Until the results came in, though, there wasn't much to say.

Back in the wagon, Harry now driving, Susan asked, "Will you swing by Charlottesville Press?"

"Sure."

Charlottesville Press on Harris Street stayed afloat, even with home printers. You couldn't get married without them. Well, a Virginian could pay for the invitations to be printed by Tiffany. But Tiffany now used Crane papers more than their own, so no Tiffany watermark. What was the point? Then again, the bride's parents, trying to save money, could print them themselves or go to someone using a laser printer. While it saved bundles, one slipped precipitously on the social scale. Much as such things shouldn't matter, they did.

Is there a Southerner, male or female, who doesn't hold paper up to the light to see the watermark? Probably, but neither Harry nor Susan nor their husbands fell into that lot. All of their mothers would be turning over in their graves if things were not properly done.

Susan—with two children of marriageable age, one male, one female—had so far been spared the expense of a blowout wedding. She was, however, in charge of the gold invitational banquet for the Multiple Sclerosis Foundation. The invitations had to be perfect. Perfect. The fees for the feast proved rather steep. Hence Charlottesville Press. The invitation had to match the elegance of the event held at Keswick Hall.

As they turned onto Harris Street, billows of black smoke curled upward. Even with the car windows closed, the smell of fire crept in.

Harry and Susan counted many friends among the business owners on Harris Street. Their worry was immediate.

Fire trucks blocked the way to Charlottesville Press.

"Oh, God, hope it's not the pet store or Chuck Grossman's business. Or Rodney," Susan exclaimed.

Rodney was Rodney Thomas, owner of Charlottesville Press.

"Harry, we've got to turn around."

"I know, but hold on one skinny minute." Harry hit the brakes, pressed the flashing-light button, stepped out of her Volvo, and ran up to Luke Anson, an officer with the Charlottesville police whom she recognized.

"Luke."

"Harry, turn round."

"What's burning?"

"Pinnacle Records. Go on, Harry. Everyone's out of the building, even the dog."

"Okay." Back in the Volvo, Harry informed Susan.

Pinnacle Records housed hard copy, some of those records going back to 1919. They also had sliding metal trays in temperature-controlled vaults for CDs, floppy disks, even removed hard drives. Two years ago, Pinnacle had developed another temperature-controlled small vault for the tiny thumb drives now coming into use.

Even though technology surged ahead, with files and backup becoming ever smaller, huge companies soon ran out of storage room, no matter how carefully they'd planned. The proliferation of materials was overwhelming. Pinnacle provided a much-needed service to many organizations. Of particular concern to some of their clients were their old papers, particularly if the paper was cheap, such as newsprint. Such articles disintegrated rapidly. Pinnacle worked with various libraries' special collections, most notably the University of Virginia, keeping abreast of the latest developments in preserving historical documents. The old inks remained as long as the paper could hold them. Experts could pinpoint the chemicals in various inks, too. It was historically vital to preserve the actual paper document. Fortunately, many companies realized this.

Pinnacle carried insurance and was supposed to be fireproof.

"Pinnacle has so much sensitive, really important material." Susan immediately grasped the problem.

"Not anymore."

11

*T*hursday, the day after Pinnacle Records burned, many law offices, medical offices, and businesses—from insurance companies to the tire dealer on Route 29—all checked their in-house records. They had used Pinnacle Records for backup, for storage, especially for materials that were old, older than computer files. With few exceptions, everyone was fine.

Safe Tire, for whatever reason, either had misplaced the files for 2002 or the computer ate them up. People who drove the usual fifteen thousand miles per year had replaced the tires purchased in 2002. However, a few customers barely put fifteen hundred miles per annum on their vehicles. Franny Howard, the owner, immediately hired a geek to comb through the computers.

People didn't expect a woman to own a tire store. Franny, smart, hired men on the floor. In the garage, she had one female employee, the rest men. She worked in her sumptuous office behind the showroom. Even with the economy downturn, Franny made money. Many people feared things wouldn't get better. Instead of buying a new car, they put a new set of tires on their old one.

Apart from Safe Tire, by the end of the day, many companies utilizing Pinnacle Records relaxed.

At four, Coop drove to the site of the fire. Rick usually drove, but he sat next to her, working a laptop computer. The state kept adding new license plates. He pulled up the latest ones to refresh his memory. Sure was easier when there was one plate and that was that.

Virginia's plate background for the last three decades was white and the letters and numerals were dark blue, easily read from twenty yards. Now plates had yellow swallowtail butterflies, the state insect. Others celebrated Jamestown, the beginnings of English settlement in 1607. Others honored war veterans, the exact war being specified. Foxhunters even had their own license plates—very pretty, too. You could get plates signifying your college. Pleasant though it was for those people willing to pay the extra dollars for the license plates with some meaning to them, this personalization created confusion.

Sheriff Shaw, Coop, and the people in his department, as well as any law enforcement officer in Virginia, simply memorized the plates. But a citizen in an accident—say, a hit-and-run—might not be able to identify the license plates on the fast-receding vehicle. The various surrounding colors and logos obscured for them the vital information, plus people in accidents were rattled as it was.

"I'm waiting for golfers to get their plate." Rick closed the laptop as Coop parked the squad car.

"The logo will read 'Put a tiger in your tank.'" Coop used the old Esso ad slogan from decades past but referred to the world's most famous golfer.

Rick laughed. "If I'd done even ten percent of the stuff that guy did, I'd be singing soprano. Helen scares me," he said, naming his wife.

"Oh, she does not."

As they both got out of the squad car, he replied, "Just a little. Helen sees things I don't. I can never tell if it's because she's a woman or if it's because she's so damned smart."

"A little of both." Coop liked Rick's wife.

A sharp odor made them cough. The ruins still smoldered. Firemen remained on duty. But this was a bit different than the usual charred timber, insulation ashes smell.

"Plastic?"

"Dunno." Rick shrugged as they walked toward Big Al Vitebsk, Pinnacle's owner, who was talking to one of the firemen.

As Pinnacle was on Harris Street in Charlottesville, this was not Rick's jurisdiction. Al and Nita Vitebsk lived in the county. Everyone knew Big Al. He was one of those guys who throws himself into any charity work with enthusiasm. For years he had headed the Easter Seals drive, as well as giving generously to the Reformed Temple, of which he was a valued member.

"Sheriff." Big Al turned to greet Rick. "Hello, Coop. Well, this is a goddamned mess."

"Yeah, came to see it myself. I'm sorry, Al," Rick commiserated.

The six-three, three-hundred-pound man shrugged. "My turn, I guess."

"I'm glad everyone got out safely."

"Even JoJo."

JoJo, a medium-sized adorable mutt with floppy ears and a coat the color of apricots, sat in Big Al's Range Rover, windows down. Big Al didn't want his best friend to rush into the hot ruins and burn his pads. JoJo was smarter than that, but if Big Al had walked into it, so would JoJo. Rescued from the pound at five months old, JoJo loved Big Al as only a dog can love. And Big Al loved him in return.

"Nita okay?" Rick asked.

"She's tough. Hell, she married me," Big Al joked.

"Got that right." Rick smiled. "Do you know how this started?"

"Right now, no. Until they can get in there, I don't think we'll know. I just hope it's not something like faulty wiring. I run a tight ship, Rick, but things can slip by or just fool you. Look what happened down at Round Hill Industries. The whole roof collapsed last winter, and the roof had been built to code in 1995. Stuff happens."

"It does, but we live in a society where blame has to be apportioned and attached to a person. I'm with you, buddy, whatever went wrong, I sure hope it isn't something like wiring."

"I hope the records in the heavy vaults survived. Once the terrible heat subsides, I'll open them. Might take a day or two. I wouldn't want to touch the locks, even with firemen's gloves." He stopped. "The old records, the ones back to the forties. I don't know."

"Those in the vaults probably survived," Rick said.

"That old paper—" Big Al shrugged, not wishing to finish the thought. "Hope some of it survived, but the heat had to impact the

inside of the vault. It's just flames can't get in. I advised everyone placing old records with me to have them microfilmed. Of course, the
newspaper has both microfilm from the old days and everything on
thumb drives. But the old pharmacy that used to be a bank on the mall,
the old stables on Main Street that were torn apart in 1919—those
records are stored here. The inheritors of those old businesses knew
records might be of some importance later to a historian, but they
didn't make copies."

"It's time-consuming, costly, and most folks think the world started
when they came into it. Tell you what, I am indebted to anyone who has
kept records. Every now and then I'll yank up a cold case, some of them
from the turn of the last century. If I had better records, I just might be
able to close the case. Even though everyone is dead. Modern technology can help you—say, if there are hair samples. Methods have improved greatly."

As the two men talked, Coop walked over, chatted with the fireman,
then reached into the Range Rover to pet JoJo.

"Glad you're in one piece."

"*Thank you,*" JoJo said, wagging his luxurious tail. "*Coop, the fire wasn't an
accident. When I came to work with Dad, I smelled a nasty odor. I think that's what started
the fire.*"

With senses beyond human imagining, JoJo may have jumped to
conclusions, but then again, because he listened to Big Al, Nita, and
their employees, he knew how critical some of the stored information
was.

12

"I just saw your husband!" Franny Howard exclaimed, catching sight of Harry standing in an aisle at Southern States.

Putting back the box of cat treats, Harry started to roll her cart toward Franny, who zoomed toward her. "What are you reading?" Franny asked.

"The label. I only buy cat food, dog food, and treats that have a high meat content. And I sure never buy anything if I know it comes from China. What scares me is how easy it is for companies to hide such vital information."

"Wasn't that an awful mess?" Franny referred to the contaminated pet food China sold to the United States a few years back.

"Not as bad as the contaminated milk." Harry wondered how Chinese authorities could miss these abuses and put up with such a flagrant lack of standards.

"They killed the executives of the company responsible." Franny leveled her amazing dark blue eyes at Harry. "And I applaud them. I don't care how brutal it sounds. What happens here? A company president hires a PR firm, spin control. Then they hire a battery of slick lawyers, you know, the kind that could get Uncle Billy Sherman's march to the sea considered trespassing? No punishment to speak of, and no accountability. There, I've had my rant and feel much the better for it. How do you feel?"

Harry burst out laughing. "You've given me a lot to think about."

"Isn't that a nice way to say 'Bullshit'?"

"Franny, you're a Virginian. You know if that's what I thought, I'd say 'That's incredible.'"

Now it was Franny's turn to explode. "Girl, I need to see more of you. Don't you need a new set of tires for that antique truck you drive?"

"Actually, I do, and I was going to bring it up. I do go off the road with it. I mean, not over boulders and the kind of stuff Jeep Rubicons do, but I am out in the fields, crossing shallow fords. It's my go-to farm truck."

"What about the dually Fair bought you some years back?"

"I don't count that. It's a dedicated vehicle. Anyway, it sucks gas like a boozehound hits Wild Turkey."

By "dedicated vehicle," Harry meant that the dually pulled their horse trailer or the heavily loaded hay wagon. The mighty machine did not make runs to the grocery store. It hauled, and that was that. Harry thought this was a good financial strategy, because the truck would last longer. A tricked-out dually, regular cab, would run forty-two thousand dollars. Add an extended cab or double doors and you tipped fifty thousand dollars. Astronomical. Her dually had better last twenty years.

"A lot of people do that. I just haul with a three-quarter-ton, no double wheels. But I don't pull the loads you do, either. Now, while I have you"—she glanced at her watch, once her mother's—"I can sell you any kind of tire you want for your F-One-fifty. 1978. Right?"

"How'd you remember?"

"If it has wheels on it, I remember. It's my business. Bring her in. I'll show you Bridgestones, Goodriches, and a pair of Goodyears. Nothing fancy. Come on to the shop. I'll give you a preacher's price." She paused. "Even with that, Harry, a good set will put you back between six hundred and eight hundred dollars."

"Thanks, Franny. I'll come on Tuesday."

"Hate to run after I've chewed your ear off, but our support group meets at two."

"What support group?"

"Cancer. I ran the five-K. Well, you didn't notice. You were at the table, and I checked in through email."

"When did you have cancer?"

"I don't know when it started. I only know when my annual checkup chest X ray showed some wonky cells in my lungs. Three years ago. Lung cancer can be a bad one, I tell you. Doesn't have the best survival rate. Anyway, Paula Benton and I are—I mean, were—friends. She was the facilitator of this group. Those people pulled me through. Now, even though I'm clear, I go. My turn to help someone else. If only I could have helped Paula. You never know. I heard they found nothing."

"Franny, I didn't know you had lung cancer. I'm so sorry. I would have done something to help."

A stern look passed over Franny's attractive features, and she touched Harry's hand. "Let me tell you something. I don't care who knows now, but I cared then. There is still a prejudice against cancer, especially— and I emphasize *especially*—if you're working in a big corporation or own a business. We'd just begun to hit the skids—the economy, I mean; I was in the process of refinancing the loan on the Safe Tire complex. I'm not so sure I would have gotten that loan if United Assets had known." She named a bank that had merged so many times it now had the most innocuous name possible.

Its headquarters was in Memphis, Tennessee.

"I had no idea."

"No one does until it happens to them. A cancer sufferer is marked. Oh, some places are better than others. I can rattle off a large brokerage house in town that stands behind its people one hundred percent and doesn't hold back on the promotions, either." She snatched a huge bag of catnip off the shelf. "I'll give this to you Tuesday. That way I know you'll be properly bribed."

Harry laughed again. You had to like Franny.

Franny continued, "I do have to run, and I am sorry if I rattled on. The last thing to die on me will be my mouth. And hey, I haven't even told you about some of my records burning to a toasty crisp in the Pinnacle Records conflagration. That's another story. A hot one."

With that she wheeled her cart around and sped for the counter checkout, waving without looking back.

Harry's eyes followed her. She thought to herself, There's a lot I don't know, and I'm terrified I'm going to find out.

Her biopsy report was due on Monday. She'd push it out of her mind, and then, like a flea you think you've brushed off, back the worry would hop.

• • •

As Harry filled her cart, Big Al was kneeling down with the fire chief, Greg Miller, outside the Pinnacle Records building. A team of three people—wearing protective clothing, because there were still hot spots—filled nonflammable containers with samples of soot, ash, debris. The containers, built to dissipate the heat, did a pretty good job, but one still needed to wear heavy gloves.

The structure stood, charred but intact. The inside, however, no longer existed, except for the vaults. The meeting rooms, the rooms where people could lock the doors and go through their files, and the front offices were all gone.

Greg pointed to the base of the building. Then he walked Al alongside, stopping at a series of small charred canisters.

"Basic but effective. Gasoline, and I think it's been enriched with something else. I don't know. The fire was deliberate."

Al's broad face registered shock and dismay. "Oh, no."

"Arson. You don't see much of this kind of thing in central Virginia."

"Why? Look, Greg, I have backup records. Why me? Wouldn't it make more sense if someone wanted records destroyed to go to the source first, not the backup?"

"Maybe they have. For all we know, Al, there's a law firm in town that's missing some highly compromising material and they don't know yet. How many companies routinely check old files?"

Big Al nodded as he retrieved JoJo from the Range Rover. "It's an election year next year."

"That would be a compelling reason if you want to run and you've got a nasty scarlet skeleton in a closet. I ask you to think about this when you can go through your own records. My hunch—and it's only a hunch—is that whoever burned you out knew the compromising records were not in the massive vaults. Pay special attention to the storage units that were not as secure."

"I see." Big Al quietly nodded, then knelt down to rub JoJo's head.

The huge man always felt better if he could touch his dog. The grounds had cooled off enough that he could walk the perimeter with JoJo.

"*Don't worry, Daddy. I'll protect you!*" the mixed breed promised.

Al stood up; his knees creaked a little. "Jewish lightning."

"Beg pardon." Greg's eyebrows raised upward.

"When I was a kid, they called arson Jewish lightning." He sighed deeply. "I hated that, and I hate this."

13

hat do I do now?" Harry sat next to Dr. Regina MacCormack as the doctor pulled up information on her computer screen.

"You have choices. I can offer my advice, but you have to make the decisions."

Harry exhaled deeply. "Tell me again what Stage One breast cancer means. Sorry to make you repeat yourself."

Dr. MacCormack had known Harry as an acquaintance for many years, and liked her enormously. The feeling was mutual. Their hobbies were so different that when they saw each other it was usually at a fund-raiser or down at the Paramount, the rejuvenated old movie theater that had transformed itself into a cultural hot spot.

Harry, with a hint of defiance, said, "I'm not going to cry."

"No harm in it, but I know you're not a crier, and I also know you'll fight."

"I will."

"All right. Stage One breast cancer means the cancer is in your breast. Although it doesn't look like it, there's the possibility that it has spread to your lymph nodes. We remove them, because they are the body's dispatch stations. However, I don't think your cancer has spread, and I've seen a lot of breast cancer. Far, far too much, really."

"It's an epidemic, isn't it? An unacknowledged epidemic."

"That's a later discussion, but"—Regina leaned back in her seat, taking her hand off the mouse—"something is wrong. It isn't just breast cancer, Harry. It's all forms of cancer. Well, I'm already getting off the track. Stage Two. The eight-year survival rate is seventy percent, quite good, and you are an excellent candidate as you have Stage One. Better survival rate."

"Do I have to have surgery?"

"I would suggest it." She paused. "The two best surgeons, I think, are Cory Schaeffer and Jennifer Potter."

"I'd have a hard time trusting myself to a man who bought an electric car."

Dr. MacCormack burst out laughing, for she knew of Harry's fascination with cars. "He's in love with that car."

"Yuck. Besides, if someone is fooling around with my boob, I want it to be a woman."

"Many women feel that way. But there are some fabulous men out there, and they are as sensitive as any woman oncologist I know."

"Cory Schaeffer isn't one of them," Harry posited.

Dr. MacCormack lowered her voice, even though it was only the two of them in her office. "He does think highly of himself. You already have a relationship with Jennifer Potter. You'll need to consult with her before your final decision, of course."

"All right."

"We can make an appointment for you," Dr. MacCormack offered. "Let's consider what's possible. Obviously, the absolute safest course is always a radical mastectomy, because everything goes. No nasty cancer cell escapes if the cancer is contained in the breast. This is such radical surgery. But I must say, it is the most complete, and you can have the reconstructive surgery done while you're on the table. Saves two surgeries. I don't think you need a mastectomy, however."

Harry slumped a little. "Thank God. I know there are worse things. I think about the men and women coming back from Iraq and Afghanistan who are blown up. This is small beans, but then again, it scares me even though I know there's a lot more bad stuff that could happen to me or anyone."

"You've got the right attitude. I knew you would. What I think will provide you with the least trauma is a lumpectomy with post-op treatment. A lumpectomy means the tumor and some surrounding tissue are removed but not your whole breast."

"That means chemo and radiation, doesn't it?"

"Depends. It is possible when your tumor is removed you may not require chemo and radiation, or you may not require chemo." Noticing Harry's quizzical look, Dr. MacCormack continued, "Based on your biopsy, the location of the tumor, it will definitely grow if unchecked. Stage One is a proper diagnosis based on the size of your tumor, just shy of one centimeter. Again, I don't think the cancer has spread to your lymph nodes, but we won't be one hundred percent sure of its size until it's out. If the tumor is over one centimeter, then you are considered Stage Two. It's not as bad as it sounds—Stage Two, I mean. We won't know until the tumor is actually removed. But—and I emphasize but—to be as safe as possible, a regimen of radiation and possibly chemo after surgery is prudent. If the surgeon missed any cells or some actually have migrated—it only takes one—the treatments will kill them."

"Might kill me, too."

"No. You're forty, strong, not overweight at all, no diabetes or any conditions that could compromise healing. You'll live through it, but I'd be a liar if I said it won't have a cumulative effect. The farther along you are in those treatments, the worse you feel. Some patients report nausea, especially with chemo, but some also feel a bit off that way with radiation. Both radiation and chemo make you tired. And I repeat, it's cumulative."

"How long must I submit to treatment?"

"Again, Harry, we won't know until we have the tumor. I hope it will be a short course." Dr. MacCormack's voice, soothing, was a tonic in itself. "Let's just knock this right out of you."

"I'm for that. Is there a course of treatment that doesn't have such awful side effects?"

"Herceptin is a new drug used to treat women with metastatic breast cancer who are HER-two-positive. You aren't HER-two-positive."

"Should I be glad about that?"

Dr. MacCormack nodded, then added, "About twenty-five percent of women with cancer have an excess of the protein which makes the cancer spread quickly. Called HER-two. You don't fall into that twenty-five percent, which I know from your bloodwork.

"However, you are premenopausal, so your body is still pumping out lots of hormones. There are drugs to inhibit the cancer getting the hormones it needs to grow. But again, you're lucky because you don't have hormone receptor–positive cancer. You've got a straightforward type of cancer. We can treat it in a straightforward way."

"Well, it's hard to think of myself as lucky at this moment, but I guess I am."

"You have no idea." Dr. MacCormack looked serious. "Again, we'll know a lot more after the surgery, and I am already assuming you will have the tumor removed."

"I will. I want to talk it over with Fair, but I will."

"He's a vet. He knows a great deal. In fact, some of what we have learned we've learned from cancers in dogs. Some breeds are especially prone, like golden retrievers and boxers. You'd be surprised how much veterinary medicine helps human medicine. An obvious example: The research and surgeries on dachshund back problems have proved invaluable for human treatments."

"Sounds like you think I should go under the knife straightaway."

"I do. I've seen so much, Harry. Get it out."

"All right."

"We'll make you an appointment to consult with Dr. Potter. We have a roster of wonderful surgeons in our area if for some reason you don't click with Dr. Potter on a patient level."

"She's been great about the five-K. I'm sure I'll be just fine with her." Then Harry laughed. "Annalise Veronese's been great working for the five-K, too. Don't want to wind up with her."

Smiling, Dr. MacCormack stood up. Harry did also. "I'm sorry to give you the news from your biopsy, but I'm glad it's not more serious. Your chances of full recovery are excellent. I do, however, think you should opt for the radiation, even if Dr. Potter thinks she's removed all the tissue. She'll think so, too. Unpalatable as it is, once it's over, you bounce back and you can rest knowing you're on the road to full recovery."

• • •

When Harry walked into the kitchen, Fair was drying a glass. He felt she would be getting bad news, and he wanted to be home. Harry would never tell her husband about her diagnosis on the phone. It had to be face-to-face.

The two cats and dog immediately knew, because they could smell the tension.

"Well." Her husband tried to look bright.

"Stage One breast cancer."

Fair dropped the glass, which shattered on the floor. He bent down to pick up the shards.

"Honey, don't." She knelt down, grabbing his hand. "I'll sweep it up."

As they stood, he hugged her. He couldn't speak. Then he found his voice. "I broke it, I'll sweep it up."

"Your hands are shaking. Let me do it."

"I'm supposed to comfort you." Sorrow filled his voice.

"I've had the whole drive back from Charlottesville to adjust. You sit down."

As soon as she swept up all the pieces, putting them in the metal trash can, she sat across from her husband at the kitchen table. "I'll tell you everything I know."

Tucker, listening, said, "If only I could bite this cancer thing, I'd kill it."

Pewter, puffed up, said, "I could scratch its eyes out."

Mrs. Murphy looked up at Harry, leaning forward toward Fair, at the table as he held her hand tightly. "Now we have to trust our human to people we don't even know."

14

"Where does the time go?" Harry leaned on the three-board fence of the pasture behind the barn.

Twilight lingered, a languid, early-May twilight enrobing the Blue Ridge with cobalt velvet.

The cloudless sky—backlit, for the sun had set a half hour ago—promised a crisp night.

Matilda, the blacksnake who lived in the hayloft, had finished her hunting and slithered back to the barn. She paused for a moment, flicked out her tongue, emitting a little hiss. This was not a comment on anything; it was more of a little salute to Harry, whom she recognized.

Like all farmers, Harry focused on weather with intensity. Too much rain, crops rotted in the field. Too little, they burned up. If one could afford an irrigation system, one could fight a drought. Nothing could combat too much rain.

Her tough sunflowers continued to grow. Her grapes, in their second year, sported leaves, ever enlarging, on the trained vines, which thrilled her. She had worried because of the ferociously cold winter, the worst winter for one hundred years. Spring, remarkably cool, was wet.

So wet, she'd rented a drill seeder only a week ago. Usually she over-seeded her pastures in early to mid-April.

Since Mother Nature was her business partner, she did as Mother dictated. Harry limed the fields in the spring. Sometimes she put down weed-and-feed fertilizer, but usually she put down chicken poop or commercial fertilizers in the fall. When the oil prices climbed through the sky, non-manure-based fertilizers skyrocketed to nine hundred percent of their former cost. This did not make the news. Agriculture economics rarely did. A frost in Florida's orange groves might get coverage, or a terrible drought in the Midwest, but the distressing effect of oil prices on your everyday small farmers wasn't news. They suffered plenty, whether that suffering was reported to their fellow citizens or not.

A nine-hundred-percent price rise is beyond comprehension.

She hadn't fertilized for two years. The price to spread chicken poop floated out of reach, too. You burn gas putting it down.

It made Harry miserable. Just thought it was the worst. She laughed at herself as she watched Venus begin her majestic ascent, shining her lovelight over all living things, fascinating Harry as she had fascinated people since they cast their eyes upward. Another hour and Harry would be able to identify the constellations.

"Why she's doing that chuckle thing people do?" wondered Pewter, sitting on the fence next to Mrs. Murphy, who sat next to Harry.

"Don't know." Mrs. Murphy put her paw on Harry's forearm.

Wedged next to Harry's leg, Tucker was determined not to let her beloved human out of her sight.

"Someone wants their chin scratched."

"I prefer tuna," Pewter replied.

"Do you ever think of anything other than your expanding stomach?" Mrs. Murphy said.

"World peace." Pewter giggled, making the odd little intake of breath that accompanies the feline giggle.

Tucker howled with glee.

"What's cookin', kids?" Harry scratched Mrs. Murphy's chin.

"If only you could understand us, you'd be laughing, too." Tucker sighed, as she often felt frustrated with human limitations.

"You know," Harry spoke to them, "what a clear crisp evening. Must be about fifty-five degrees, and it's seven-thirty. Glad I wore my sweater. Of course, you all are always dressed just right for the weather." As she rubbed her hand over Mrs. Murphy's back, her undercoat shed out.

"*Murph, you shed too much,*" Pewter grumbled, as some of the undercoat landed on her lovely gray fur.

"*You shed as much as I do.*"

"*Do not. No one sheds as much as you do. You're like a dalmatian.*"

"*Pewter, you're trying to start something.*" Tucker stood on her hind legs to get closer to Pewter.

Harry—even on her two legs—recognized the signs of Pewter gearing up to be a bad girl. Sometimes she'd taunt the others. Sometimes she'd be asleep, wake up, shoot straight up in the air, race around the house, then pounce on Tucker. The dog suffered endless abuse from the cat, who would wrap her front legs around the corgi to wrestle her to the ground. Truth be told, the dog loved it. Tucker would growl, but she'd flop down as though the cat really had thrown her. Sometimes Mrs. Murphy joined in, but usually she watched, because with her Pewter sometimes unleashed her claws, if only for effect. Still, it made the tiger cat mad.

"You know"—Harry folded her hands together as Venus, bright now, seemed a pure beacon in a deepening sky—"I fretted so during the oil crisis, which corresponded to the tail end of those wicked drought years. My hay burned up in the fields, too, from that unremitting heat. Thought it couldn't get much worse."

"*We remember.*" Tucker dropped back down.

"*We remember because you kept us up at night, walking the floor.*" Pewter relished the negative detail, as always.

"Now I wonder if the rains will water down my grapes, so to speak. Remember, this is the second year, so I can harvest them and sell them to a vintner. Boy, I hope I can make a little money. I must have been out of my mind to put in a quarter acre of grapes. Hardest work ever, and there's so much to learn."

"*They look good,*" Mrs. Murphy hopefully meowed.

"Now this. Before, I worried about my crops; now I'm worried about myself. I know I'm going to live. Really, you all, I do."

"*Of course you're going to live!*" the two cats meowed in unison.

"*You can't die, Mom. I couldn't live without you.*" Tucker's soft brown eyes looked so sad.

"Sounds funny, but I believe I'll know when I'm going to die, and it's not now. But I am so scared of being cut and then radiation. God, I don't want to do it."

"*You're doing it,*" Tucker firmly ordered her.

"I feel betrayed by my own body, and then I think about Paula Benton. Dead, sitting on the stool at her potting shed, head down on the table. She was about my age. I don't know. Dumb things are running through my head."

"*That's natural,*" Tucker consolingly murmured.

"*Certainly is. Dumb things are always going through her head.*" Pewter giggled again.

"*Pewter, you're a pill tonight.*" Mrs. Murphy rubbed her cheeks against Harry's arm.

"*Hey, I love her. But she is what she is, and humans can't help it. They're, well, limited. And I think she does know when she will die. This isn't her time, but from what I hear everyone saying, sounds like she'll be pooped out before the treatments are over.*"

As the sky turned Prussian blue, Harry looked back at the farmhouse, her birthplace. The light went on in the living room. She saw the glow through the kitchen window. Fair would be building a fire, since the temperature would dip into the low forties tonight.

What a wonderful man, she thought. Just a good guy. She needed this time to herself. Harry thought best when it was just her and her animals.

Tomahawk, her old Thoroughbred, still in great shape, lifted his lovely head to watch a great blue heron fly high overhead. "*Going late to the nest, aren't you?*"

"*Fishing was too good to leave,*" the large, beautiful bird called down in his harsh voice, so at odds with his body.

Shortro, a five-year-old Saddlebred, given to Harry by Renata de Carlo, a client of Joan Hamilton's at Kalarama Farm, also followed the bird, its huge wingspan impressive as he dipped lower, his beautiful colors more visible now in the twilight. "*Can you imagine flying?*"

"*Sort of,*" the older horse replied. "*I don't think anyone below me would much like it.*"

It took Shortro a minute to get it, then he laughed. Both horses walked over to Harry to have their heads rubbed. Mrs. Murphy, on ex-

cellent terms with all the horses, daintily stepped onto Tomahawk's back.

Harry observed her four-footed friends and thought how fortunate she was to have them and how lucky she was to have her human friends, too.

Last week she'd told Susan the minute she received her results. Tonight all her close friends and even a few close acquaintances had come out to the farm with food.

Even Aunt Tally, at one hundred years of age, arrived with her best friend and former William Woods University classmate, Inez Carpenter, D.V.M. As Inez was a mere ninety-eight, she rubbed this in.

Inez hired Fair shortly after he graduated from Auburn University College of Veterinary Medicine. As one of the nation's best equine vets, specializing in reproduction, she had taught him so very much, and his association with her had also enhanced his own reputation. Inez did not suffer fools gladly. Her unique skills garnered her a reputation in what was once an exclusively male field. Young women vets worshipped Inez as a groundbreaker. Also, throughout her career, Inez was happy to help a young vet who showed promise and was dedicated. While she was as happy guiding a male as a female, she understood the barriers the women faced. Her low-key, sensible approach prevented many a meltdown.

Inez had been going to live with Fair and Harry this year, as she had lost a lot of money in the stock market. Also, age was taking its toll. But Aunt Tally threw a major hissy, so Inez had moved in with her.

In the living room, Harry asked her how she liked rooming with the ultra-rich Tally Urquhart. Inez answered, "I've sat down in the lap of luxury, and I don't want to get up again."

Franny Howard showed up, a surprise. Susan had called her. Harry had bought a set of BF Goodrich all-terrain ten-ply tires the day after her diagnosis. She had not said anything, even though Franny would likely have been helpful. Harry was reticent to talk about herself. She'd talk about the weather, farming, books, horses, world events, but she talked about herself only with Susan, Coop, BoomBoom, and, of course, her husband.

The four tires would have cost $796, and Franny, true to her word,

gave her a preacher's price and knocked off $150. At the farm, this rau-
cous evening, Franny gave Harry all the information she needed if she
wished to join her support group. She offered to pick her up and drive
her, too, if it was a punk day.

Harry's consolation dinner turned into a lively party. Aunt Tally
belted out some tunes from old musicals. Tucker sang along, too. Harry
forgot for a while that her operation would be early Monday morning.

Now, after her walk, she'd had her fill of the starry sky. Even with her
sweater, Harry felt the night air's chill. "Going in."

Tomahawk showed his teeth, smacking his gums. "*Good luck. We love
you.*"

The animals echoed this, all of them: "*We love you.*"

Hearing their murmurs, although not understanding, breathing in
the beauty of the night, tears filled her eyes. She wiped them away, but
they kept coming. "I do so love this life, and I love you all."

15

*T*hat same Friday evening, Al Vitebsk sat at his cleared dining room table. Nita perched across from him, computer up and running. Al used a yellow legal pad. White bankers' boxes were stacked in two large groups. The group to his left had been reviewed. Those remaining on his right would take days.

Big Al kept his own advice. He put his own backup records for Pinnacle Storage into a self-storage unit in Waynesboro. His records, along with so much else at Pinnacle, had been destroyed.

He spent hours at the building with JoJo and his employees, ascertaining what had survived. Surprisingly, even with the intense heat, much of the material in the vaults remained intact, including old handwritten records. Stored outside the vaults in heavy metal trays lined with fire retardant, the floppy disks had melted. All those trays looked like rectangular candleholders filled with an odd wax. Any disks not in the vault suffered a similar fate. The thumb drives, in smaller, thick trays, also had incinerated.

Rental prices depended on the amount of space the records took up as well as the actual physical type of storage. The thick vaults carried the highest price tag. The price decreased according to the reduction of space and the manner of storage. A simple file cabinet was cheap but offered no protection against fire or flood.

Each type of storage carried its own waiver. The file-cabinet policy stated in bold print that those cabinets offered very little protection. Each renter signed a contract.

Big Al painstakingly combed through each signed waiver, which also included the type of stored materials: paper, floppy disks, disks, thumb drives.

Nita entered this on the computer as Big Al read off the information in the waivers. JoJo slept, his head on a fuzzy bear toy. The dog tried to stay awake to help, but hour after hour of two humans sitting opposite each other, with little to no movement, sent JoJo into dreamland.

Nita looked up from the screen. "Two four- by two-foot vault trays, locked. Cantor and Fowler." She named a small, good law firm.

"Right. All records survived."

Reaching into the banker's box, his big hands grabbed a thin folder on top of three fat ones. He flipped it open. "Paula Benton. One four-drawer file cabinet, locks on each drawer." He sighed. "All gone."

"Do we notify her next of kin?" Nita, glasses pinching the bridge of her nose, removed them.

"Yes."

Nita checked Paula's name with a red pen. "We're going to have to draw up form letters for each type of storage unit."

"I know. I know." Al shook his head. "That was a loss. Paula."

"Yes, it was."

"Let's hope some of her stored materials might be on her home computer, but," he read, "yearbooks. Paper files. Some floppy disks."

"Ah." Nita put another red check by Paula's name. "Naturally, honey, I will personalize the form letters. The last paragraph will list what you have on the waivers."

"The crew can help."

By "crew," Big Al meant the four people who worked in the building, their hours meticulously arranged so Pinnacle always had two people in it during business hours. No one worked at night, although there was a cleaning service that vacuumed, mopped up each evening from seven to nine. There wasn't much to do, as Pinnacle Records didn't generate much foot traffic. Still, Big Al wanted the place to be clean. For one thing, he believed dust destroyed records. Even the big vaults collected small amounts of dust. Each time those heavy doors were opened, dust entered. He'd unlock the vaults once a week and stayed while they were cleaned. They received the least traffic. Not many people visited their records or checked them out. If they did, they retired to a twelve-by-ten room with a long table, where they could place their boxes or papers to examine.

A few regulars would cross the threshold about once every two weeks. Big Al and Nita knew Pinnacle Records was not secured to store jewelry, money, or drugs. However, the closely knit couple also knew there had to be drugs or money kept in some of the storage units. There was no way for the couple to inspect what was stored. The contract stated that if a bill had not been paid in three months, they could remove and destroy records. A few times they had to do just that. However, renters with a pile of money or a càche of OxyContin tended to pay on time.

Neither husband nor wife ever went through the stored records. Each felt that would constitute a violation of trust.

There was no way to screen out anyone storing contraband. In Charlottesville, Jamaican drug gangs had moved in. But no Jamaican came to Pinnacle Records. And these days a drug dealer did not faintly resemble the stereotype beloved of cop shows. In fact, one of the biggest drug dealers was an eighty-two-year-old, well-dressed, well-connected matron. She was shrewd, at the center of a good network, and could not be touched. Her social position was unassailable. She had become tremendously rich. No surprise.

Thankfully, since the fire there had been no lawsuits filed against Big Al. Both husband and wife knew if someone had stored money or drugs, they would never file a suit. Accidents happen, and the contracts were clear as to the Vitebsks' liability, but that wouldn't stop an ambulance chaser from convincing someone the Vitebsks had been negligent.

JoJo let out a loud snore.

Nita wistfully said, "I wonder when either of us will sleep that soundly again."

Big Al rested his chin on his fist for a moment. "Whiskey helps."

"You." She smiled at her husband of thirty-two years.

"Babydoll, we'll get through it. It's a great big mess. It will eat up hours and hours of our time. We're still keeping our people on payroll, so it will eat up money, too. Can we rebuild the building? No. Can we rebuild the business, yes, and I will oversee construction of a new building. I think I can build a near-impregnable building unless it gets a direct hit from the Taliban."

"I know you can." She thought for a moment. "But right now I'm tired. I don't want to give up, but I'm lacking in enthusiasm."

After a long pause he said, "Yep."

An hour later, their eyes aching, they finally stopped for the evening.

Before turning off her computer, Nita said, "How many boxes do you have left to go through?"

He counted. "Eleven."

"You finished up the L's."

"Tomorrow we start with the M's, and so many last names start with M or S. Or maybe I just think so, but those are fat folders."

"Well, everyone who paid for the vaults has come out okay. And the others, depends."

It was ten P.M. already. Big Al fixed himself a double whiskey and soda. Nita sipped a little sherry as they slumped in their living room club chairs, so comfortable.

"I'm almost too tired to take a shower." Big Al petted JoJo, who was now on his lap.

"You've taken a shower every night since I married you."

He grinned. "I figure if I smell like a rose, you might be interested."

She laughed at him. "Al, if either one of us loses our sense of humor, then we should worry."

Halfway through his whiskey, relaxing at last, Big Al mused, "Odd, isn't it? Records. A way to hang on to information, but maybe a way to hang on to the past."

"What made you think of that?"

"Paula Benton's contract. She'd written 'Yearbooks, high school! The past.' And she'd come in the week before she died. Signed in. Signed out." He shook his head. "Her past burned up. Once her class is gone many years hence, those old yearbooks would be interesting only to a historian who might want to know something about that particular high school. Life really is fleeting."

"In her case, far too short."

16

"Harry, supper's ready."

Harry, grooming her gray pony, Popsicle, yelled from the barn, "Okay." She kissed Popsicle's nose. "I'll see you tomorrow, and we can go down to the creek, where all the beavers are."

"Good enough."

As she led Popsicle into his stall, Champ, the family's big tricolor collie, rose and stretched, following behind.

"Harry!"

"Mom, I'm coming."

The nurses in the recovery room noticed Harry's eyes moving. She was murmuring something.

Bill Menegatto walked over. Thirty-four, and usefully strong, he said, "She's coming round."

Violet Smith, older and pretty strong herself, bent over. "It's a struggle to fight your way out of anesthesia. Maria Kimball said she thought the operation was a success. She's seen enough of them."

Maria Kimball was Dr. Jennifer Potter's nurse in the operating room. The two made a good team. Maria sensed what Dr. Potter wanted even before she asked. She'd seen the young oncologist open up a patient only to confront a raging cancer, far worse than the tests had indicated. Imperturbable under pressure, Dr. Potter could make split-second decisions. Any specialist in oncology knows one can't always save a patient, but you can generally give that patient more time with their loved ones. With the vicious cancers, such as ovarian, sometimes a doctor could extend a patient's life using a drug like Avastin. A small percentage of people did survive gruesomely aggressive cancers, but most didn't. Dr. Potter took those cancers as a personal affront, as did Maria Kimball. Both women hoped for and worked toward the day when these diseases would be eradicated. If not eradicated, then made less lethal.

Jennifer Potter often discussed cancer with Cory Schaeffer. They pored over cases and new research, as well as not only current litigation involving physicians but legal action aimed at the giant pharmaceutical companies.

Cory believed the nomenclature of cancer was misleading: lung, breast, colon, etc. He felt the disease was maddeningly complex. It might present itself as breast cancer, but did it truly start with those cells? Or was there a trigger elsewhere in the body?

Jennifer Potter believed that cancer created pathways through the body or followed established routes. How and why had yet to be determined, but she believed the answer would be found in gene study.

The two oncologists would agree, disagree, toss about ideas. Both were passionate about their work.

While Cory haunted Annalise's autopsies, Jennifer honed in on studies of the genetic sequence of tumors, a relatively new field.

Harry and others like her were well served by doctors whose life's work was battling cancer.

Feeling as though she were being pulled back by an undertow, Harry knew nothing of this. She heard her mother's voice and smelled Popsicle's wonderful odor, Eau de Cheval, loved by horsemen, less admired by others.

"Champ, Champ, come on, Mom's worried the food will get cold."

The magnificent collie put his cold nose in her hand, and they ran from the barn to the house, snowflakes falling on both their noses.

"Mom." Harry threw open the door, at which time another door opened.

She saw lights overhead, which fuzzed up. She heard voices. They weren't her mother's voice or Champ's. Which way to go?

Meanwhile, sitting outside the recovery room, tired even though they hadn't undergone an operation, Fair and Susan waited.

Susan had already texted Harry's battalion of good friends who had sense enough to leave her husband and best friend in peace. They'd show up one by one or in pairs once they knew the length of her hospital stay or when she was coming home.

The Reverend Herbert Jones, pastor of St. Luke's Lutheran Church, would be one of the first. He'd offered a small prayer service in the chapel off the main nave at St. Luke's for her friends. He didn't know if it was his memory, but he felt there were so many more cancer cases these days. He had inaugurated special prayer sessions and short readings of the Gospels to offer comfort last year. This service expanded to other crises, drawing back people who had drifted away from the church.

Mrs. Murphy, Tucker, and Pewter lay around at home, wondering, worrying. Not until Fair walked through the door would they really know. He wouldn't have to open his mouth. Everything about him would tell the truth, especially his smell. Human sorrow, stress, loss, anger, fear, and happiness gave off signature smells.

With Herculean effort, Harry pulled herself into the present. A moment of feeling lost was overtaken by a wave of nausea. As she hadn't eaten or drunk anything, there was nothing to come up. She felt awful, though. Her mind slowly focused like a camera's lens, spiraling inward very slowly.

At last, she knew where she was and why she was there. She did not, however, know the outcome of her operation.

Tears rolled down Harry's cheeks, not because of the operation but because she'd seen and heard her mother, touched Popsicle, felt Champ by her side. She'd loved them so, and they had loved her. Her mind played tricks on her as she came out of the anesthesia, but her heart had not. If only the creatures, the people you love, could go through all of life with you. But one by one, the Angel of Death leaves his calling card, and those called cross the bridge.

She felt cold but couldn't quite get her fingers to work to pull the sheet tighter.

In the recovery room, Bill leaned over her, did it for her. The nurse looked into her eyes.

She looked right up at him and blinked.

"You're doing just fine." He smiled.

She smiled back and closed her eyes, although not asleep. She felt an exhaustion she'd never felt before. She wondered if her mother, Popsicle, and Champ had visited her to give her hope and direction. Irrational as that thought was, it gave her deep comfort.

"Love never dies," she whispered.

Violet, who knew Harry in passing, was nearby with another patient who was still out cold. She turned. "What?"

Harry opened her eyes. "Violet, love never dies."

Violet put her hand on Harry's shoulder, the warmth flowing through the sheet. "I know."

• • •

As Fair finally came through the door back home, he was grateful to the doctor. In fact, to everyone at Central Virginia Hospital who had helped Harry and who had been so kind to Susan and him.

"He's exhausted, but he isn't scared," Tucker observed.

He pulled a cold Sol out of the fridge, popped the cap, sat in the kitchen, and just drained it. He hadn't eaten. The taste of the crisp beer picked him up a bit.

The two cats sat on the table.

"Girls, I forgot." He rose, opening two cans of Fancy Feast.

"Thank you." Mrs. Murphy minded her manners.

Face in the bowl, Pewter forgot hers.

Then he fed Tucker, who licked his hand.

He thought about drinking another beer, but he needed to get up early in the morning to take Harry home. He took a shower and crawled into bed. Mrs. Murphy snuggled on one side, Pewter on the other.

Tucker curled up on the sheepskin rug on his side of the bed. Fair liked to sink his feet into the thick rug when he first got up.

His head hit the pillow. He was out.

Tucker called up to the cats, *"We've got a lot of work ahead of us."*

Pewter, sleepy herself, replied, *"While she's recuperating, at least she'll stay out of trouble. Easier for us."*

Mrs. Murphy whispered, *"Don't bet on it."*

17

*A*nnalise Veronese was at the Lampo dealership on her day off. A soft spring breeze sent tiny blossom petals across the lot, many falling to outline windshield wiper blades.

Tired of hearing Cory Schaeffer trumpet his electric car, Annalise came to see for herself. She knew a bit about motors, since her father ran a gas station.

The salesman—Sean Hedyt, young, twenty-four, with the latest haircut and sporting the stubble fashionable among young men—was personable and smart enough not to try the hard sell.

No one was going to sell Annalise anything. Show her. She'd make up her mind.

"So, tell me, Sean, how many volts does the battery have?"

"Four hundred forty volts at forty amps. You can cruise for three hundred miles and then the four-cylinder engine will take over."

Annalise knew that at four hundred forty volts, less than one amp would fry a person. "What are the safety measures?"

"Well, the Lampo is in the top third for crash tests. The front end absorbs most of the impact."

"No, I don't mean that. Sorry not to be precise." She smiled at him. "What are the safety measures concerning the power from the battery?"

"There's a bypass safety relay, a series of relays, to shut down power from the battery in the event of a crash."

"And what if corrosion occurs in the relay? Perhaps the battery wouldn't shut down."

Surprised that he was talking to a woman who knew her beans, he swallowed. "Ma'am, that's why you have to follow the service schedule. But you should do that regardless of what kind of car. It's a lot easier to keep things running smoothly than to fix a problem."

"I worked in a gas station as a kid. You're one hundred percent right."

This pleased him. "Would you like a test-drive?"

"Not right now. I'd like more literature to study the car. It's all so new. I want to make sure I understand it, and I'd like you to pop the hood."

"Be glad to." He opened the driver's door, leaned down, and pulled the release to the left of the steering wheel, down low in the driver's footwell by the door.

He turned on the car and then joined her. They both peered down.

"Amazing." Annalise whistled. "Quiet."

"I'll confess that took some getting used to. When I drive, I listen for the engine."

"And you really listen when it's a manual shift, which I love. This is truly amazing. I don't know if the idea will catch hold, but it does seem to me, who loves a big gas engine, that we have to find some compromise." Annalise felt a leaching loss even at the thought of bidding the internal combustion engine goodbye.

She took the brochures, bade Sean goodbye. She liked him, but then, if you don't like a car salesman, you aren't going to buy. Likability ought to be the first quality a dealer looks for in an employee. You can always cram the knowledge about the vehicle in someone's head, but you can't make an individual personable.

She drove her old quirky Saab to the Volkswagen dealer, where she tried a diesel Jetta, which got forty-four miles per gallon on the open road. She could feel a slight diesel thump, but as she hit sixty-five on I-64, the engine felt smoother. Dawson English, the salesman sitting next to her, was relaxed, because the woman could drive. The small machine handled very well, but going from zero to sixty left something to be desired: It took 9.8 seconds.

You can't have it all, she thought to herself.

Dawson said, "You ever drive competitively?"

"Loved it. I'd be happy driving go-carts. I never had the money for the big leagues. My father and I sprinkled garage fairy dust on a few cars. We did pretty good at local tracks. I still like to drive the quarter-mile races, but it's so expensive now."

"Everything is," he agreed. "You're a doctor. I sell a lot of cars to doctors who want good gas mileage but don't want a crossover car. What do you think about healthcare reform?"

"I have no idea how it's going to turn out, but I think the only people who can honestly deliver healthcare reform are doctors, nurses, and the hospital administrators."

18

*P*eering out from under her umbrella, Thadia Martin said, "Rain, rain, go away, little Thadia wants to play." She was waiting for a break in the rain to make a dash for her car.

"So they say," replied Dr. Cory Schaeffer, also under an umbrella, a navy blue one. "How's it going?"

They were in the hospital parking lot, close to the emergency room wing.

"Good. More and more keep coming through the door. Eventually the hospital will see that my rehab groups make money. Then I'll ask for another assistant."

"How many groups?"

"Right now five. I keep them at ten people. It's difficult, because there's such a need—a need for more counselors, more space. I've also been trying acupuncture. Need a special room for that."

"Really?" He took her by the elbow. "Raining harder. Let's step under the overhang."

They walked back to the hospital, ducking under the protective overhang. It was quiet but for the pounding rain. They closed their umbrellas.

Thadia raised her voice to be heard over the downpour. "Acupuncture helps. I don't know why, but it does. I got the idea from reading papers from Fenway Health."

"The organization in Boston?"

"Right. They're cutting-edge on so many things; curing addictive behavior is just one."

"I'll have to look into that." He raised his voice. "How are you doing with the vitamin therapies?"

"Works for some. Not for others."

"This all comes back to body chemistries. Cancer changes the body chemistry. I put some patients on a vitamin regime. I can't say it provides a cure, but it sometimes provides a rollback: a slowing down of the cancer's proliferation. I really will have to look into acupuncture."

"People around here act like we're practicing voodoo." Thadia grimaced.

"If we did, we'd probably have more patients and would definitely have more fun." He reached over, giving her arm a light pinch. "I can see you with a python wrapped around you. Thadia, Voodoo Queen of Crozet."

"Worth a try." She smiled. "Hey, not every patient responds to conventional treatment. If voodoo works, I'll do it."

"Me, too. Paula Benton, before her death, cussed me out."

"Why?"

"I was getting to that. She didn't say I was practicing voodoo, but she did say she didn't think central Virginia was prepared for alternative treatments and therapies."

"If she meant people's attitudes, she was right," Thadia responded.

"I don't know. People aren't as backward as they might appear. Paula told me to stick to surgery and let other people worry about what comes after. I took offense at that."

"Tear her a new one?"

"No. I told her if she wanted to go toe to toe with me, she should go to med school and emerge with her M.D. Then it would be a fair fight."

"Bet that pissed her off."

"Did."

"Thought you liked Paula. She was good-looking," Thadia went fishing.

"She was." Cory stared off into the distance for a moment, then snapped back. "I enjoyed working with her. I didn't like when she'd question me. Nurses don't question doctors. She thought she knew more than she did." He shivered. The temperature was dropping as fast as the rain. "But she was good."

"Nosy." Thadia couldn't resist a little jab.

He shrugged. "Speak no ill of the dead."

"I guess." Thadia spoke louder due to the downpour. "I don't know why she was so opposed to trying new things, but the one thing she said, which I thought had some merit, is that we might give people false hope with alternative treatments. They haven't been rigorously tested and don't conform to the scientific method."

"Some do. I have reams of tests with control groups for new drugs, like Crizotinib, which can be used to shrink lung cancer tumors. So what if the test group is only five hundred patients instead of fifty thousand? It may be a life preserver in a stormy sea. If someone is desperate and has the genetic anomaly for which Crizotinib is effective, why shouldn't they try new approaches? As long as patients understand it's a new approach. Studies, too. If a patient agrees to this. Good."

Wryly, Thadia remarked, "My clientele can help you there. They're so used to popping pills or sticking needles in their arms, they'll volunteer."

"Body chemistry." Cory spoke louder, too. "I had this discussion with old Izzy Wineberg."

"He's getting old."

"He ran the five-K, in good order. I'll give him credit for that. He's always telling me what it was like before this hospital was built."

"He does vacation in the past. Anyway, what was the discussion?" Thadia leaned toward Cory, the picture of receptiveness.

"We were talking about how each patient is an individual. He was complaining that so many young doctors miss the whole person. He's right. This started with us joking about how two different bodies, if opened, would not conform to the drawings in *Gray's Anatomy*. One person might have their heart on the right side of their body. Another could have one less rib than the normal number, or two more. The human body is variable, and so is chemistry. In fact, I think blood chemistry is the most variable of all."

"I know. Many of us are missing something, usually serotonin."

"Cocaine or alcohol supplies it."

"Right. It's a bit more complicated. Family background factors into it, the person's outlook on life, how much responsibility they're willing to accept for their actions."

"Back to Paula. Did she say why, other than false hope, she opposed a lot of what you're doing?" Cory inquired.

"She thought it was wrong to charge for treatments that haven't yet been proven effective."

"What?"

"Her argument was if someone can kick their habit, it may not be because acupuncture or whatever helped. It might be something else, since there's a medley of treatments and I can't isolate one from another."

"I don't know what got into her." Cory peered out from under the overhang. "This rain isn't going to end anytime soon."

"No." Thadia reopened her umbrella, preparing to go to her car. "None of it."

"Meaning?"

"Hostility toward new methods."

"Ah." He reopened his umbrella with a whoosh. "We have to keep keeping on."

As Cory splashed through the puddles, now all over the paved parking lot, for the rain was unrelenting, he had the strange sensation that he was being followed. When he peered out from under his umbrella, though, he saw no one. He opened the door to his Lampo, keeping his left arm outside, then turned, closing his umbrella. His left arm was soaked. As he closed his door he thought he heard another door close nearby, but he couldn't see anyone behind the wheel of a car.

He shook off the odd feeling, started the silent machine, and drove home.

19

*T*uesday, Harry sat in the tack room. It was 7:30 A.M. The sound of horses eating from their feed buckets made her feel all was right in the world. Mrs. Murphy, Tucker, and Pewter patrolled the aisles. The possum, Simon, after a night's rambling, was asleep in his nest in the hayloft. The great horned owl, another night creature, slept in the cupola. Matilda, the blacksnake who wintered in the back of the hayloft, burrowed in old hay that wouldn't be used for feed, was slowly waking.

Fortunately, Harry had no need for a drain tube. The incision was low, two inches long. Tonight she'd change the dressing with Fair's help. She refused to take painkillers. It hurt, but not so much that she couldn't function. The greatest irritation was not being able to throw hay or lift anything more than ten pounds, as she might rip her stitches. Her focus now was in healing fast, getting the stitches out, and getting back to her old routine. She could, however, still use a hoe. She could mow or ladle out sweet feed. These activities improved her mood. She didn't feel completely useless.

"I'm *going back in the tack room.*" Tucker felt the aisleway was free of varmints, thanks to her presence.

The cats greatly enjoyed the sounds of scurrying-away mice, for they could hear their little claws, and they took full credit for the intimidation. After all, whoever heard of a corgi catching mice?

Seneca Falls Library
47 Cayuga Street
Seneca Falls, N.Y. 13148

"She's fine," Pewter called over her shoulder.

Tucker paid no attention, slipping through the animal door in the closed tack room door.

"Hello." Removing a bit from a bridle, Harry smiled.

"Mother, you should pull a jacket over your sweater. It's chilly."

Harry had no idea of her dog's concern, but she reached down to scratch those glossy ears.

A small electric wall unit kept the tack room warm. Harry dialed it on at night before retiring, keeping the temperature at sixty-two degrees. A sweater kept her warm enough. The frosts had vanished right around April 15, along with everyone's money. By mid-May, the night temperatures hovered in the high forties, low fifties, although occasionally a night could get cold. In the morning, a light frost would silver the western side of the hills, the northernmost pastures, only to evaporate when the sun at last reached them.

Today the mercury would climb into the middle sixties, perfect for outdoor work. Stitches or not, Harry was determined to knock out some chores. A farmer doesn't make money sitting on her nether regions.

What Harry had not foreseen was how tired she would get, even at the beginning of the day. She forced herself to keep going, having been up since 5:30 A.M. Fair had an early-morning emergency: A horse roared through a fence, cutting up its leg. So many horse injuries were fence-related.

She reached into the small refrigerator and pulled out a Coca-Cola, gulping it down.

"I don't know what's the matter with me."

Tucker wisely noted, *"Your body's been under assault. Sleep heals. Why don't you go back to bed?"*

The phone rang.

"Hello."

"Harry." Big Mim's voice sounded startlingly clear. "How are you?"

"I'm fine. How good of you to call."

"Well, I've been through it. As soon as Jim and I return, I'll visit, but do take care, and don't try to do too much. You're bad that way." In her mid-seventies, called the "Queen of Crozet" behind her back, Big Mim had known Harry since she was born.

"Well, I'm bored already, but I won't be stupid. If I don't take care, the healing will take that much longer."

"What about chemo and radiation?"

"A short course of radiation. Start in two weeks."

"Just get it over with, and don't be surprised if you get burned. Radiation does burn."

"How's Austria?"

"Beautiful, as always. We're in the Alps now. We stayed in Vienna for a week. Really, it is the most civilized city, and whenever I return I wonder why I stayed away for so long. However, I've discovered my German isn't as serviceable as I'd hoped. That's what I get for not taking a brushup course. Once you're up and running, check on my horses. I know my team does a fabulous job, just fabulous, but you're so good that way."

"Thank you. Fair was over there last week."

"No problem, I hope." Big Mim's voice rose.

"No. He wanted to check on Mind Game's foal," Harry said, mentioning one of Big Mim's best flat-racing mares who had foaled in late January. The sire, Tapit, stood at Gainesway Farm in Kentucky for fifty thousand dollars. While that stud fee was completely out of reach for Harry, Big Mim could easily swing it. A shrewd breeder, Big Mim knew Tapit to be a bargain. She also knew, given the percentage of winners to the percentage of runners, the Tapit-sired stud fee would climb once the depression was over. "Growing like a weed and so correct, Big Mim. Breathtaking."

"If she has her mother's mind and her father's constitution, then I've got everything. If ever a horse was aptly named, it's Mind Game. To change the subject, how is my aunt?"

"As you would expect."

"I see." Big Mim lived in fear of what Aunt Tally would do next, since the old lady felt at age one hundred that the rules of propriety no longer applied to her.

Actually, Tally had felt that at twenty as well.

"What time is it there?" Harry asked.

"One-thirty."

"You sound clear as a bell," she marveled.

"When cellphones work, they are incredible. Well, Sugar, do take care. Jim and I are thinking about you. Oh, one more thing. Miranda."

Big Mim was referring to Miranda Hogendobber, the woman with whom Harry formerly worked at the post office. In many ways, Miranda was like a second mother to Harry. The good woman, a contemporary of Big Mim's, was down in South Carolina, where her sister was dying of cancer. What she thought would be a short trip had turned into an extended stay. The breast cancer had proved so aggressive, it baffled Didee's doctors.

"Spoke to her last night," Harry said. "I don't think her sister has long to live."

"Oh, dear. Well, I'm sorry to hear that, but Didee has had her three-score and ten and more, as have I. If we go, it's in the nature of things. If *you* go, it's far too early, so *do* what the doctor says."

"Yes, ma'am." Harry said goodbye. She knew once Big Mim came home, she'd watch Harry like a hawk. The elegant older woman had been a friend of Harry's mother, and would consider it her duty to make sure Harry behaved.

●　●　●

As Harry considered her good fortune at having such wonderful friends, Dr. Cory Schaeffer arrived early at work. Like Dr. MacCormack, his office was in another of the modern buildings off the main circular drive. He'd often arrive early to enjoy the quiet. Much as he loved his children, three of them at the breakfast table could wear a guy down.

He didn't flick on the waiting room lights, not wanting anyone to think the office was open for business. After unlocking the front door, he strode down the short hall to his private office. Putting his key in the lock, he was surprised the door was unlocked.

With concern, he pushed it open. His office, the desk, the shelves, looked just as immaculate as when he had left them. Breathing relief, he thought he'd locked his private office door, but perhaps he'd been interrupted somehow and forgot.

He walked behind his desk and stopped cold. In the center of his specially made desk—to the tune of $5,355—rested the scrubbed base of a skull. He looked around. Except for this macabre offering, all was in order. He touched the bone: cool, smooth.

Quickly he swiveled over to his computer and switched it on. He typed in the password to his private files; a busty babe appeared, then up came the lists. Also undisturbed.

Sweat beads appeared on his forehead. He reached into his coat pocket, pulled out a cotton handkerchief, and wiped his brow.

Someone had been in his office. Did he or she have a key? He got up and ran to the front door. No sign of forced entry. Three people had keys: himself, his assistant, and his part-time nurse for in-house procedures. But then he remembered there was a fourth: The cleaning service had one. Its employees were bonded.

Someone had easily entered his office and placed a skull fragment on his desk. That someone knew Cory could not call the sheriff's department.

He grabbed the edge of the desk to steady himself. He was shaking like a naked man in Antarctica.

20

*I*n the basement under the westernmost spoke of the Central Virginia Medical Complex, Harry, Toni Enright, and Franny Howard stood outside the room where the cancer support group met.

Voice low, Harry asked the other two, "What does the group do when someone dies?"

Toni replied, "We go to the funeral, of course." She also lowered her voice. "It's obvious that some of our number won't be with us for long. We do what we can, and we draw closer together because it's a reminder to everyone."

Franny then added, "Babs Hatcher, as I'm sure you noticed, hasn't long."

"I did, but she seems . . . settled. I can't think of another word."

Toni nodded. "We've lost two of our number in the last year. That's why we could take you. Luckily, you should be around for a long time, but Babs's ovarian cancer, well, you know. She's as prepared as one can be, and she sets an example for everyone else."

Harry, who said very little in the group other than what her cancer was, asked, "Toni, have you had cancer?"

"No. Central Virginia encourages the nurses with oncology experience to be with a group. We all do it, and it's a part of my job that I love."

"Do any doctors ever come by?" Harry inquired.

"If the group asks, they do. Or if a new treatment is available. The doctor gives us a talk about it. There's so much happening with new drugs, new ideas, one person can't keep up with it."

"It's a nice group of people." Harry turned to Franny. "Thank you for telling me about it."

Toni said, "Ladies, I have to go. Harry, I hope we see you again."

Before Harry could reply, the next door opened. Laughter spilled out from a conference room into the hall. Thadia Martin walked out.

"Harry Haristeen? The real Mary Minor Haristeen, attack forward for Crozet High?"

It took Harry a moment to recognize Thadia. "Thadia, yes, yes, it's me."

Thadia, never one for subtlety, asked, "Are you all right?"

Obviously, she knew the cancer support group met at the same time as one of her drug rehab groups.

"I am now."

"Good. There are vitamin therapies, you know, that can help people who are recovering from cancer. Well, they can help a lot of things. I get a lot of my people on these new strategies."

Toni, shoulders tensed, interrupted, "Thadia, what works for recovering addicts and alcoholics will not necessarily work for cancer survivors." She forced a professional smile. "With all due respect."

Thadia ignored Toni, spoke directly to Harry. "Dr. Schaeffer is really on the cutting edge."

Harry quipped, "As a surgeon, I expect he is."

Toni pointedly said, "Thadia, if you'll excuse us."

Toni then walked back into the room, hand under Harry's elbow. She shut the door behind her. Two other group members, in deep discussion, sat together. Franny followed in, too.

"She's not your fav." Harry smiled devilishly.

Toni scrunched up her face. "No. She's so damned pushy."

Franny supported Toni's assessment. "That never gets a woman far in these parts, and the wonder of it is that Thadia was born and raised a Virginian."

"Some people lack the patience for the dance of politeness." Harry laughed. "Even back in school, Thadia was a bulldozer. She got away with it as far as she did because she's pretty."

"Amazing she kept her looks after all those years of self-abuse." Franny folded her arms across her chest.

Franny changed the subject. "Toni, how's your rattletrap doing?"

Toni laughed. "I'm going to trade it in." She held up her hands when she saw the excitement on Harry's face. "Don't know yet, Harry."

"Have you seen Alicia's new Mustang? G-o-rgeous!"

"As is Alicia," Franny added. "Before I forget, Toni, who has taken Paula's place in the evening support group?"

"Violet Smith. She's not an oncology nurse, but we're shorthanded. Everyone is. Here we are, this unbelievable medical complex, and there's no money for hiring. I'm sure Will"—Toni named the hospital administrator, Will Archer—"can find money for a star, but I'll give him credit, he hasn't hired any new doctors. I hope we pull out of this economic nosedive fast."

Franny, ever the shrewd businesswoman, simply said, "It's a W dive."

"What?" Harry leaned toward her.

"They're calling it a double dip, but that's not really accurate. It's a W. First, you go down one side of the W. We come back up a bit, right? Then you go down again and the second side of the W is a hell of a lot worse than the first. The forecasters, the government, no one wants to even hint at it, because that will stall out the tiny recovery we're experiencing now. Anyway, let's not talk about that. I can't stand it. Back to Paula's group. Are they all right?"

Toni shrugged. "As best they can be. Here we are, trained to deal with such matters, and she goes." Toni snapped her fingers. "No one expected that."

"She's missed." Franny then handed Harry a bag of catnip. "I promised. Sorry, I didn't have any when you came in to get your tires. Said I would, but sometimes it's one damn thing after another."

"Thank you." Harry opened the plastic container for a hit of high-powered catnip. "The kids will love it.

"Toni, did Paula have any enemies?"

Franny rolled her eyes. "Harry."

"Well, Toni worked with her. Who knows what happens at the hospital."

"Thadia." Toni uttered the name.

"Why?" Harry asked, and now Franny was interested.

"Oh, the usual drama with her. She came to me after a meeting once—everyone had left, thank God—and she wanted to know what I knew about Paula and Cory Schaeffer. I told her the truth. Nothing. But she went on and on. She was convinced they were having an affair. They weren't. I think I knew Paula as well as anyone around here, and she wasn't interested in Cory Schaeffer. For one thing, she wanted time to herself."

"The divorce?" Franny said.

"More or less. She was over it. That's why she moved here, but she said so many times, 'I never really took care of me.' She was focusing on herself—not in a self-centered way, in a healing way. Paula wasn't having an affair. She didn't want one, and Cory wasn't her type. Paula liked manly men. You know, linemen, farmers, garage mechanics."

"Strange," Harry replied, "that Thalia concocted their affair."

"I'm telling you, Thadia was fuming. I told her to calm down. If she wasn't such a chemical mess, I'd have given her a hit of Jack Daniel's Black."

Harry and Franny laughed at this, then Franny said, "Double shot."

"She could probably knock back two and keep going," Harry remarked. "Even in high school, Thadia could drink everyone under the table. I remember once I asked her if she liked Saint Anne's, and she said, 'The drugs are better than at Crozet High.' I mean, she could be funny when she wasn't vicious."

"Chemistry. I hope the day comes when we can identify in childhood those people who are prone to alcoholism and drug addiction." Toni lowered her voice. "Look, the truth is some people can drink and some can take drugs in moderation. This idea that one toot or toke and you're captive to the weed or coke is bullshit, and we all know it." She held up her hands. "Okay. There may be a few people out there who are lost with one swig. People don't immediately turn into a raging cokehead, so they think they're all right, so they drink more, they toot more, and then the trouble begins. We all know the road to ruin after that. If we'd just tell people the truth, but you know if a doctor publicly said what I just did, or a sheriff, they'd lose their jobs."

"You're right about that. Nothing should ever disturb American hypocrisy." Franny deplored the current state not just of affairs but of behavior.

"Wonder if there was more to Paula setting off Thadia."

"Oh, Harry, people are their most irrational about sex and about their children. Thadia kept saying she was going to confront Paula. I told her to drop it. No good would come of it. Plus, Paula wasn't sleeping with Cory. End of story."

"Ever notice how some people can't learn?" Franny mused. "Look, I give Thadia credit for cleaning up. Other than that, she's still a two-legged disaster."

"Yeah, but at least we didn't elect her to public office." Harry grinned as the other two laughed.

Less guarded than usual, Toni threw this out: "Actually, Cory is having an affair, but Thadia, who is so crazy about him, has missed it completely."

Harry's jaw dropped. "You're not going to tell me?"

"No. It will keep you busy." Toni slapped her on the back, then left the room.

"She's got your number." Franny laughed.

21

ud and John Benton had selected real estate agent Julie Bendel to market their daughter's house. The next day, Julie asked Harry to accompany her to the site.

Julie Bendel, a petite fireball, put a special lock that realtors use on the door. She liked the house, as did Harry, who'd never walked all through it. Even in this difficult market, it would be an easy sell. Paula's remodeling preserved the integrity of the farmhouse while enhancing it. She kept the old wavy handblown glass in the windows, but upstairs in the main bedroom she'd installed a large skylight, which let the light pour in. Wisely, she'd also installed louvers for the skylight, to shut off the burning sun in the summer. The floors had all been refinished, revealing rich variations in the color of the heart pine. The marble countertops in the kitchen, Paula's one concession to flashiness, brought the room to life.

"You okay to go to the barn?" Julie asked Harry.

"Yeah, I made myself go back there when we packed up the house."

"I wanted you to look at this with a horseman's eyes. You're conservative with money, and whoever buys this will probably be a middle-income person. I think it's a great property for horses."

"Is." Harry walked in step with Julie.

Before reaching the barn, Julie stopped. "The distance from the back door of the house to the barn door is enough to keep the odors at bay but not so far that a trip in bad weather is a mess. I see that as a selling point."

"Sounds about right." Harry mentally measured off the distance, which she figured to be about fifty yards. "But if whoever buys this has good stable practices, it isn't going to smell, anyway. Keep it really clean, toss a bit of cedar shavings in with your bedding."

"I'll remember that." Julie pushed back the big sliding doors as they entered the barn. "So?"

Harry, peering into the stalls, walked along the center aisle. "Packed earth. That's what most stall bases are, but if the new owner wants to make their life easier, he or she will dig down about a foot and a half, put in various layers of stone, various sizes, I mean, just like a layer cake. The top six inches pack down with masonry sand. Put Equigrid over that. Expensive. Fill it with masonry sand."

"Why?"

"It keeps the horse from digging holes. Takes a lot of time to keep filling them back up, but you have to. If you don't, it's not good for a horse to stand on uneven ground. Out in the pasture, an animal can keep moving. In a stall, they can't. Think what you'd feel like if you stood for six or eight hours with one foot in a hole."

"Gotcha."

"The rough-hewn heavy oak boards for the stalls and the dividers are great. Originally, marine oil was slapped on them. That's why they aren't brittle, even though no horses have been in here for years. If the new owner power-washes everything, lets it dry, then reapplies marine oil, it will be good. The only real expense is the floors, if they want to incur it. You can put down the Equigrid yourself, but it runs around one thousand dollars for a twelve-foot-by-twelve-foot stall. The other thing, and this really is important: Have the new owner check the wiring. If it's old, rewire the whole structure. So many fires are caused by faulty wiring, and there's nothing more horrible than hearing horses scream as they burn to death."

"God, Harry." Julie's face registered dismay.

"Well, one has to think about these things. If you take animals into your care, it should be done properly. I mean, would you have children and not feed them, clothe them, make sure they sleep in safe bed-rooms?"

"After five children, you know the answer." Julie smiled.

"I can understand a woman having the first one; it's the second and the third I question." Harry poked her.

"You sort of forget the pain in between the deliveries. Anything else?"

"No. It's a serviceable barn, set so the wind hits the back. The fences need painting, but they're in good order. This is a very attractive hold-ing for a horseman."

"Okay. Next. Ready?"

"Yeah." Harry followed Julie into the potting shed.

"Now, she used the old tack room and one stall to make this. How difficult would it be to convert it all back?"

"The tack room is pretty much undisturbed. All Paula did was take down the saddle racks and bridle brackets. She left the wooden floors and the small baseboard heater. What must come down is that plastic barrier she put up on the stall wall. She also cut a door into the side of the tack room. That should be filled in with heavy oak to match the original wood. If you can't find rough-hewn oak, they'll need thick pressure-treated pine."

Julie opened the door into the area where Harry found Paula. "Okay?"

"Julie, I made myself come here. I'm fine."

"Sorry." Julie stepped down into the potting shed. "Earthen floor."

"Good. A new owner won't have to rip anything up if they want to turn this back into a stall, and if they don't, it's a nice little shed. You have to remove the glass out of the back stall door, obviously. And if they keep it for a potting shed, no need to fill in the door to the tack room."

Paula, a practical person herself, had kept the outside Dutch doors. She pinned back the top one, putting glass into the opening, which helped her force her bulbs, such as hyacinth. Four evenly spaced rows filled the space so the pots received lots of light.

A two-foot-wide piece of planed pine ran from one end of the stall to the other, facing the back door. As the wood was smooth, Paula could use it as a makeshift desktop. It was here that Harry had found the well-liked nurse.

"I wonder why she didn't put shelves under this," Julie noted.

"Probably didn't need them. She had plenty of room, and how many bulbs do you need to force if you aren't a commercial nursery?" But Julie had piqued Harry's curiosity, so Harry knelt down to peer under the wide top. "Hey, everyone missed this."

Julie knelt down, too. "Looks like an old cartridge box."

"It is."

On her hands and knees, Harry grabbed the sides to back out with it. "Not heavy."

Once out from under, Harry and Julie popped open the wooden box. Most old cartridge boxes had a wooden top the same thickness as the sides. Affixed with a simple latch, it kept the ammunition dry. Given the weight of cartridges, these boxes needed to be sturdy. Artillery ammunition was so heavy it took two men to carry those boxes. Even a Remington box like this, fully loaded, took muscle to move.

Inside were a few bulbs in Ziploc bags. A white tab marked each bag, identifying the fall bulb.

"What in the hell is this?" Julie pulled out a yellow cylinder that was more than a foot in length, with perhaps a ten-inch diameter. The thickness of one cylinder wall left a somewhat narrow interior.

"Here." Harry took the cylinder and flipped the metal fastenings on each side, designed to keep the top as tight as possible.

The inside of the cylinder was a thick wall to keep the contents cold.

"Harry, what is it?"

"Breeders use this to ship semen. It's filled with liquid nitrogen, which, as you know, is incredibly cold. The semen is in narrow straws. You overnight it to wherever. Semen loses motility pretty rapidly if improperly preserved. When you figure that some stud fees can run a hundred thousand dollars or more, the container is critical." Harry paused. "Not to belabor it, but Thoroughbred people still use live covers, so they rarely have need of a cylinder. These containers are used by some of the Warmblood breeders, Saddlebreds, quarter horse breeders who are at the top. People want to AI mares, hence the cylinders. The

Saddlebred, quarter horse, and various Warmblood registers do not demand a live cover."

"I had no idea."

"No reason why you would, Julie. I just know about it because of Fair."

"Right."

At that moment, Harry wished she had her animals with her. Something was off-kilter here. She trusted their senses more than her own.

"Paula was no horseman."

"No, but she was a nurse. Is it possible to ship human semen this way?"

"Well, I'm sure you could. I don't know a whole lot about that. Fair and I use the old-fashioned method."

At this, both women cracked up, then Julie said, "Always worked for me." Then she studied the cylinder, holding it in her hands. "Could someone run a business on the sly?"

"Sending out stolen semen?"

"Yes. Isn't it a whole lot of paperwork, tests, endless crap, for a woman who wants to become pregnant without marriage? Or without a man, I should say?"

"I think it is, but Julie, Paula was not a reproductive specialist. I know people can fool you, but I don't think she was the type of person to be involved in the black market."

"What was her area?"

"Surgical nurse."

"Could you send tissue samples in this?"

"I don't see why not, but there's no reason to use a cylinder used for horses. And given technology, doctors can send pictures of tissue to another doctor halfway around the world."

Julie closed the lid. "This business about artificial insemination. Who do you ask for, Brad Pitt?"

Harry laughed. "I'd ask for Henry Kissinger. Imagine the mind."

They both laughed. Julie knelt down to push the cartridge box back. Harry knelt with her.

"Think her parents want the bulbs?"

"No. Julie, if the farm is sold by late summer, the new owner can plant these. If not, I'll come back and put them in. Do you mind if I take the cylinder home? I'd like Fair to see it."

"Not at all. It's a sure bet I won't be using it." Julie inquired, "Is it easy to get one of those?"

"If you know anyone with a good stallion, it is. And this area is filled with reasonably priced good stallions. Smallwood is just down the road." Harry cited Phyllis Jones's establishment, noted for the now-deceased Castle Magic, but his male progeny continued the blood.

Show people particularly flocked to Smallwood, but central Virginia had something for everyone. After all, Secretariat had been bred right outside Richmond.

As the two women walked back through the growing grass, the afternoon sun brought the mercury up to sixty-eight degrees. There was a lovely breeze, and Harry felt that tingle, that challenge to figure out a mystery. Why would Paula Benton have a shipping cylinder?

Toni Enright had tweaked Harry by telling her Dr. Schaeffer was having an affair, but Harry rarely became intrigued by sexual peccadilloes: They were all too common. But this intrigued her.

22

Driving rock blared from the speaker system, but it still didn't drown out all the grunts and heavy breathing. At six in the morning, the serious bodybuilders and athletes hit Heavy Metal Gym. Some people, like Harry, could work out early. Others, needing time for stiff muscles to awaken and warm up, as well as their minds, had to wait until lunch hour or after work. But there's no way for a hard-core workout at lunch, so those people with a goal beyond simple fitness had to overcome the morning fatigue, much of it mental, to rev up and start moving iron.

Noddy Cespedes, a former successful bodybuilder now in her forties, walked with Harry between the rows of sweating gym members. "How long before you can perform your usual farm chores, anything that involves lifting?"

"Three more weeks. No muscle was cut. Well, obviously not. It was breast tissue. Dr. Potter advised giving myself time. The incision is only two inches."

"Jennifer took care of Mom," Noddy stated. "Do what she tells you. But you're in good shape. You don't need to work out unless you have specific goals."

"I do. I know my radiation, which starts tomorrow, will make me tired. If I can do something new that would help me not lose muscle,

I'd like to do that. I need to push myself through this. And once I'm a hundred percent, I will really need to play catch-up on some farm chores. I can't afford to be weak."

The other trainer was Kodiak Jenkins. That was his real name, for his parents were old hippies and thought Kodiak was a great name. It was, but anyone over forty hearing it always took a moment to adjust. Kodiak, also a competitive bodybuilder, stood behind a handsome young fellow on the bench press. When the kid pushed the bar to its height, Kodiak watched carefully. The young man, perhaps late twenties, not well built, already fat around his middle, would be transformed if he stuck to the program. Both trainers respected anyone who worked in an office, anyone going soft, who decided to reverse the inevitable slide to obesity.

Since Noddy could bench-press two hundred pounds and sported gorgeous triceps in perfect balance with her biceps, the male body-builders and athletes listened to her just as they listened to Kodiak. The gleaming trophies in her office bore testimony to her skill.

One thing both Harry and Noddy had learned about men was that if you prove yourself, the sniping and disrespect usually ends. This is not necessarily the case with other women. Sometimes it is, sometimes it isn't.

Harry, though well built, had never lifted weights. Her wonderful body came courtesy of tossing sixty-pound alfalfa bales, riding twelve-hundred-pound horses, and sometimes having to hold them—which means you have twelve-hundred pounds in your hands. A farmer's work develops a strong body, unless that farmer hits the bottle or eats too much fried food. Harry shied away from both, although she sure missed her mother's fried chicken.

"What brought you to Heavy Metal instead of a fitness center?" Noddy asked.

"I've seen you in a bikini, and I can't envision myself in a group of people all wearing leotards. I'm just not the type." Harry smiled. "You know the one thing that really bothers me? First of all, I feel guilty saying this, because I really loved my grandmother, but the back of her arms got a little flabby. She wasn't really overweight or anything, but this little swing of flab. I will do whatever it takes to avoid that. I don't care if I have to do five hundred push-ups a day."

"Not that many." Noddy smiled back. "But if you can work up to one hundred, terrific. Like sit-ups, push-ups you can do anywhere, and I tell ·you, they work. Eventually you'll get to the point where you can do one-armed push-ups. I truly believe aging is a disease and you can fight it."

"I do, too. My horses taught me that." Harry watched Jim O'Hanran, a beautifully proportioned man, sixty-three, pull down a frightening load of weights on the lat machine.

He wore a bandanna around his forehead to soak up the sweat and terry-cloth wristbands for the same purpose.

Heavy Metal Gym catered to dedicated types. The other gyms in Charlottesville, all good, had tai chi classes, Pilates, all manner of things, as well as special Nautilus cambered weight machines. Again, all wonderful stuff. At Heavy Metal, you pounded York barbells, the best of the best in weights. If a York barbell said twenty pounds, it was twenty pounds, perfectly balanced. One can generally assess a gym by its equipment. Serious: York barbells. Fun and good: everything else.

Five-K winner Mac Dennison labored under the Smith machine. The decades-old Smith machine focuses on quads, a difficult muscle to work, one requiring total concentration and megawatts of energy. Quad exercises could make you puke, they were so tough.

Noddy was intrigued by Harry's statement. "What did horses teach you about aging?"

"Mother hunted on a dark bay Thoroughbred mare until the mare was twenty-five. That's old. But Hedy—the mare, Mom named her for Hedy Lamarr—never really aged, because even in the off-season Mom would walk her out, a little trotting. God, how I tried to keep up with my pony, Popsicle. But Hedy never sat down and grew a fat butt. That's my point."

"It's the truth. Use it or lose it. So tell me this, what's the long-term goal?"

Harry hesitated, for she didn't want to seem vain. "I turned forty last August. No Botox. No face-lift. Can't afford it, anyway. But I don't want to sag. Farm chores don't work your entire body the way you all work here. I walk, bend, throw hay. If I'm going to fight old age, I need more than that. I'll live with wrinkles. I won't live with fat."

"Harry, I'd love to work with you. We aren't expensive. This is a basic gym. But will you allow me to call Jennifer? First of all, I like her so much for what she did for Mom. It'd be good for you to talk to her. And I want to make sure I am doing right by you, what medications you might be on, your radiation schedule. Just think what would happen to Crozet if I messed you up." Noddy laughed.

"Oh, Noddy, as long as Aunt Tally and Big Mim are upright, Crozet is fine. But sure, go ahead."

Noddy walked to her small office, her trophies on the shelf and plaques on the wall. Harry kept in step.

"I don't know if you know, but a lot of the doctors and nurses from Central Virginia, Martha Jefferson, and University of Virginia Medical Hospital work out here. I'm sure glad for the money, but with what they spent on construction—especially Central Virginia, since Martha Jefferson and UVA Hospital have run out of land—you'd think they'd build a huge gym for their personnel. Make life easier."

"Never thought about that."

"Paula Benton was a regular. Can't believe she died." Noddy paused. "She'd come in with Annalise Veronese—who is serious, let me tell you—and Toni Enright. No distractions. Those girls hit the iron. Paula would say she needed the energy boost after working with people all day. Annalise says she doesn't have that problem."

•   •   •

At that early hour, as Harry and Noddy talked, Annalise Veronese carefully cut into the body of an eighteen-year-old man. Cory Schaeffer assisted. While Annalise had staff, she always called Cory if someone requested an autopsy of a patient who died of cancer. Cory, if his schedule permitted, rarely missed the opportunity to study the disease's effects. Also, to remind himself of how organs looked at different stages of a human's life regardless of cause of death. Again, abuse was a factor, but an eighteen-year-old man—those organs should be textbook-perfect, healthy.

Annalise expertly removed kidney, liver, heart. Cory carefully packed them in large light blue shipping containers. Each of these organs would save someone else's life. There was a desperate need for them. People died waiting.

Nothing that could be useful was left. She carefully replaced the skullcap, meticulously pulling the hair over the cut line. The top of a human skull, properly sawed, lifted off just like a cap.

This young man would be traditionally buried, so that line must not be visible. She also put a tiny little thread through each eyelid, fastening it down, for she'd removed his eyes, again something that would help another human in need. But the last thing a family member needed to see was an empty eye socket if for some reason the lid rolled back. Annalise took no chances.

Once finished, she left the body on the table. Her assistants would be in within the hour. They would again wipe him down, put him on the gurney, and deposit him in the hospital morgue. For most autopsies, the corpse was carefully washed down before, as well. If foul play was suspected, this couldn't be done, nor could anything else be done, until law enforcement people had checked the body. Even so, not being doctors, they could and did miss things—a tiny little needle pinprick, for instance.

Her first year on the job, Annalise performed an autopsy on a healthy man. No apparent cause of death. She found a needle mark at the base of his skull. Someone, with supreme skill, had hit the exact right spot to drive a long, sturdy needle up into his brain.

Annalise was very observant.

As she and Cory washed up, she said, "For the last years—ever since the helmet law was passed and the cops cracked down—we've had a hard time. There weren't enough organs for those in need. Now that kids are doing this car surfing, things are picking up."

"Yeah. People mourn the kid, of course." Cory tossed the long rubber gloves into the stainless-steel trash can. "Yet someone else rejoices because they've got a chance to live."

"I guess it's the old saw: One man's loss is another man's gain. Still, you'd think these kids would have more sense."

"Part of human development. Those crazy years between fifteen and twenty. Sixteen seems to be the worst. Kids, especially boys, take really stupid chances."

"Never was any good at psychology. Hated taking it, too." Annalise toweled off. "Not one thing can be quantified, but that's another discussion. Did you ever think why it's the boys who die?"

"Testosterone."

"There's a convenient explanation, but you can't prove that, either. Besides, Cory, hormonal arguments have been used for about a century and a half to keep women disenfranchised. Let's not do the same thing to men. Two wrongs don't make a right."

"No," he thoughtfully replied. "But three will get you back on the freeway."

Laughing, they left the room, stepping into the small anteroom near Annalise's office. She didn't need another larger plush office, as did other doctors. Annalise's patients never set up appointments.

"I think the reason boys and young men die as foolishly as they do is a man has to prove he's a man. A woman has nothing to prove. So all one man or a group of boys have to do is taunt one another. You know, he wants to drink white wine and one of the guys at the table says, 'Would you like a box of tampons with that?' That sort of thing. So it's the way men control other men. Make them insecure, and they'll really do stupid things." Annalise put her hands on her hips.

Cory considered this, his handsome features composed. "I agree, but don't you think you compete with other women?"

"Sure, but competing for me means I want to win at something. Not proving I'm a woman."

"Yeah, yeah." He smiled broadly. "Being beautiful, you have no competition."

"Ha!" She kissed him on the cheek.

"How's everything else?"

"Good. It's been a slow couple of weeks. Not too many harvests. But business is steady."

"I'm operating Thursday morning, if you'd like to observe. Do you good to observe living tissue," Cory invited her.

"I'll be there." Annalise, a circumspect individual, looked around even though she knew no one would be there for another fifteen minutes. "Any more pieces of skull on your desk?"

Cory had called her about this once he'd settled down. "No. But it worries me."

"I'm not happy about it, but if I were you," she wryly said, "I'd be a lot more worried if it had been a fresh set of male genitals."

23

A sea of asphalt dotted with colored metal gumdrops was how the vast parking lot of Central Virginia Medical Complex might appear to someone with an imaginative streak. To Mrs. Murphy, Pewter, and Tucker, it was just ugly. No grass, rocks, or snakes—although bugs crawled on windshields. Animals burrowed in the greenbelt surrounding all this. Birds flew overhead and made nests in the Bradford pears that lined the streets.

"*Boring,*" Pewter complained.

"*She'll be out soon.*" Tucker curled in the fleece-lined bed Harry had put in the back of the Volvo.

Harry had outfitted the station wagon for her animals' pleasure as well as her own. She kept the second row of seats down. The XC70 had no third row, a wise decision. With those seats flat down, Harry covered the cargo area with a heavy rubber mat, better to handle those wet, muddy paws. She put down three very cushy beds, fastening them to the mat with small double-eye hooks. She'd put small U-fasteners in the heavy rubber to hold the double-eye hooks. The beds wouldn't slide, so the thick, heavy-duty carpet on the cargo area would be protected. She could haul the heavy rubber mat out to wash it. Always organized when it came to physical spaces, she felt quite proud of herself. The animals liked it but still rode up front with her.

"*Cool day,*" observed Mrs. Murphy, intently watching out the window.

Happy to make polite conversation, Tucker agreed.

"*If it's cool, why does Harry put the windows down a crack? I don't like it,*" Pewter grumbled.

"*Fresh air.*" Mrs. Murphy noticed a chipmunk shoot across the beltway road.

"*Bother.*" Pewter vacated her bed to crawl in with Tucker. "*You take up so much space.*"

"*It's my bed, Fatso.*"

"*Oh la.*" The gray cat ignored this, curling her back to Tucker's white stomach.

• • •

As these edifying conversations were taking place, Harry lay down for her first radiation treatment, the killer beams focusing on the former tumor site marked with ink.

The process, explained to her in detail, caused no pain, but she needed to remain still on the special table. Staying motionless was more difficult than Harry had anticipated. She wanted to scream and run out of there. The nurse told her the first treatment wouldn't be so bad. But in case nausea developed, there were drugs for that. A slight possibility existed for burns on her skin, which would be uncomfortable.

Harry refused drugs. She wanted her mind to be clear. What she'd do down the road, she didn't know. She'd find out when she got there, but the first treatment was okay, apart from staying still.

The support group had prepared Harry. Medicine, with its many protocols and restrictions—courtesy of one's government—could be as baffling as a peasant landing in the court of Catherine II of All the Russias. There were way too many complications, too many forms to fill out and papers to take home and read. Basically, all the forms boiled down to one thing: letting the hospital off the hook, should something go awry. In turn, the hospital feared gargantuan lawsuits if so much as one bent needle was used or someone was not properly swabbed, according to a potentially litigious patient.

Harry hated all of that. As she lay on the padded table, oddly grateful for the interlude on a busy day, she felt as though she'd stepped through a door into a prison without walls. Her body no longer belonged to her. The hospital accepted her body and the money in her purse. She was told what to do and when to do it. The insurance companies would try to kill her with paperwork, calls, and the need for intense documentation of every little thing done to her. She pitied Jennifer Potter. If Harry, a patient—well, actually a number—faced towers of paper and constant concerns about liability, what did her surgeon face?

Harry paid little attention to medicine. Although married to a vet, she exhibited zero curiosity about human medicine. Thrilled with the miracles stem cell treatments did for horses, she didn't give it a thought for people.

Yet here she was in the cancer factory. She still didn't really care. If she hadn't been married, she wouldn't submit to radiation. Thanks to his medical knowledge, Fair had insisted, as did Susan, BoomBoom, Alicia, Rev. Jones, Franny, and every single person with whom she came into contact. Part of her felt she'd caved to the pressure. Part of her figured she'd get through it and then everyone would shut up. She'd be forty-one in August; she hoped she had a lot of life left.

If nothing else, cancer introduced her to her own mortality. Intellectually, she knew she was eventually going to die. Now she knew it emotionally, and it was okay. She didn't want to go now, but she was a farmer. She'd lived with nature in a way few Americans did anymore. She accepted death, including her own. When that Dark Angel knocked on her door, she prayed she would accompany him with dignity. She resolved during that first radiation session that once done with this, she'd avoid this or any hospital if she was ill and the survival chance was less than fifty percent. If injured, sure, let the doc fix your bones or whatever. Injury is different from illness. She hated being ill. She could put up with injury.

"How do you feel?" asked Corrine, the nurse.

"Okay." Harry smiled up at her. "Did you always want to be a nurse?"

Corrine nodded. "I used to bandage my dolls."

The two laughed, and Harry understood why men fall in love with their nurses.

Once finished and back outside, Harry flipped up the collar of her fleece-lined denim jacket. Hard to believe it was full spring. If the dogwoods—now in full bloom—weren't in sight, she'd think this was early April. You never could know about the weather in central Virginia, or maybe the fickleness of the weather was true in most places.

As she reached the Volvo, she clicked the open button.

"Harry."

The voice made her turn around and brought the animals to the windows.

"Thadia." For years Harry hadn't seen her, and now twice in short order. She wasn't sure she liked that, but being a Virginian to the marrow of her bones, she appeared thrilled at the sight of Thadia Martin.

"I'm on my way to lunch," said Thadia. "Would you like to join me? We could talk about women's lacrosse. Saint Anne's is always a power."

"Thank you, but I have to get back. Just had my first radiation."

"Ah." Thadia's brow furrowed. "I was hoping you could help me."

Here it comes, Harry thought to herself.

"Do jockeys, show riders, or polo players use performance-enhancing drugs?"

"Jeez, Thadia, I've never seen any evidence of it. Or even heard of it, either. Yes, the big-money riders, some of them, have battled the same demons a lot of people battle, but drinking and drugging, especially before riding, would be a real death wish."

"Why?"

"Correct me if I'm wrong, but doesn't cocaine speed you up?"

"Certainly speeds up your heart rate," Thadia said.

"And alcohol is a depressant, a downer?"

"Yes."

"Okay, then, when you ride, you have to be perfectly in tune with your horse. It's like dancing. If you're flying high, it isn't going to work. You'll rush your jumps or do something stupid, or you'll set off your horse and the animal will refuse to do as you ask."

"Really." Thadia was incredulous. "I never fooled with horses. Half the girls at Saint Anne's did, but that wasn't the half I ran with." She smiled ruefully.

"Horses are very emotional animals. They sense a great deal about you. Like I said, you need to get in tune. And it's kind of like with people. Some you get along with better than others, but if you're out of it or flat-out crazy, they know. They don't like it."

"But aren't a lot of horses on drugs?"

"Depends on the venue. Are they on drugs foxhunting? No. Again, that would be a death wish. Flat racing." She whistled. "Unfortunately, it's a dreadful mess. Every state has different standards. Most of the drugs for horses abused by their trainers or owners don't correspond to, say, cocaine for the horses, but they mask pain or inhibit bleeding—stuff like that. And, of course, there's always steroids."

"Bodybuilding for horses?" Thadia had never heard of that.

"For some medical conditions, steroids are appropriate. However, the horses loaded up on them aren't being treated for those conditions. Steroids do to horses what they do to humans. They make them bigger, stronger, faster. In short, a better athlete." She stopped. "Do you have people in the recovery groups who abused steroids?"

"Not many. And I can't say that was their primary problem. A lot of athletes fall into evil habits." She half smiled when she said that. "Pressure—too much too soon—and a lot of them don't come from stable backgrounds. Well, since we were talking of horses, forgive the pun."

Harry stated with conviction, "Horses have more sense than people. We screw up their body chemistry and the poor animal has no choice."

Thadia nodded. "I read somewhere, wish I could remember, that if you tested a thousand Americans, about eighty percent would show positive for trace amounts of cocaine."

Harry's eyes opened wide. "What!"

"They aren't users. It's on our money."

"Oh, my God." Harry's hand came up to her face. She'd never thought of anything like that.

"You can see, I got my work cut out for me. Also, when times are hard, people drink more, drug more, abuse women, children, and animals more."

"That's horrible."

"The problem is men. They lash out. Women internalize their misery. They'll hurt themselves, which in turn hurts others—it's just not that obvious. Can you name one woman who's picked up an assault rifle and gunned down innocent strangers?"

"No."

"But I bet you can name some who have committed suicide."

"Sure." Harry hated that thought.

"Most of the work I do with the men in my groups is getting them to face their problems without taking it out on someone else or escaping via the bottle."

"Well, you have to do that with the women, too." Harry was ever suspicious of gender statements, even though occasionally she made them herself.

"I do, but it's different. What really upsets me—and this gets back to drugs again—people, medical people, explain the violence of the men by latching on to physical explanations. Their hormones, the male brain. Blah, blah, blah, blah. Hey, there's the male brain in France, too. They don't have the problem of domestic violence to the extent that we do. It's culture."

"Yeah, I agree with you. And our culture also encourages all the drug use. Doesn't matter if a doctor's pushing it on you or the guy on the street corner."

"Actually, Harry, the guy on the street corner corresponds to the streetwalker. Bottom of the barrel, because usually both of those jobs, if you will, are people who are paying for their habit. It's the pushers in the country clubs that never get caught. The pusher in the big corporation, say, in personnel. It's so easy."

"Given your history, I can understand your anger."

"What I'm angry about is our duplicity. Either legalize the crap or ban all of it. After all, the biggest drug is alcohol. It's crazy. Our War on Drugs is a great recipe for failure, for ensuring that the brightest make fortunes and pay not a penny of taxes. It ensures that we have millions of poor people in prison, maybe they had a lid of marijuana. But the rich kingpin is untouchable. It's so sick."

"Thadia, I can't say I share your passion about this, but then I don't have your history. Do I think it will change? If the American people want it to, it will, even though the bigwigs you're talking about can buy our senators and congressmen, can sway the churches with giant contributions, and probably the media, too. I trust the boots-on-the-ground American. My fear is Americans too often wait until it's a crisis squared before we do anything."

"Well, we're already pretty damn close. Anyway, thanks for talking to me about people in the horse world."

"You can cross out performance-enhancing drugs, because they won't enhance performance. I'm pretty sure about that, but as to cocaine and booze, after the show—well, most horsemen carry a bit of pain."

"You?"

"I have my share. I take Motrin when it gets to me. The ground is pretty hard." Harry laughed.

"It was hard when I hit it playing lacrosse, and I was closer to it than someone falling off a horse," Thadia remembered.

"All part of the game."

"You take vitamins?"

"Susan—you remember Susan Tucker—gave me a bottle of Centrum when I turned forty. I actually take it."

"She was the best midfielder I ever played against."

"Now she's a good golfer. Her handicap is four, and she's determined to get it down to zero."

"You're a good natural athlete."

"You, too, but there wasn't a path for us. Team sports, I mean. I was lucky because I had horses. Now girls have the hope of a future in professional sports if they play basketball. Still not much else, though, besides golf and tennis."

"And the skills you and I had, well"—Thadia shrugged—"golf and tennis are too tame."

"Not the way Susan plays." Harry laughed.

"Not to be pushier than I already am, but talk to your cancer support group about vitamins. They can really help."

"I will."

As Thadia turned to leave, Harry considered how lucky she was that she hadn't gone down that gilded path, which turns to molten lead fast enough. Thadia—the pretty party girl, the good athlete, the girl everybody wanted to date—looked ragged, old, and gray in the face yet there was still something pretty about her. She'd lost her muscle tone by age thirty, every job she ever had, and all her friends. Much as Harry admired her comeback, she didn't particularly want to be her friend, didn't want to see much of her.

And she wouldn't. This was Thadia's last day on earth.

24

*H*arry had promised herself after her operation to try one new thing per day. It might be as quiet as reading Wilfred Owen or, like today, riding a different breed of horse with an acquaintance made on trail rides.

"Like sitting in your easy chair." Harry smiled after jumping a three-foot-six-inch coop on Sparkle Plenty.

Following on Overdraft, her eight-year-old, Sue Rowdon enthused, "You can see why I love my Irish Draughts."

"Can. Takes up my leg," Harry noted.

Accustomed to riding Thoroughbreds and her one special Saddle-bred, Shortro, the barrel of the Irish Draught meant she couldn't reach as far down with her leg. Sparkle Plenty—five years old and 16.2½ hands, the flashy chestnut she was riding this morning—moved so smoothly she didn't feel that she would pop off.

"Aren't you surprised at how cool it's been?" Sue asked.

"The humidity creeps in by this time of year. I try to get all my outside chores done by noon. Go out again about five or six. The killer time is around three to five, don't you think?"

Sue replied, "Yeah. I like fall. I'm not built for hot weather."

Harry liked all four seasons, and changed the subject. "You battled thyroid cancer. I was just getting to know you when it was over. What did radiation do to you?"

"Unlike you, Harry, I drank mine. Actually, cancer turned out to be lucky for me. It was my dentist who found something wrong. I'd been so tired. He urged me to go to my doctor. Well, my body was making antibodies against my thyroid. I say lucky because I survived. My immune system—compromised before the cancer, which I didn't know— came back strong when it was all over, thanks to good doctors."

"I can't imagine drinking radiation crap." Harry grimaced.

"Gave me vertigo. I couldn't move without throwing up. I never want to go through that again." Sue whistled.

"I don't like what I have to do. Can't imagine not being able to stand up, walk, or ride."

"You know, Harry, you go through what you must. I thought our ride would get your mind off cancer and"—she smiled—"onto Irish Draughts. I knew you'd never ridden one. I always bred and rode Thoroughbreds. As the years crept up, I decided I wanted a breed I could ride when I'm ninety."

"Think you found it." Harry smiled.

"Me, too."

"Would you consider joining our committee? It's work, but it's not too overwhelming until the week before the race. And it's a great group of girls." Harry switched gears and hoped.

"No men?" Sue arched her eyebrow.

"Dr. Cory Schaeffer is the nominal head. The oncologists, they're all so busy, they do what they can. Jennifer Potter even shows up for meetings sometimes. And so does Annalise Veronese. She says she sees the damage cancer does and she wants to help." Harry paused. "You don't have to answer me now."

"I'd love to be part of it. Give me my marching orders."

"I will." Harry grinned. "I'm so glad you said yes. The best part is dinner after the real work is done. Everyone takes a turn, and we meet once a month until just before the race, then it's once a week the last month before the five-K. You will laugh until you cry, the stuff that comes out. Alicia got us all laughing at the last meeting. She'd clipped a silly report from *The London Sunday Times*. So now everyone is clipping stupid stories for our next meeting—the aftermath meeting. We made a lot of money on the race. Of course, having the BMW raffle was a big help."

"Don't you all have a dinner?"

"Next month. I'll be sure to get you and Rick tickets. It's a black-tie affair. God, I hate them."

"Oh, Harry, you look good in an evening gown."

"If only I could figure out how to walk in one."

"The female dilemma!"

"Revenge would be to make the men wear an evening gown."

Sue giggled. "Fair Haristeen, six foot five inches, in a strapless. Oh, my Gawd."

"It's the heels. I'd pay to see him tottering in!" Harry envisioned Fair in four-inch heels, towering over everyone at six-ten.

"Men wore high heels at the Court of Louis the Fourteenth."

"Gross. People see Louis the Fourteenth as such a great king. I figure he's the one who set the stage for the French Revolution." Harry disliked overadornment, regardless of the century.

"Could be. Come on, let's canter," Sue said, as they rode into the far rolling meadow at the back of her land, Wild Hare Farm.

Tucker, who'd been trotting with them, picked up speed as well. Other dogs would have run to the side or up front, but Tucker—bred to herd and to keep a sharp eye on cattle—ran behind the horses. If anyone strayed out of line, she would nip them right back. Corgis have an important job in this world.

· · ·

Back at Sue's barn, Mrs. Murphy and Pewter sat on a sweet-smelling hay bale. The F-150, parked in the drive, had all the windows down. Harry used the Volvo for town errands. Loath to run up miles on it because she wanted to drive it for a good ten years, she used the truck for country visits, hauling feed bags. So accustomed to firing up her beloved truck, Harry couldn't quite get used to driving the Volvo for as many chores as she might.

Mrs. Murphy looked out the front door of the barn. "*Yellow swallowtail.*"

Pewter followed the flight of the beautiful insect. "*Easy to catch if they light on the low blooms of a butterfly bush.*"

"*That's why Mom cuts those off.*"

"*It's not fair. There must be millions of yellow swallowtails and black swallowtails in Virginia. If I kill a few, it's not going to hurt the population,*" Pewter sensibly replied.

"*Hurts her.*"

"*Murphy, she's such a softie. Insects.*" Pewter puffed out her chest. "*Six legs! Who cares what happens to something with six legs?*"

"*She does. Haven't you heard her lamenting about hive collapse?*" Mrs. Murphy lifted her right paw to lick it.

Pewter emitted a little puff of air. "*Every word. She said her mother and father remembered the same thing in the 1940s. It's happening here again and in Europe. She said tests show certain chemicals in the bees. Well, I bet those chemicals weren't there in the forties. How can anyone know what goes on in an insect's brain? Especially humans. They don't even know what's going on in their own brains.*"

"*Aren't we Mary Sunshine today?*" Mrs. Murphy tartly said.

"*All I want are a few butterflies. As it is, Harry's put the bluebird boxes so far from the house. I'm not going all that distance to sit under them.*"

"*She'd never forgive you if you killed a bluebird or an indigo bunting. I do think she'd reward you if you killed that blue jay that's been dive-bombing her lately.*"

"*I will kill that bird if it's the last thing I do.*" Pewter puffed out her magnificent gray chest even further.

"*I'll help you. Hateful. Hateful bird.*"

"*I just wish she weren't such a softie, our mom,*" Pewter again lamented.

"*She can't help it, but you have to admit, Pewts, she's cool in a crisis.*"

"That she is," the gray cat readily agreed.

• • •

Good thing, for Harry at that moment encountered one.

The large meadow ended at a cul-de-sac, the end of Sue and Rick's property. One could see the edges of an upscale subdivision east of this. The dirt road, which went nowhere, would someday probably be part of another subdivision. For now, the farmer who owned the adjoining acres, a good neighbor, hung on to them. But age was creeping up on

him. Sue feared she and her husband wouldn't have the money to purchase the good pastureland if he sold due to infirmity. The last thing she
wanted was a subdivision hard up on her own farm.

A deep drainage ditch also created a barrier at the easternmost edge
of the land, curving toward the cul-de-sac.

A 1992 white Corolla sat in the middle of the cul-de-sac, nose
pointed west, toward the Blue Ridge Mountains. The driver's door hung
wide open. Someone sat behind the wheel, forearms bent at the elbow,
elbows leaning on the steering wheel.

From a distance, this looked odd.

"Something's not right," Harry remarked.

The two women, walking the horses as they'd finished their bracing
canter, picked up a trot toward the car.

They rode up onto the road.

Tucker immediately warned, *"Dead!"*

The two horses snorted.

"Oh, my God." Sue grimaced.

Harry dismounted, handing her reins to Sue. "Got your cell?"

"Harry, don't go over there."

"Call the sheriff's department. Tell them Thadia Martin is dead at the
end of Pheasant Lane, the dirt road off Barker's Crossing Road."

Accompanied by Tucker, Harry walked to the open door. Thadia, in
rigor mortis, did not yet smell terrible. The night had been cool. The
stink would come up by midday. If they hadn't found her in two days,
the odor would have been unbearable to all but vultures and dogs.

"Harry, don't touch her." Sue was aghast.

"I won't. I don't want to destroy evidence, but as we're the first ones
here, I should look."

Sue tried to avoid looking at the macabre sight of a woman in her
early forties, hands straight up, jaw wide open, eyes bulging. She
couldn't see Thadia's legs under the steering wheel, which prevented
them from becoming as bent as the arms. A body in rigor mortis is difficult to remove. That would be the ambulance team's problem.

Sue marveled at Harry's matter-of-fact approach. She did not marvel
that Harry knew the deceased. Harry knew everybody.

Harry touched nothing. She carefully looked for a sign of struggle.

No struggle, but Thadia's throat had been neatly slashed. Blood had spilled on her blouse; some had spurted on the windshield. Startling though this sight was, Harry's curiosity kicked into high gear. She walked to the passenger door, did not open it—again, for fear of destroying fragile evidence. She peered in the window to see if she could get a view of Thadia's right side.

A small carton, which she reckoned to be six inches square, rested on the passenger seat. Thadia's purse was in the passenger-side footwell.

Harry walked close to the hood and peered in.

Thadia wore a short-sleeved buttoned blouse, her sweater thrown in the backseat. Harry noticed her bracelet. She returned to the driver's side. The bracelet had slipped down to her elbow. Harry could clearly see it was a scarab bracelet and one scarab was missing. She'd not noticed the bracelet on Thadia before, but then one doesn't wear the same jewelry every day.

"Harry," Sue called.

"Coming." Under her breath, Harry muttered, "Shit."

Tucker, hard by Harry's leg, looked up and stated, *She never had a chance.*

25

The chill dissipated while Harry and Sue waited for the sheriff's department. Given that there was a nasty accident on Garth Road, it took Rick and Coop a half hour to reach Pheasant Lane.

Rick slammed the squad car door. Furious at the delay, he merely nodded at Harry and Sue while walking to the corpse. Upset herself, Coop first questioned her neighbor, then Sue.

"Look at her throat, Coop," Harry instructed after telling Coop all she observed on first finding Thadia. "Neat work."

Sue had less to tell, although she had taken note of the time they'd found Thadia: 10:13 A.M.

"You two can leave now. I know where to find you." Coop waved them off.

"One more thing, she's wearing a scarab bracelet. One is missing. I still have the one I found in Paula's driveway, if you want it," Harry said.

Tucker wished she could communicate with the humans. Fear, a powerful perfume, lingers. A dog can detect such an odor even after dogs pass. There was no fear odor on Thadia. That meant either she wasn't afraid of her killer or the killer struck in a nanosecond.

Coop joined Rick, leaving light footprints in the dirt, for the dampness still clung to the road, the dew just melting on those fields and roads now touched by the sun.

He looked up at his partner. "Given the rigor, I'd say she was killed last night. It was forty-eight degrees at my house, cooler here. That factors in."

"No sign of struggle." Coop exhaled.

"No stranglehold or someone reaching out, face-to-face, to throttle her." Rick stood back. That would leave small bruise marks. There were none. He again put his head into the driver's side. "Just one clean cut."

"Wish the photographer would get here."

"Me, too. I'd like to get her body into the cooler. And I want the fingerprint team here pronto."

A fly buzzed near Coop's head. She shooed it away. "Nothing touched her. No nibbles. For a night hunter, this was a free lunch."

"True, but there's so much game out there now. The flies are discovering the body."

"Rick, I read somewhere that a fly knows you're dead two seconds after you breathe your last."

"Luckily, she breathed her last at night. I'm hardly a fly expert, but I think they're daytime insects. Ever think about it, the stages of death, I mean?"

"Sure," Coop replied. "As law enforcement officers, we have to. The condition of a corpse, the time of exposure, all that stuff."

"No, I mean, who discovered the body first? It's usually not a human. It really is a fly or an insect. Then, if the body's left out, the buzzards find it. The other carrion eaters come round. And then there are the bugs that burrow under the body so it will eventually collapse into the earth."

"Pretty revolting."

"To us. If you and I were vultures, this would be a beautiful sight. And you know, if those carrion eaters didn't exist, the earth would be choking with dead. There'd be Alexander the Great and piles of humans on him. There'd be old bears from the 1400s and mountains of little grasshopper exoskeletons." He shrugged. "Be a goddamned mess."

"You're right."

They waited, silent. A crunch in the distance announced someone's arrival. Turned out to be photographer Charlotte Lunden driving up.

Rick waved as she parked behind them.

"Be a minute," she called out as she stepped onto the road.

Leaning back in, she plucked out her camera.

"Come on. You've seen a lot worse." Coop led her to the body.

As Charlotte took photographs from every angle, also paying attention to the vehicle in case any evidence at all might be there, she coolly commented, "Good shape. That's a plus."

"Yep," Coop replied.

"Two deaths in less than two months of women who both worked at Central Virginia Medical Complex." Charlotte kept snapping.

Coop nodded. "That had crossed my mind."

"People have heart attacks in their twenties. Paula's death appeared natural." Charlotte adjusted the lens.

"Yeah. And her autopsy didn't show a thing."

"Curious." Charlotte, who'd been leaning over the old car's hood, stood up and checked her camera. "Bet you when this one's opened up, her heart will have scar tissue."

"How do you know her?"

"Class behind me at Saint Anne's. She'd played lacrosse and field hockey. I ran track. Just couldn't get into anything where you swung sticks." Charlotte laughed. "Thaddy ran with the rich kids, the drug crowd. Every school has one. Scared me then, and scares me now."

"A pity. What kids have to deal with. All I worried about was trigonometry."

Charlotte took photos through the passenger window, then moved to shoot a few at an angle from the back window on that same right side. "Coop, it's like everything else in this life. You make choices. She made those choices with her eyes wide open. Thadia and the coke crowd mocked the rest of us. We ranged from uncool to no cool to clueless."

"I reckon she paid for it. Maybe the ultimate price. Right now, I'm clueless."

"Hey, Coop, how many times have I seen you and Rick figure it out, finger the killer? You will this time, too."

"Damn well better." Coop made a note to remember that Charlotte was uncommonly observant.

• • •

Two other uncommonly observant creatures, Harry and Tucker, along with Mrs. Murphy and Pewter, headed back to their farm. As it was the first day after her first treatment, Harry had wanted to do something out of her normal routine and to ride the horses Sue Rowdon so loved. Harry had seen them in the show ring, in the hunt field. They could all jump. She had looked forward to the morning. She'd promised herself, along with a new workout program at Heavy Metal, to do something new every day. Grateful that this something new hadn't occurred when she was farther along in her treatments, she couldn't get the cut throat—a clearly visible bifurcated windpipe—out of her mind.

Tucker had filled in the cats as the humans untacked and washed the horses. They were furious to have missed such an adventure. For Pewter, this was twice she'd missed out on something big. She pouted at Sue's barn, pouted in the truck, and pouted at her own barn.

Harry called Noddy Cespedes at Heavy Metal even before calling Susan.

"Noddy, it's Harry Haristeen."

"Oh, Harry, I'm looking forward to working with you tomorrow."

"Me, too. Is Thadia Martin a member of the gym? Forgive me for asking about another person." Harry carefully did not spill the beans.

"No."

"You know who she is, though?"

"Only because she sometimes comes in to watch Cory Schaeffer box. It embarrassed him. I stayed out of it. I think he told her he'd like to keep his training matches private. I never asked."

"Don't much care, either," said Harry. "But isn't it odd that a surgeon would take such risks with his hands?"

Noddy thought a moment. "I guess. I just figure whoever comes in here knows what they want and the bodily risk. He was on his college team. I guess he figured the workout, the concentration needed for boxing, rejuvenated him."

"Painful sport."

"Harry, it's the most complete sport there is. Think about it, you're out there all alone, pitted against another human being in your weight class but with different skills. You have to figure out your opponent as he's trying to figure you out. You have to be in fantastic, unbelievable condition to go fifteen rounds, even ten. Here they stick to three. Cory is good, a very balanced fighter. Younger men all want to spar with him."

"Hmm. You have any women boxers?"

"A few. Slowly but surely, women will pick it up. Like I said, to box you have to be in splendid condition, and it's the best, and I mean the best, thing you can do for your hand-eye coordination."

"Really."

"Trust me. The best. If you're a serious baseball player or tennis player, even if you don't want to take a punch or throw one, you work the speed bag, then the big old heavy bag, run like a boxer runs to get in condition, you'll be doing yourself a big favor."

"I never thought about that."

"No one does. Oops, gotta go. My noon client just came. A real success story. Overweight at seventy-two. Made a commitment to be healthy. He's already lost thirty pounds in five months. No pills or crank diets, either."

"You're a miracle worker."

"Well, thanks. I'm not. I just unlock the potential in everyone's body."

After hanging up with Noddy, Harry sat at the kitchen table, drank a Coca-Cola, and thought about the situation.

She called Susan and discussed it with her. Susan predictably told her she was engaging in her favorite sport: meddling, then jumping to conclusions.

Irritated as one can only be irritated by a spouse or best friend, Harry thumped to the barn followed by her other three best friends.

Even Pewter kept her mouth shut. She knew Harry was one step ahead of a running fit.

All the horses were out in the perfect spring day. Harry vented her thwarted energies on cleaning the barn. That took just one hour, because it was pretty clean to begin with.

Dusty, she stomped her boots, shook herself, then walked outside, lifted the back of the Volvo, whistled for the kids to jump in. She set off for Central Virginia Medical Complex.

"*On a mission,*" Mrs. Murphy said and sighed.

"*Yeah, well, maybe I don't want to be on it with her,*" Pewter said, nodding.

"*You jumped in the wagon,*" Tucker said.

"*Only because I couldn't bear to be parted from you, Bubble butt,*" the gray sassed.

Mrs. Murphy laughed, and Tucker, who hated being called Bubble butt, couldn't help it. She laughed, too.

"All right. What's going on back there?"

"Nothing," all three replied in unison.

Confused but motivated, Harry wanted to talk to Toni Enright before news of Thadia's murder reached the medical complex. What nagged at her was the scarab. Did Thadia kill Paula? How? Did someone who loved Paula figure it out and kill Thadia? Harry was making herself crazy.

"Stick to facts," she said under her breath.

Harry didn't know Toni Enright's work schedule, but she knew where her small office was, shared with other nurses. Toni wasn't there, but two nurses mentioned she was in the operating room. Harry left her cell number and asked if they'd give it to Toni.

On her way to her husband's clinic, the phone rang. She pulled to the side of the road, a two-lane paved one, not heavily traveled. It was Toni. Harry told her Thadia was dead. Neither the sheriff nor Coop had told her she couldn't.

Toni, voice rising, asked, "Did you see any evidence of drugs?"

"There was a small carton on the passenger seat. Don't know what it contained."

"Nothing in the backseat?"

"Her old sweater."

"God, I hope she's not full of drugs."

"Why?" Harry naïvely asked.

"It will just kill the people in her recovery groups. Say your prayers, Harry. Say your prayers that she was drug- and alcohol-free. This is just terrible!"

"Maybe I shouldn't have told you."

"You did exactly the right thing. I've been in the operating room, so Thadia missed her morning groups and I didn't know. I'll get a few other nurses; we will inform all her groups and call the people who are in the morning groups. Harry, some of these people are very fragile. They need to be informed in as supportive a way as possible."

"I understand." She was beginning to, at any rate.

"Why was she murdered?"

Harry told her what she'd seen.

"I just hope one of her old associates"—Toni said "associates" with dripping contempt—"didn't reappear. She was in jail, remember?" Then Toni sighed. "She cleaned up. She tried to make amends. It was a bad end. I'd be a liar if I pretended to like her. I tolerated her. But she really did a good job with her groups. Too much drama for me, but that's me."

"Toni, that's all of us except another ex-addict. I think most of those people feed on drama."

"They certainly create enough of it."

"Like politicians," Harry crabbed.

"I've noticed lately that you're spewing venom in that direction."

"I am. I feel betrayed by elected officials. They're officials, not leaders. Hell, I feel betrayed by my own body."

Toni waited a moment. "Look to yourself first."

"I'm sorry. I'm upset. First, I found Paula, and now Thadia. I need to keep my mouth shut."

Toni replied, more kindly now, "It's been two nasty shocks. You did the right thing in calling me. I need to contact her groups."

"Toni, before I let you go. You said Cory Schaeffer was having an affair. Thadia was on him like a tick. Do you think his mistress could have killed her?"

A long pause followed this. "No. She's not that stupid, and I don't think she loves him. He's her boy toy."

After disconnecting, Harry drove to the clinic, where she told Fair everything.

Mrs. Murphy, Pewter, and Tucker always enjoyed visiting the horses who were recovering from surgery in their special stalls.

As Harry's husband advised her to relax and try to put this unpleasantness out of her mind, the cats and dog walked outside in the sunshine.

"She's got the wind in her sails," Mrs. Murphy said.

"It's her nature, just like it's your nature to chase mice and my nature to herd cows, horses, humans." Tucker sighed. "What worries me is that with each of her treatments, she'll become weaker. In the past when she's made a mess of it, her strength and her quickness helped."

"And we saved her ass," Pewter bluntly put it.

"What do we do now? She's going to get into it. Two young women dead from the same workplace. Something's not right. It's no coincidence," the corgi posited.

"Double murder." Pewter tossed this off.

The two women's deaths meant nothing to Pewter. As far as she was concerned, there were way too many humans on the earth anyhow. But she did love her human, and, although loath to admit it, she was worried, too.

They sat watching the beautiful deep blue barn swallows, with their russet breasts, flash in and out of the barn. Purple martins, tree swallows, and barn swallows, all of the same family, could zoom about at such speeds, and they could execute turns almost at a right angle.

"Well?" Pewter asked.

"Well what?" Tucker replied.

"What are we going to do?" For once, Pewter had dropped the blasé act.

"We'll do the best we can," Mrs. Murphy quietly said, then ducked as a barn swallow flew right for her.

"Banzai!" the beautiful bird shouted.

"We have to survive these barn swallows first." Tucker laughed as she moved out into the small paddock, followed by the cats.

26

When Harry arrived at Heavy Metal Gym the next morning at 5:30, the weight room teemed with people. A smaller room off the weight room had mats on the floor for stretching. In the boxing area, two young men did rope work; another hit the speed bag.

Dr. Annalise Veronese and Toni Enright were already there. Harry flopped down and took her orders from Noddy. Chitchatting was at a minimum, because everyone here attacked their exercises seriously. Two bodybuilders arrived at 5:45 A.M. They, too, stretched. Easy as stretching appears compared to a three-hundred-pound bench press, it took concentration. It bored Harry, but she trusted Noddy's wisdom.

"Hold that for one minute," Noddy commanded.

On her back, left knee to the ground over her right side, Harry started to sweat. By the time she finished twenty minutes of stretching, she knew why the bodybuilders carried towels with them. She wiped her sweat off the mat.

"We'll concentrate on your core. I'll give you isolated exercises for your arms, back, legs, but today it's your abs and obliques. We'll work on strength, twisting for flexibility. Given your riding, there are times when you need to swivel in the saddle. Well, I've put together a program for you."

"I don't have any weights at home."

"The exercise program uses the floor, chairs, and a low tree branch for you to do chin-ups. If you don't have anything low, then buy a bar and put it up in a doorway. In time, you might want to work on a body-builder's schedule. That means you isolate the muscle groups, and for three consecutive days work each one, take a day off, then back again. You always begin with stretching, and you end with running or the stationary bike. You can possess the best core strength in the world, but if you haven't wind or stamina, what good is it?"

"Right." Harry was beginning to realize there was a lot more to this than was at first apparent.

However, she was enthusiastic. All the more so when she saw how much Annalise and Toni were accomplishing.

"On your back." Noddy pointed down. "Now bring your legs up a foot off the floor; keep them straight. Arms out to your sides straight. Fold yourself together so you're on your butt. Back's off the floor. There. Now hold it."

After one hour, plus twenty minutes for the stretching, Harry felt exhilarated even if tired. She headed for the locker room.

Annalise showered, dressed, and applied light makeup in the mirror near her locker. She stepped into her jeans, putting a pocketknife in one pocket, a list of chores in the other. She looked over at Harry.

"How'd you like it?"

"It's harder than I thought, but I thought it was great."

"I didn't hear about your finding Thadia until last night. You have an odd knack for finding dead people."

"Let's hope this is the last. Will you perform the autopsy?"

"No. Richmond has one of the best forensic pathology departments in America. They'll do the work."

"I don't know how pathologists do it."

"Most people don't," Annalise answered in good humor. "A pathologist is always right but a day late. There may be something we can take from the dead that will help the living."

"Forgive me if I'm asking this the wrong way, but how did you get interested in dead things?"

The attractive doctor laughed. "I didn't think of it quite that way. When I was little we had such a wonderful family doctor. That was the beginning, but I didn't know I had an interest until biology class. I loved dissecting things, just loved seeing how everything fit together. Once I got into med school, it all fell into place. I feel like a detective when I'm working. I enjoy the challenge."

Harry changed the subject. "Don't you find it odd that two women who knew each other, both from Central Virginia Medical Complex, have died, one clearly murdered?"

"It is unfortunate. And yes, it is odd."

Toni returned from the showers, towel wrapped around her. She twirled the combination lock for her locker. "Talking about recent events?"

"Yes," both women said.

"Jigs for Coke," Harry quickly said.

In the South, if two people say the same thing at the same time, the first who utters the words "jigs for whatever" gets it.

"All right." Annalise laughed. "Do you want money for it so you can drink one on the way home, or do you want one on different terms?"

"Medical skills *and* negotiating skills. We're lucky to have you," Toni teased.

"Now." Harry grinned.

"All right." Annalise opened her purse and pulled out a five-dollar bill.

"That's too much," Harry protested.

"You might need more than one. You had quite a workout."

"I feel great."

The well-built, strong physician added, "Wait until the second day."

"We'll see." Harry then turned to Toni. "How'd it go—telling Thadia's groups, I mean?"

"A mess. Some got hysterical, others cried, others sat like stones. They're lost, and we've got to find a counselor fast, a really good rehabilitation person."

"Won't be easy." Annalise slung her purse over her shoulder. "She was an odd duck."

"Nicely put," Toni responded.

"Well, speak no ill of the dead," Annalise advised.

Harry felt that she'd heard that before recently. A flash of disquiet was followed by telling herself it was a stock phrase thousands of years old.

Maybe the ancients knew more than we did. Who is to say spirits should not be propitiated? Is there such a thing as the unquiet dead?

"Harry." Toni spoke louder than usual.

"Huh?"

"Where are you?"

"Sorry, my mind traveled back to my Latin teacher." Harry's reply was almost true.

"If you're going to vacation in the past, couldn't you pick a more exciting time?" Toni laughed.

Harry mused, "Athens and Rome. They make us look so dull."

"Then you and I better make up for it." Toni lightly punched Harry's arm.

27

*I*sn't it late for this?" At Fair's veterinary clinic, Harry watched as her husband carefully put the two straws of equine semen into the cylinder of liquid nitrogen. A sponge in the bottom of the cylinder had been filled with the liquid nitrogen; the sides of the cylinder helped maintain the temperature. He closed the lid, snapping it shut.

"Hey, hand me that pen, will you?"

Harry picked up a Pilot G2-07 medium-point black. Fair used this ballpoint because the ink wouldn't wash out. Given the value of the semen, the last thing he wanted was for a shipment to go astray or for a careless FedEx employee to get the label wet. He had to admit he'd not met any careless FedEx employees, but Fair's motto could have been "Better safe than sorry."

He wrote out the address on preprinted FedEx labels. Then Harry held the cylinder as he affixed the labeling pouch and inserted the label, keeping the top copy for himself just in case.

She read the label: "Rosehaven. Fair, that's Paula Cline's operation in Lexington, Kentucky. Since when is she breeding Warmbloods?"

"She's not. Paula is a Thoroughbred girl." Fair smiled, thinking of the woman they'd gotten to know because her son attended UVA some years back.

It was serendipity. They'd met at a college baseball game, sitting next to one another, and were surprised to find each other involved in the horse industry. Then they discovered they were both friends with Joan Hamilton and Larry Hodge of Kalarama Farm. Like all people in that situation, they marveled at how small the world was or, in the parlance of the day, our collective six degrees of separation.

Fair explained, "Paula promised a friend she'd take care of this. Brie Feldman wants her stallion crossed with one of Paula's Thoroughbred mares, the one with Forty-niner blood."

Harry tried to be circumspect in public but was considerably less so in her husband's presence. "Well, that's just stupid."

"I don't know."

"Oh, come on, Fair, why ruin a beautiful Thoroughbred shoulder? Warmbloods are too straight up."

"Harry, you were born around Thoroughbreds, and so was I, but even you have to admit that Warmbloods can jump the moon and most people are more comfortable with their temperament."

"Slow." Harry tapped her forehead.

"Amend that slow to mature. Anyway, Brie has made a good living with her Warmbloods. She goes to Germany annually to visit the Holsteiner Gestüt"—he used the German name for breeding station—"and she's brought back very good horses."

Harry, slightly peevish, said, "She can't hold a candle to the late Virginia Klumpp."

"Virginia really was special, but remember, it was Virginia that guided Brie. Give her a chance, Harry."

Harry burst out, "Oh, Fair, all these wonderful people have left us. I miss Virginia. What a generous, funny, funny woman. Hell, I still miss my mother and father, and—"

He put his strong arm around her. "What's up, Skeezits?"

Hearing her childhood nickname, she slumped against him. "I don't know. I'm getting as crabby as Pewter."

As Pewter reposed on the counter in the reception room, an instant comment flew out of her mouth: *"I resent that!"*

"Oh, shut up, Pewts, you are crabby." Tucker, head on paws, rolled her eyes. *"I calls 'em as I sees 'em. You and Mrs. Murphy don't."*

"We have the sense to shut up." Mrs. Murphy defended herself and Tucker.

"Right." Tucker smiled.

"Well?"

Harry sat down as Fair double-checked the cylinder. "It's the scarab," she said. "It preys on my mind. Pewter found it in Paula's driveway when I found Paula. And then, God knows why, I also ride up on Thadia, and there's the bracelet with a scarab missing. Coop picked it up, the tiger's eye I kept. It fit in the bracelet perfectly."

"I found it." Pewter raised her voice.

"Honey, I expect most scarab bracelets come with small-, medium-, and large-sized stones. That the stone fit may be important, may not."

"Probably." She then blurted out, "There's that rictus smile that mocks one. It's horrible without being gross, if you know what I mean. I will never again think of Thadia without thinking of her in death, that frozen open jaw."

"All mammals get it if they go into rigor mortis. I never thought of it as mocking. I sure have thought of a skull's smile. Hard to miss, plus horror movies have burned it into our brain." He continued to keep his arm around her shoulders. "I'm sorry, baby. You've been through a lot."

The report from Thadia's autopsy was that her heart did have scar tissue consistent with cocaine abuse, but the muscle showed no signs of disease, the valves were healthy, her arteries clean and clear. Her heart was just fine—as were her lungs, kidneys, liver, and brain. At least the people she had been counseling could keep on track, keep trying, knowing that Thadia hadn't fallen back into her old bad habits. The small cardboard box had contained OxyContin, but none was in her bloodstream. The hospital administrator, Will Archer, did not tell anyone about the OxyContin. He had enough trouble as it was. He asked Rick to keep it out of news reports, which the sheriff did.

"Two." Harry held up two fingers.

"Harry, just let Coop and Rick worry about this."

"Paula had a familiar scent, but not so familiar we could identify it." Poor Tucker tried one more time to get through to her people.

Pewter looked over the counter. "Describe it again."

"Not bad. Faint. Like an old banana, but not really." Tucker strained for some telling detail.

"She's right. It wasn't an odor that would snap your head around like gasoline," Mrs. Murphy chimed in. "Or like a lot of perfumes humans slap on."

"*An assault on any dog's nose.*" Tucker laughed.

"*Calvin Klein's Obsession isn't so bad.*" Mrs. Murphy found it very interesting.

"*Isn't so good, either.*" Tucker wrinkled her black nose.

Pewter lifted her head. "*Better than decay, which you so adore. Can you imagine a human describing your ideal odor? 'Deep, meaty smell with hint of toasted fingernails and deteriorating ligaments, with a dried coagulated blood finish.'*"

At this, all three animals howled with laughter.

"What gets into them?" Harry laughed, too.

"Honey, we're better off not knowing."

"I guess, but sometimes I feel left out. Fair, I think they experience life more fully than we do, I really do."

His lustrous blue eyes met hers. "If you and I didn't have to pay bills, fill out endless income and other government tax forms, listen to the nightly reports of misery, terror, natural disasters, and murder all over the world, we might come close to their enjoyment."

She seized on one word. "Murder. Did Thadia kill Paula?"

"If she did, she left no trace. Sugar, I doubt Thadia killed Paula. She was weird, had fried a lot of brain cells, and was terminally immature, but I don't think even at her drugged-out worst, Thadia was a killer."

Harry leaned against the counter, her face low so Mrs. Murphy could rub her cheek on hers. "Maybe."

"Honey, what's the motive?" He now leaned on the counter, too.

"Thadia was consumed by jealousy. She thought Paula was sleeping with Cory Schaeffer. Thadia was obsessed with him, according to Toni Enright. Toni's not one to get in the middle of people's stuff, but Thadia didn't hide her feelings, at least to Toni."

"The real question is, did she hide them from Cory?"

Harry stood up straight. "I am such a dolt. I never thought of that."

"You never think of how aftershave soothes razor burn, either."

"What's that supposed to mean?"

"It's subjective. You and everyone else sees the world through their own eyes. You have to make an effort to think about how it looks or feels to be someone else. I wonder what it's like to be five-six."

"I'm five-seven, thank you very much." Harry stretched her height and the truth a tiny bit.

"Of course. But you see what I mean? If you can turn your questions upside down or inside out, you might come up with an answer."

"That will throw her for a loop." Pewter giggled, a little puff of air being exhaled.

As Harry grappled with this, Fair called the 800 FedEx number for a pickup.

"Is there a cheaper way to send semen?"

"Uh-huh. Fresh cooled. But that only works if the vet or tech pulling the semen understands the rate of cooling. It's a lot less expensive if you know what you're doing. Now they've got these Styrofoam boxes for fifty bucks for shipping. They're insulated, and you can use cans of water. It's easier than liquid nitrogen, but the drawback is you've got to impregnate the mare within forty-eight to seventy-two hours. I know the Standardbred people use the Styrofoam boxes all the time. I prefer the blue boxes if I'm to send out fresh cooled semen, but those are three hundred dollars. Here's the other problem: If your box sits on the tarmac on a hot day and isn't promptly loaded into the hold of the plane, you can lose your investment. What I'm sending today is five thousand dollars' worth of sperm. To one of the great Thoroughbred farms in Kentucky or Florida, that's chump change."

"Hey, don't forget Pennsylvania's coming way up in the horse world, as is West Virginia. Remains to be seen about New York. The legislature seems not to care if they harm the Thoroughbred industry." Harry knew a lot about the economics of horses because of her husband and because she grew up with them. Like so many East Coast people, she forgot about all the good Thoroughbreds in California.

When Harry was young, Maryland was one of the great states of the equine industry. Blind legislators in less than a decade had destroyed a century and a half of labor, gutting the lifeblood of many a Maryland country resident. Those who held state office in New York, Pennsylvania, Florida, California, or Kentucky determined who would eat and who would go hungry. Kentucky had its troubles despite a brilliant, horse-friendly governor, Steven Beshear.

"It's pretty much a muddle." Fair placed the yellow cylinder by the front office door in case he wasn't there when the delivery driver arrived.

"I wish I could get those two bodies out of my mind."

"I do, too. I have something that might help. Came in the mail here today. I was going to wrap it up, but you need it now." He handed her a cardboard box, eight inches by eight inches.

Harry took her penknife out of her jeans' pocket to slice open the flaps. Green Bubble Wrap enclosed the gift. She slit the Scotch tape, then peeled off the Bubble Wrap.

"Oh, wow." She kissed him. "Can't wait."

Fair had bought her the DVDs for the television series *The Tudors*.

"I don't want to watch a bunch of people in puffy sleeves." Pewter was disappointed. "He could have ordered some little fake furry mice with that."

"Be glad he didn't order the Miss Marple series." Tucker didn't much feel like watching something about the sixteenth century.

"Why?" Pewter wondered.

"Miss Marple is a fictional detective, English, and she solves clever crimes. It would only inflame Mom," Tucker said.

"I know that." Pewter sniffed. "I've read over her shoulder. I don't understand why people need to make up things. Why can't they focus on real life?"

Mrs. Murphy rose, stretched, and offered this thought: "Their senses, except for sight, are so poor. They can't take in as much information as we can. They don't know as much real life. They try. But the made-up stories help them. They collect them from humans long dead. Calms them."

"Twaddle," Pewter pronounced judgment.

"If only they knew what we were saying, I'm sure it would help much more than their made-up stories," Tucker teased her.

"It would."

"Whether it would or not, I actually wish Mom would be watching All Creatures Great and Small instead of The Tudors." Mrs. Murphy heard the FedEx truck coming down the paved drive. "That was fast."

"In the neighborhood," Tucker reasoned.

"Back to Miss Marple." Pewter's curiosity was aroused.

The tiger sighed. "Miss Marple had the sense to keep her mouth shut. Mother, and I truly love her, but sometimes she can be a fountain when she needs to be a well."

28

*N*ervously sitting in the small booth with the fabric curtain, Harry waited for the results from her first mammogram since the surgery. She knew if she was called back for a second set of images, it wasn't good.

Nurse Denise Danforth called outside the booth. "Harry."

"Yep." Now clothed, Harry pulled the curtain back.

"You're good to go. No abnormality at all after your surgery."

"Thank God." Harry exhaled.

Denise, late thirties, put her hand on Harry's back. "You caught it early, girl. Good for you, and good for Regina MacCormack for getting you into surgery pronto. When she retires, what will we do?"

"Regina still makes house calls."

"The only people who do that these days are thieves." Denise smiled, then added, "Charlotte told me you were cool as a cuke when they found Thadia."

Charlotte Lunden, Denise's sister, had photographed the deceased Thadia Martin. The Charlottesville area remained a tight community, so many people had known one another all their lives. Denise had graduated from high school three years before Harry. They were tied by geography and generation. Some families had five generations alive and breathing who knew other families of five generations.

"I didn't think about it."

"A terrible end to an unhappy life." Denise walked Harry down the long aisle to the waiting room.

"So it seems," Harry murmured.

"Being a nurse, I see so much: people who have brought their conditions upon themselves, those who had a misfortune drop out of the sky. Seeing how people handle this is a privilege. You wouldn't think that, but it is. The smallest, most unassuming woman can have the greatest courage."

"I'm seeing that in my support group."

"Glad you're going."

"Denise, I'm a medical idiot. I know a lot about equine health but next to nothing about human health. I had no idea that one out of eight women will be diagnosed with breast cancer in her lifetime."

"True." Denise opened the door for Harry. "I pray they find a cure, even if it means I'll probably be out of a job."

"Oh, Denise, we need nurses so badly. You can work anywhere in America, anywhere in the world, I bet."

"I'm staying right here." Denise hugged Harry.

Once outside the building, Harry stopped, breathed deeply. Spring's signature fragrances filled her. An Appalachian spring assaults all the senses. This spring seemed more vivid than any other, or perhaps she appreciated it more.

At ten in the morning, the mercury reached sixty-two degrees, low humidity, the air a touch cool, with a light breeze. It couldn't have been more perfect.

The Volvo sat in the crowded parking lot, the windows down two inches because the kids had hitched a ride. No matter how she tried to keep Tucker in the house, the intrepid dog found a way out, only to blaze down the driveway, barking furiously. Once she'd picked up the corgi, all thirty pounds of her, she'd usually turn back to fetch the cats. If Tucker got to ride and they didn't, destruction followed.

Walking toward her, Annalise Veronese waved. "Good morning."

"Hey, how are you?"

"Good. Just attended an incredible lecture sponsored by the Virginia Historical Society about the medical advances springing from the War Between the States."

"Annalise, since when did you start calling it the War Between the States? I thought you were born and raised in Vermont."

Annalise laughed. "Yes, I was, but I've lived here long enough to watch my P's and Q's. Say, how do you feel after that workout with Noddy?"

"Pretty good." Harry then added, "But you were right about the second day. I feel muscles I've never felt before."

"If you stick with her program, she'll keep mixing it up so you don't get bored, and you'll be super-fit. How's everything else?"

"Just had my first mammogram after my surgery, and I'm fine."

"That is wonderful news. You must be a fast healer, too. I was surprised you could do the push-ups and stuff," Annalise complimented her. "You'll beat it."

"Thank you." Then Harry informed her, "Susan makes a paste, I have no idea what's in it, for the horses. Heals up flesh wounds so fast I used it on myself. I keep asking Susan what's in it, and she says it's a family secret. I hope it doesn't have mouse droppings in it."

"Harry, you'd know."

They both laughed. "If you ever want to attend any of the special medical lectures, like today's, let me know. As I recall, you like reading history."

"I do. Regina was telling me she has to put in seventy hours each year to keep her license current. Is it the same for you? I thought perhaps not."

"Same. You'd be surprised at how much there is to do in pathology to keep current. All of medicine is changing so rapidly, thanks to the technological advances. Harry, something as simple as pollen—now, I'm not a forensic pathologist, as you know, but if there is pollen in the nostrils or lungs of a corpse, it's possible to trace where that person had been. Often murder victims' bodies are not left at the murder site. It fascinates me. I know people think we cut open dead bodies and that's about it, but some of the biggest advances in medicine come from pathologists." She held up her hand and smiled. "You're on the end of an unasked-for lecture, but I am so passionate about what I do. Karl Landsteiner, who was born in Vienna in 1868, a pathologist, was the first doctor to distinguish between different blood types. Do you know how many lives have been saved by that once we knew how to perform transfusions?"

"No. I know so little about any kind of medicine."

"It's one big detective story. I'm going up there now to perform an autopsy on a twelve-year-old who died of a brain tumor. I've asked Cory and Jennifer to attend. We are seeing a disturbing uptick in brain tumors in the young. A researcher in Sweden reports that anyone using a cellphone before age twenty—and that's everyone, and they use them nonstop—that individual has a four to five times greater chance over a nonuser of developing a brain tumor. University of Pittsburgh Cancer Institute researchers report an increase in brain tumors in Americans under thirty. No warning about the dangers! The cellphone industry is at stake, and until the public demands changes, nothing will be done. In fact, it will be denied. Same with computers. We know they cause certain types of health damage, the eyes being the most obvious. Billions in revenue could be lost, so what's life compared to profit? Sometimes I wonder how long it will take for citizens to realize we have poisoned ourselves. Even plastics aren't as safe as you think. Every day I see the damage from all forms of pollution, from the chemicals—even from antibiotics in the meat we eat, to say nothing of hormones, which are even worse. We're awash in chemicals. Lung cancer is the leading cause of cancer death. Right? It's not all from smoking, Harry. It's the great American way: Blame the victim."

"I don't know why we're like that," Harry puzzled.

"It's the very air we breathe, and it's a result of those polluting industries belching out filth. I see what these substances do to the human body. Year after year, I see the man-made damage."

"Annalise, a lot of that has been cleaned up."

"Harry." Annalise reached out to her. "A lot hasn't. What's worse, we don't really know the life span of those particles released in, say, 1937. I didn't mean to take up your time, but I so care. I try not to let emotions affect me when I do my job, but I can tell you, looking at a twelve-year-old will affect me. Then I have to put it out of my mind and go to work. Maybe I can contribute something that will repair damage, slow injury, retard aging. I won't contribute on the level of Dr. Landsteiner, but I can do something to help."

"It's good you're passionate about your work. If people love their work, they're happy. We spend more time with our co-workers than we do with our families, most people." Harry mentally exempted herself, since she farmed.

Annalise touched Harry's hand. "You've been patient with me. Thanks. I can go a little over the top, but I see—literally—so much unnecessary damage to the human body, and I know there are many things that can be done to enrich life, to ease suffering. Our government—I don't care who's in charge—is bought off by the lobbies. If it threatens profits, forget it. The real threat to public health, apart from government, is the intertwining of the pharmaceutical giants and medicine."

"Things like stem cell treatments? Sure works for horses."

"That's not a result of pharmaceutical research. The problem there is it's a religious issue for some. A small but powerful group of anti-anything activists can hijack government and medicine. And they have. Your husband can perform treatments as a vet that I cannot. Until recently, hospitals didn't even allow acupuncture. Now there's evidence it releases enzymes that help to blunt pain, to heal. Human growth hormone, another substance produced by the body, drops off after age twenty-five, and if I could give it to people according to their age, I truly believe we could prevent aging. Aging is a disease. But here I am, one physician in central Virginia, no powerful friends, lacking great wealth. Who will listen to me?"

"I am."

Annalise smiled broadly. "So you have. I guess I needed to let it all out. Too much going on."

"Always is."

Annalise spontaneously leaned over and kissed Harry on the cheek. Then she headed for the hospital.

As Harry climbed into the Volvo, she saw Cory walking through the parking lot. He jogged to catch up to Annalise, and they walked to the entrance together.

Three faces looked up at Harry, whiskers forward in anticipation.

"*I thought she'd never shut up,*" Pewter moaned.

"Gang, I am so naïve. What have I been doing all my life?"

"*You were the postmistress of Crozet before they built the big post office,*" Tucker said. "*You were the best postmistress in the world.*"

"*Don't gild the lily, Tucker.*" Pewter lifted one dark gray eyebrow.

"*She was.*"

"*That means you've worked with other postmistresses,*" Pewter argued.

"*Miranda.*" The dog named Harry's friend, who had worked with her.

Miranda Hogendobber's husband, George, had been the postmaster for decades. When he passed away, Harry, fresh from Smith College, had fallen into the job, assuming it would be temporary.

When the new post office was built—quite a nice one, and much needed—she was told she couldn't bring her pets to work. No one much cared at the old, cozy PO. Furious, Harry resigned to take up farming full-time. Much as she missed that regular paycheck, she'd never regretted it.

Harry's eyes followed the two doctors, engaged in an animated conversation. Then Cory pushed open the large glass door for Annalise, and they disappeared into the hospital.

Mrs. Murphy jumped into the passenger seat, leaving Pewter and Tucker to fuss at each other in the back.

Absentmindedly, Harry reached over to pet the tiger cat once she'd started the wagon.

"Good news." Harry ran her forefinger under Mrs. Murphy's chin.

"*Good.*" The cat purred.

"All right. We're off and running. Who knows what else the day will bring."

29

he whole thrust of where we are now with cancer surgery," Cory Schaeffer spoke to Harry's support group, "is to get survival rates equivalent to those where women have undergone a radical mastectomy. We've accomplished that for the early stages of breast cancer." Sitting on a chair, he crossed his right leg over his left, holding his right ankle. "As many of you know, there is now tissue-targeted therapy, which we're using with those breast cancers that overexpress ERBB-two. Tremendous advances have been made in tissue-targeted therapy, as well as endocrine therapy. Tests now are far more sensitive than they were even ten years ago. We can use aromatase inhibitors for women, almost always postmenopausal, with hormone receptor–positive breast cancer." He took a deep breath. "What I do is remove your cancer, then advise treatments based upon the tumor, the stage of the cancer, and your body chemistry. My great hope is that one day we will be able to prevent breast cancer. We will be able to develop a vaccine just as we have for smallpox."

Tired from her second radiation treatment, Harry listened, but much of it went over her head.

He continued, "An immunologist at the Cleveland Clinic in Ohio believes breast cancer is a preventable disease. I do, too. Clinical trials of a vaccine could begin within the next two years. It's tremendously exciting."

At ease in front of a group, the handsome doctor forgot that his audience—unless they had the receptor-positive breast cancer or something rare, such as inflammatory breast cancer—might not understand the technical terms.

When Toni Enright asked for questions, many were for clarification.

Franny Howard asked the most interesting question. "Dr. Schaeffer, you mentioned a vaccine. Does that mean you think cancer is a virus?"

"Some cancers, yes. This is an issue often discussed by oncologists. Obviously there are different kinds of cancers, and they may be caused in different ways."

Now more alert since the discussion was less technical, Harry asked, "If cancer is a virus, then wouldn't people close to you come down with it?"

"In fact, Harry, they do. We all know of families where cancer runs through all the generations. Is it genetic? Probably, but there has to be something that kicks it off. This disease is so complex, we don't know. Can you give it to someone else like the common cold? Probably not, but we don't know. Some oncologists believe when we can cure the common cold, we will cure cancer. One thing that makes cancer work easier for doctors is it isn't disguised as something else, the way syphilis is."

Listening intently was Emily Udall, a young woman in Stage Four cancer. She'd been diagnosed with early-stage breast cancer when pregnant. She had delivered a healthy daughter, but her cancer exploded. Emily knew her time on earth was drawing nigh. But she fought on, more for her baby and her husband than for herself. She wanted to make certain she left them in as good an order as possible, but she feared her disease would reappear thirty years later in her beautiful baby girl.

Franny reached for Emily.

Emily put her hand over Franny's, then removed it and raised it. "Dr. Schaeffer."

"Emily." He was her surgeon.

"How early should my daughter begin getting tested?"

If only he didn't care so much about his patients. Wretched that he couldn't save Emily, couldn't save any woman diagnosed with cancer when pregnant, he said, "I'd begin checkups once she gets her period. And mammograms once her breasts develop. With your family history, this is critical, and we can fervently hope that by the time Teresa reaches adolescence, we will be far more advanced than we are today."

Emily's grandmothers on both sides of her family had developed breast cancer. Her mother also died from it.

The questions continued, and Cory did his best not to be so technical.

Watching Emily, Harry realized that what Regina and Jennifer told her was the truth: She had been lucky. Bad as it was to be diagnosed with cancer, her chances were excellent. She knew she wasn't a deep thinker. Her interests weren't superficial—she loved art history, she loved history, and, of course, she loved farming—but Harry hadn't considered the giant questions of life. She'd not given much thought to her purpose, to the direction of her nation, to the fragility of both democracy and life. In a strange way, she was becoming grateful to that invader of her breast. How could she sit near an attractive young mother, her chances nil, and not ask profound questions?

Perhaps the most painful was: Am I living a full life? Am I reaching out to others, be they human or animal? Am I doing one thing to make the world a better place?

She snapped back to the group when Cory and Toni agreed to disagree.

"He has more faith in these things than I do. But he's the doctor." Toni smiled.

For all his sometimes arrogance, Cory wanted to ease suffering as much as he wanted to cure cancer. "A regimen of vitamins, staying away from too much salt and sugar, and exercise can help. I actually think in some cases faithfully taking care of yourself through diet, supplements, and even walking a mile a day can jump-start the body's healing." He became animated. "Your body wants to be healthy. Again, we don't understand the interplay between good health habits and disease as much as we should. The emphasis in Western medicine is always on disease, not health. We are woefully behind with preventive medicine, but I believe your body wants to live, to be healthy. How can I or any other doctor explain how a person dying of lung cancer sponta-

neously heals? An X ray reveals no dark mass. And that person lives another twenty years. While these events are considered uncommon and
exceptions that prove the rule, I don't think they are. I think, however,
whoever that individual was, they triggered the body's deepest mecha-
nisms to heal. Sometimes I think we—by 'we' I mean modern medicine—interfere with that. And I am the first one to be dazzled by
technology. Yet what are we missing? What am I missing?"

Harry never expected Cory to show a streak of humility, to openly
question himself. She thought of Annalise's passionate outburst yesterday. Maybe a sensitive human being can't work every day with the
Emilys of this world and not be touched.

Cory handed everyone a sheet of paper with simple vitamin sugges-
tions based on what type of procedure the woman had undergone,
which treatments they were in now.

Harry's sheet listed a multivitamin, vitamin E, vitamin C, and potassium.

"Harry, I spoke with Jennifer. You had cancer light." He half smiled,
handing her the paper. "So this is my short list, but you might want to
speak with her yourself. Noddy told me you're working out two days a
week now. With your farmwork, that's very positive."

"Thank you for taking the time to do this for each of us."

"Half of your group are my patients. I'm delighted they are in this
group, and Toni will keep everyone going."

Harry looked up at him. "There must be times when this is hard on
you."

He waited, then lowered his voice. "It is. I tell myself every woman I
see is a legacy. She is teaching me for others, and I truly believe in my
lifetime I will see a vaccine or possibly a preventive measure, such as
taking a pill every morning if you're at risk."

"I hope I live to see it, too."

"You will," he confidently predicted.

After her meeting, Harry drove to the GNC store in the mall. She
bought each of the vitamins Cory suggested. She now had an arsenal to
accompany her Centrum.

When she arrived home, she kissed her pets and carried the small
bag into the kitchen.

"No time like the present." She opened the bottles, grabbed a Coke, and counted out one pill each.

"That's the smell!" Tucker barked loudly.

"What are you making noise about?" Pewter, miffed that Harry hadn't brought treats or toys, complained.

"That's the smell, much stronger, that I smelled on Paula!"

Mrs. Murphy leapt onto the table. She batted over the bottles, then knocked Harry's pills, like tiny hockey pucks, onto the floor.

"Hey!" Harry quickly grabbed the white plastic bottles, for she'd turned her back.

Mrs. Murphy stuck her nose in each bottle. *"That's it."*

Pewter, mouth agape, was too surprised and curious to continue complaining.

"What is it?" Tucker called up, her nose on an oblong pill.

"Potassium." Mrs. Murphy then knocked that bottle on the floor, the pills scattering all over the place.

"Murph!" Harry lunged for the bottle.

The cats and Tucker grabbed what pills they could, ran outside, and spit them in the grass.

"Oh, my God, will we die?" Pewter realized what she'd done.

"We'll know soon enough," Mrs. Murphy calmly replied.

Harry, livid, blasted outside only to see those pills ruined. "I could just kill you all!"

"We might have saved you the trouble." A mournful Pewter regretted her moment of bravery.

By 8:00 P.M., all were fine. At 5:30 A.M., the usual rising time, the three got up hale and hardy.

Pewter, thrilled to be alive, said, *"Looks like you two were wrong."*

"No, we weren't." Tucker stoutly spoke up.

"Pewter, the potassium smell was the exact same smell." Mrs. Murphy sat next to the only dog she loved.

"Why did it kill Paula and not us?" Pewter asked, reasonably enough.

"I don't know, but I hope we find out," the tiger cat answered.

30

*F*lopped backward over a large plastic ball, Harry did sit-ups, hands clasped behind her head, all while trying to keep the ball steady.

"Crap," she muttered under her breath as she rolled off. Another tough early-morning workout.

"Butter butt, you slid off." Noddy offered zip sympathy.

"Tell me why I'm doing this again?"

"Pride." Noddy lifted one eyebrow. "You want a few more? To look sexy for your wonderful husband, to strengthen your body while it struggles with an invader."

"Oh, right." Harry put her two feet flat on the floor and scooched up on the ball.

"This is one of those great core exercises. It works so much. I know you can feel it."

"Yep." Harry started again. After doing three sets of ten reps, she gratefully stood up.

"Assume the position." Noddy pointed to the ball.

"I did them."

"Yes, you did, and now you're adding a twist, literally. You only have to do one set. Right elbow to left knee. Left elbow to right knee."

Harry found this more difficult than a regular sit-up. Gritting her teeth, she was determined not to slide off. She managed, standing up, dripping with sweat.

"Need a break?"

"One sip." Harry toweled off, picked up her bottle of water, un-screwed the cap, and took a swig. Water never tasted so good. "All right. What next?"

"Take heart. You're very nearly finished for the morning."

"Oh, thank you, Jesus." Harry rolled her eyes. After all this, beating cancer and figuring out why Paula and Thadia died should be a cinch.

"Last one. Then you do some warm-downs, as I think of them. Okay, grab two dumbbells."

Harry walked to the rack, picked them out. Gray mats covered the floor. A smaller, volleyball-sized ball with two rubber handles was there, as well as two medicine balls on the floor.

From here, she saw the main room of Heavy Metal Gym. Out of the corner of her eye she could see Annalise pulling down one hundred pounds on the lat machine. Toni Enright was there somewhere, but Harry couldn't see her.

"When do I graduate to the real weight room?" She faced Noddy.

"Don't think of it as graduation. You build muscle there. You build some here, too, but the purpose of these exercises is to make you strong and supple. This can improve reflexes, especially the explosive exercises."

"Do I need firecrackers?" Harry asked. She wondered whether if Thadia had had better reflexes she wouldn't have ended up with her throat slashed.

Noddy smiled. "You perform each exercise very quickly, usually four sets of ten for each exercise, twenty seconds in between. You'll start some of those next week. You haven't been at this all that long. Don't be impatient."

"Right." Harry sighed.

"You're doing good. You started in pretty good shape, an advantage. Now give me those dumbbells."

Noddy knelt on the floor, then got in a push-up position, her hands on the dumbbells. She dipped low, one good push-up, torso straight, then she pulled the right dumbbell up to her chest, a rowing motion. After returning the dumbbell to the floor, she repeated the same se-quence for her left side.

"Got it?" Noddy handed the dumbbells to Harry.

"Got it." Harry dropped down, fired off ten.

This was easier than the big ball until she had to do four sets. Still, she liked it better than struggling to keep her balance. It felt good to make her mind a blank. Maybe working out would help her look at things with a new perspective.

After that, Harry did some more stretching, then on to the stationary bicycle, another exercise she disliked. She didn't mind running in the open fields on the farm, nor did she mind bicycling down the farm roads, although she preferred riding a horse. To sit there—pedaling and going nowhere—tried her patience. But she did it. Once she'd put in twenty minutes, she gratefully retired to the locker room. She couldn't remember a shower feeling so good.

Few women came in at this early hour. She'd hoped she'd catch Annalise and Toni, but they'd wrapped up their workout and already left.

On Harry's way out, Noddy came out from her small office. "Hey, Toni left this for you."

Harry took the magazine, opening it to the page marked by a paper clip. "That was nice of her."

It was a glossy women's magazine. Harry rarely read them, but this one had a roundtable discussion of five women who had various types of cancer.

"You know what I find about people who have recovered from anything, illness or injury?" Noddy asked.

"What?"

"Most of them renew themselves," Noddy said.

"Yes, it's true. I'm asking myself questions I never asked before, and hey, I'm here."

"Exactly." Noddy smiled.

Driving home, Harry opened the windows to breathe in the sweetness of spring. Once on Route 250, she put them up again as her speed picked up.

Difficult as those workouts were proving to be, Harry found that once home, she burned through her chores, feeling much more energetic. She also found that her concentration was improving.

"I wish she'd take us to the gym." Tucker followed behind as Harry ladled out sweet feed.

"*Someone would complain about allergies.*" Pewter also followed, making frequent stops to check for anything left on the aisle floor that might prove edible.

"*There are shots for that.*" Mrs. Murphy walked ahead of Pewter.

"*Well, what did people do before the shots? What did people do when George Washington was president?*" Pewter batted a piece of molasses along the aisle floor. "*They sneezed and lived with it. Now everyone has a condition. Wimps. They run to the doctor for a shot or a pill. If you ask me, those allergy doctors should give us a percent of their wages for sending people to them.*"

Simon, the possum, hearing this, peeped over the edge of the hayloft. "*You woke me up.*"

"*It's not my fault you're a nocturnal creature.*" Pewter exaggerated her sashay.

Mrs. Murphy climbed the ladder to the hayloft to catch up with Simon. Pewter and Tucker remained below.

The perfect morning with low humidity added to Harry's returning energy. The exercise helped, but also the effects of the radiation were wearing off. She had two more treatments. All she could think about was being done with it.

Then she'd need to go in for six-month checkups. More money spent.

She couldn't help but fret over the cost as the bills came in for use of the operating room, from the anesthesiologist, the post-op room, the hospital room, the surgeon's bill. That bill she gladly paid, for she liked Jennifer and was relieved at her small scar. It could have been so much worse.

She knew she'd spend the rest of her life enduring checkups, blood tests, and mammograms. On one level, she didn't care. If it wasn't for Fair, Susan, and her friends, she'd probably bag it. She'd be in more danger from their anger than from the cancer recurring.

Walking back from her grapes—happy as she could be with how healthy they looked at this early stage, dew on the leaves—her three best friends in attendance, she saw Coop tearing down the driveway.

Tucker's ears pricked. "*Wonder if she has treats.*"

"*She usually doesn't,*" Pewter replied.

"*Yeah, I know, but I'm just in the mood for a bone or cookies,*" the intrepid dog said.

Harry reached Coop's Dodge just as the lanky blonde stepped out. "Hey, neighbor."

"Hey back at you. I brought over all the registration papers, the figures for T-shirt sales, pink wristbands. Here's the final accounting for the race, plus all the registration papers."

"I thought Nita was doing all that."

"She did. That's why everything is tidy, simplified, and down to the penny. I ran into her at the post office, and she asked me to take the papers to Cory. She was going to do it, but the insurance people want to go over the Pinnacle Records site one more time. I meant to do it, then I forgot I unloaded the truck and saw the red folder. So I figured I'd pick you up and we could drop it off together, then go over to the nursery on Route One-fifty-one, Jeffrey Howe's place."

Immediately interested, Harry eagerly agreed, because she wanted to plant Leyland cypress. "I bet it takes months or even a year before Al and Nita get a check from the insurance company. They need it to rebuild."

"The company has to establish that the Vitebsks didn't set the fire themselves."

"Coop, that's absurd. Surely John Watson doesn't believe that." She named the owner of Hanckel-Citizens, a local insurance company.

"Of course he doesn't, but he finds the best, cheapest insurer, and those companies are gigantic. So they send their own team. I talked to Marsha Moran about it," Coop said, mentioning a member of the Hanckel-Citizens team. "She said it was standard procedure. John and Marsha will also be at the site to be sure that the investigators understand that Al and Nita are people of good character."

"With so much of what we do in the hands of giant corporations or the government, I'm surprised anyone cares."

"Hey, John and Marsha do. You're sounding like a cynic."

"Oh, just a tad. Let's go in my truck. Then the kids can come along."

"Oh, pile in." Coop opened the door to her vehicle. "What's a little cat and dog hair?"

"*Hooray.*" The cats jumped in.

Tucker, lifted up with a grunt by Harry, grumbled, "*I don't shed that much. Your old mohair sweaters shed more than I do.*"

Cory lived some miles behind the Miller School. The road, parts paved and parts not, would lead you to an I-64 ramp. He and his wife had built one of the very expensive houses within four miles of the interstate.

Harry loved looking at the countryside, which was easier to do when someone else was driving. "You going to leave this at Cory's door?"

"Nita said this is one of his consultation days, so he might still be there. Isn't she something? She put everything in that plastic red folder. Have you ever noticed how much easier it is to find stuff if it's in colored paper or a colored box?"

"I have. She's smart, Nita. Cory doesn't do but so much—well, he can't really for the five-K, but he is our titular head, and he should have copies of everything. When did they do that?" Her attention was diverted by a large new feed shed for cattle.

"This year. I don't come down this road often."

"Me neither. Good design. I get more excited about barns, sheds, kennel designs than I do house designs. I really try to read the house magazines, but it's all so fussy."

"Well, Harry, it's another way for people to show off."

"I suppose."

At Cory's driveway, they turned left off the road just in time to see him get into his green Lampo. He did not see them.

There was suddenly a startlingly bright flash, and Harry saw the physician jolt violently upward in his seat.

"Oh, my God!" she shouted.

Coop pressed the gas pedal, fishtailing up the long crushed-gravel drive, flopping the animals back in the seat. She skidded to a halt behind the Lampo.

As the two women opened the car doors, they ran toward the electric car but didn't dare approach it.

Cory Schaeffer was banging back and forth in the seat. His body would hit the seat, then lurch furiously forward to smash his chest against the wheel. His face was twisted and barely recognizable. He was being fried at 440 volts at forty amps.

"Coop, if we touch anything, we'll be electrocuted."

Coop ran back to her truck, grabbed her cell, and immediately called 911. Then she called the Lampo dealer. Completing that call, she closed the door of the truck because she didn't want the animals to get out. Coop, regardless of the crisis, had presence of mind, which was partly her personality and partly her law enforcement training.

Harry had turned away from the dreadful sight. "I can't bear it."

They could hear him thumping back and forth. Worse, they could smell the fat in his body frying.

"The battery goes for over three hundred miles. Can't stop this."

"I called Barker Rund, the Lampo dealer. He's on his way," Coop said.

"What can he do?"

"All dealers have a skeleton keyless entry. He's bringing it. If he hits it, the car will turn off. He's on Pantops Mountain. I called to get him a sheriff's escort. They should be here in fifteen minutes, twenty at the latest."

"Have you ever seen anything like this?"

"No. I've seen some pretty terrible things, but nothing like this. Thank God the kids are in school. Can you imagine if they witnessed this?"

"I don't see any other car, so let's hope his wife doesn't get home until she's picked them up from school. My God, this is like the electric chair."

"Worse."

Coop called it to the minute that Barker Rund with his head mechanic, escorted in a squad car by Sheriff Shaw, arrived. To their credit, neither the dealer nor the mechanic puked. Barker hit the remote, the motor stopped, and the hideous remains of Cory slid down the seat.

Rick, tough, gulped. "Coop, go down and block the driveway until the ambulance arrives, will you? Even if his wife comes home, don't let her up here."

Harry sat in the truck with Coop as she turned and drove down the drive.

Back at the horrible scene, Rick asked Barker, "Can he be removed without danger?"

"Yes, now he can. But to be sure, we'll drain the battery. It's far too heavy to lift out."

"Barker, you're sure?"

"I'm sure. The circuit is broken. And Tom grabbed a tester just to make certain there's no leak."

Tom was the head mechanic.

Rick, still unconvinced, followed the men to the car. "Barker, how could something like this happen?"

"I don't know. I really don't know. Jesus Christ, Sheriff, do you think I'd sell cars if I thought they were capable of doing this to someone?"

Rick, knowing Barker was shaken, soothingly said, "I know you wouldn't."

Working as fast as possible, the body was removed before Mrs. Schaeffer and the children got home. Rick took pictures with his cellphone. They may not have been protocol, but being the boss means you know when to drop protocol without jeopardizing a case.

The car was towed to the dealership. The mechanics found out what had happened easily enough. Someone had direct-wired the battery to the metal frame of the driver's seat. When Cory turned on the car, he was instantly electrocuted. The pain had to have been ferocious. He could have felt it for only a second or two, but he did feel it.

•   •   •

Later, Harry was home, Fair with her, when Coop called.

"I'm sorry to call so late, but I thought you'd like to know that a yellow cylinder like what you found at Paula Benton's was in the backseat of the Lampo."

"What in the hell is going on?" Harry blurted out.

"I don't know. Are you all right?"

"Yeah. Well, as all right as I can be. What about you?"

"Same. I keep thinking I will have seen everything in my line of work, every humiliation and violence to which the human body can be subjected, and then there's something new."

After talking a bit more, Harry hung up. She told Fair the news.

"Not one of them was a horseman," he replied.

"This is so bizarre. But if there's one thing life has taught me, it's that what seems bizarre always makes sense once we find out the killer's reason."

"If only *she hadn't said 'we,'*" Tucker wisely noted.

31

*A*nnalise finished harvesting organs from a young suicide. Done, she left her assistant to sew up the body, peeled off her gloves, and washed up.

As she stepped outside, Toni Enright walked into the anteroom, a grim look on her face.

"What's the matter?"

"Cory's dead."

"What?" Annalise stepped closer to Toni. "How?"

"Electrocuted by his Lampo."

"Oh, no." Annalise swayed.

Toni caught her, maneuvering her to a chair. "Sit down. This is a terrible, terrible thing, and the staff has had too many shocks these last weeks."

"I told him not to buy that damned electric car! I warned him that no matter what they tell you—and I went to look at one, too—that much voltage isn't safe. It can never be safe. A gasoline engine might seize up, but it won't take you with it. The gas tank might explode in an accident, but your chances are good to get out without bad burns if you have your wits about you or aren't comatose behind the wheel. But these things—why, why didn't he listen to me?"

"Listening was not his strong suit," replied Toni, her voice kind. "He thought he knew more than he did about a lot of things. Maybe we're all like that."

"I grew up with cars. I explained everything to him. I told him that at four hundred and forty volts, it would take less than one amp to kill a person. He blew me off, saying that was impossible. The bypass safety relay and backups provided ironclad safety. They're too new. You never buy the first year of any car model, because the bugs haven't been worked out yet. In something this new, you're nuts to buy one." She dropped her head in her hands.

Toni leaned over, put her arm around Annalise's shoulders. "You did all you could."

Tears running down her lovely face, Annalise strangled a wail. "The man couldn't even change a spark plug."

"No, but he was one hell of a surgeon."

Annalise nodded in agreement. "Fervent."

"Pardon?"

"Fervent. He truly wanted to cure cancer. The hours that man spent with me here, and Jennifer, too, examining the ones who died from various cancers." She wiped her eyes with the palms of her hands.

Toni walked over to the counter, plucked out some tissues, brought them back. "Here. You need to hold it together."

Annalise wiped her eyes. "Mascara."

"You look like a raccoon. Here, let me fix it." Toni fetched more tissues, wetted them at the small sink, then cleaned under the pathologist's eyes. "You'll need a reapplication."

"Have a tube in my bag. Toni, how did you find out?"

"Izzy Wineberg took the call from Sheriff Shaw. Couldn't find Will Archer," she said, naming the hospital administrator. "Izzy came down to our department. We are being told department by department, and I think Izzy will oversee a notice to go out by email, as well as for a printed bulletin."

"As the most senior physician, he's the best choice."

"Yes. I don't think there is a doctor here more respected than Izzy. But here's the thing"—she again wiped a speck from under Annalise's eye—"the cops think Paula Benton's death, Thadia Martin's death, and Cory's may be linked."

Annalise's eyes opened wide. "Nothing was found to have caused Paula's death. And Cory's, I told him! I told him!"

"Annalise, lower your voice."

"Oh, Toni." She put her hands to her face, dropping her head back, exposing her swanlike neck. "I doubt they're all connected."

"It does seem a stretch, but Izzy doesn't know the details. They're treating Cory's death as murder."

"What?"

"According to Izzy, the car was, I don't know the terms, anyway, hotwired."

A long silence followed. "It couldn't be. Rachel knows nothing about cars," Annalise said, naming Cory's wife.

"Did she find out?"

"No. At least he didn't think she did." A deep breath followed. "Look, if she did, I wasn't the first. I seriously doubt his wife would kill him. Hit him with a frying pan, yes, but kill him, no."

"Did you love him? All the times we talked about covering your tracks, I never asked."

Annalise looked directly into Toni's eyes. "I loved him, but I wasn't in love with him. We shared a passion—more for medicine than each other—but it was good. We pushed each other to learn more, look more deeply. And we were both always figuring out how to invest, utilize our resources. That doesn't sound romantic, but it drew us closer. Everyone thinks doctors are rich. Well, I make a much better living than someone in a computer pool, but the expenses are considerable, and there's all those school loans to repay. We talked about everything. I will miss him."

Toni looked through the large glass window in the door. "Your assistant is washing up. You don't know what kind of emotions will well up, so do your best: Repress." She squeezed Annalise's shoulder. "Pull it together. Bad as it is, it would be much worse if you had been in love with him."

Annalise rose to walk with Toni to the outside door. "Maybe. He was my friend before he was my lover. Lovers come and go, Toni; a friend is forever."

"You might be right." Toni hugged her, then slipped out the door.

• • •

Izzy Wineberg fielded calls, soothed some shaken staff members, and was grateful when he had a moment to himself in his private bathroom in his large office. He washed his face, then held a washrag, wrung out, to his face.

Rising like a comet in the medical world, Central Virginia Medical Complex wouldn't be brought down by what now appeared to be connected deaths. Ten years ago at the old hospital, there had been murders, related, as they usually are, to money. It's always love or money. He patted his face dry with a fluffy towel, courtesy of his wife of forty-six years. She filled his life with all manner of thoughtful objects and events.

On the subject of wives, he knew Cory had cut a wide swath through the hospital nursing staff, and probably outside, as well. He was that kind of guy.

Izzy faced two immediate conundrums. The first was: If he told Sheriff Shaw about Cory's conquests, would the sheriff raise the issue with Cory's wife, Rachel? What a wretched time for a woman to learn her husband suffered from chronic infidelity. Then again, maybe she knew. But Izzy doubted it. He'd seen them together many times, been a guest at their home. But people can be marvelous actors, he reminded himself.

The second problem—thornier—would need a deft touch. Paula and Cory had worked together. Thadia had not, but one could hardly miss the fact that the woman was besotted with the surgeon. Physicians solve mysteries. You can't cure a patient until you know what ails him or her. Using all the skills that had served him well in his profession, Izzy discarded extraneous information, concentrating on symptoms. His conclusion: Cory Schaeffer was central to this string of murders.

32

The fruit-bearing trees dropped their blossoms, and tiny little bumps of peaches, pears, and apples gave hope for a good crop. The dogwoods, too, lost their beautiful white or pink blossoms. Trees began to fill out, the light spring green already turning a shade darker.

Daffodils and tulips faded in their place while, like blaring trumpets, irises opened. There were small, intense Japanese irises, bearded irises in lavender, a maroon iris with a peach interior. There was every shade of purple imaginable. Along with the early irises, the azaleas created luxurious oceans of color. It's a rare Virginia residence lacking in azaleas or irises. People will haul in sand to give those azalea bushes the right soil.

Some years the azaleas and irises did not bloom in sync, but this year they did, and Harry marveled at the color around her house and in the big wooden half buckets in front of the barn. Eventually those buckets would give way to the ever-hardy geraniums and petunias.

Kneeling, she weeded out her flower bed by the back door. She'd have another radiation treatment at the end of the week, so it'd be better to get this task done now. She knew she'd be even more tired than she was the last time.

In her support group, she learned not only about what cancer does to the body but also what the treatments do. A combination of chemo and radiation seems designed to kill cancer cells and very nearly the patient. Grateful that she had to face only radiation, she joked with those sisters about losing their hair, their appetite, and their energy. Thankfully, nobody lost their sense of humor.

One of the girls quipped, "God made hair to cover imperfect heads."

Some invested in good wigs, and those without funds were helped out by an organization that makes wigs for indigent cancer patients. Others wore baseball caps and said, "The hell with it."

Harry didn't know how she'd handle that. She knew what she faced wasn't nearly as bad as what so many of the others had. Still, she felt it: the slide in energy; the gusts of irritability, which she took pains to hide; and sometimes the sorrow of it. Yes, she was doing great, in good shape, but the idea that her body had fooled her troubled her.

She'd repeat over and over to herself the mantra of her support group: I have cancer; cancer doesn't have me.

The long rays of late-afternoon sun brushed the barn, the fields, the old handblown glass in the windowpanes. Harry thought of this as soft light, almost liquid light, and like most country people, she felt one of the compensations for winter's harshness was the magical quality of the light, no matter what the time. But now, mid-spring, one waited for late afternoon.

"Coop," Tucker barked, for she heard Coop's truck turn off the road far away, onto the gravel farm drive.

Coop pulled up next to the barn.

Harry stood up, dropping a handful of persistent weeds into the blue muck bucket. Dusting off her knees, she walked toward the tall blonde just stepping out of her truck.

"Hey, neighbor."

Coop smiled. "The place looks great."

"Thank you. I couldn't stand looking at those weeds one more minute."

"You're much better about weeding than I am." Coop sighed. "Got a minute?"

"Of course. Come on in and let me wash up." Harry peeled off her gardening gloves, putting them on a high shelf inside the screened-in porch, because if Tucker could reach them, she ran off with them.

In the kitchen, as clean as possible, given that she'd been gardening, Harry asked, "Your pleasure, madam?"

"Iced tea, if you have it."

"Sounds like just the thing."

Harry reached into the big double-door fridge and grabbed the handle of a full jar of unsweetened tea. Heavier than she thought, for she was weaker than she realized, she had to use both hands to get it to the counter.

Coop noticed, rose, and poured the tea. "You'll come back."

Frustrated, Harry plucked out a lemon from a bowl on the counter and sliced it. "I know. If I weren't going to Heavy Metal, it would be even worse. It comes, then goes. I don't mean it comes out of nowhere. I've noticed a definite schedule. Exhaustion after radiation. That turns into tiredness the next day, and each day away from the treatment, I improve. And it's the same way for, I don't know, strength. But the effects last longer. One last treatment. Really, Coop, I've been lucky."

Coop put the jar back in the fridge, and they both walked to the rough-hewn kitchen table.

The cats jumped up on the counter to eat from their large crunchie bowl. Harry filled it once a day, doing the same for Tucker.

"Brought you this." Coop plucked a small jar of potassium tablets out of her back jeans pocket.

"Good you did before you sat down." Harry opened the jar, for Coop had slit the plastic covering. She knew Harry's grip hadn't been as strong since the treatments.

"*What!*" Both cats looked up.

Before any of the animals could respond, Harry popped a vitamin into her mouth.

"*Oh, no,*" Tucker wailed.

"Tucker, calm yourself."

The three animals stared in horror, waiting for Harry to keel over.

As the two humans chatted, Pewter finally said, "*Maybe it's not the same smell.*"

"It is!" both Tucker and Mrs. Murphy shouted, which brought quite a rebuke from Harry.

Fifteen minutes passed.

"*She's fine,*" Pewter pronounced.

"*Maybe it takes a long time,*" Tucker worried.

"*We ate them,*" Pewter rightly said.

"*Our systems are different.*" Mrs. Murphy stopped eating, baffled.

"*It is the same smell,*" Tucker insisted.

"*Obviously, there's something we don't know.*" Mrs. Murphy intently watched Harry.

"*Maybe it was used in combination with something lethal, or maybe it's the way you take it,*" Pewter logically offered.

"*The problem is, anyone can buy this stuff.*" Tucker lay down by Harry's chair. "*We can't isolate the killer through the smell.*"

"*Maybe, maybe not.*" Mrs. Murphy, as curious as any cat, hated not knowing something as much as Harry did.

The two humans talked, unaware of the concerned conversation swirling around them.

"Did you know that rottweilers are being studied to understand long lives?" Harry pushed a piece of paper toward Coop. "Fair showed me this at breakfast."

"Huh." Coop read that a thirteen-year-old rottweiler is the equivalent of a one-hundred-year-old human.

"The study comes out of the Cancer Foundation in West Lafayette, Indiana. Isn't that something? The old rottweilers escaped cancer, renal failure, all that stuff. It will be fascinating to see what's discovered."

"On the subject of long lives, I came by to drop off your potassium and to talk about short lives." She then conveyed Dr. Isadore Wineberg's conclusion.

"He's right, but, Coop, is it possible that Thadia killed Paula? She had some provocation in her own mind, at least, and the scarab fit into her bracelet. Then someone kills her."

"Anything is possible." Cooper squeezed more lemon into her tea.

"Cory's spectacular demise supports Izzy's idea that Cory is at the center of all this."

"Well, he's paid for it."

"Which means someone is still out there." Harry thought. "Any other clues you're willing to share?"

"No. Well, there is one thing, and it's a long shot. The fire at Pinnacle Records. Paula rented a file cabinet there, so her records were destroyed. Big Al said she went in a few days before she died. They have to sign in and sign out. She deposited a file in the cabinet. They're locked. It probably has no bearing at all on the deaths, but it's all we've got."

"No. You have the yellow cylinders. Paula had one. Cory had one."

"Right. I've thought of everything. Too small for organs. Really too small for the amounts of cocaine that would make one rich. I'd estimate the cylinder might hold eight thousand to ten thousand dollars' worth of cocaine if wrapped in plastic, compressed."

"That's a lot of money."

"Not in that business, Harry." Coop finished her tea, got up, poured more for her and Harry. "More lemon?"

"No, thanks."

"I don't think Cory would be dumb enough to risk his license for ten thousand dollars a pop."

"But if he had a thing going for years, it sure would add up."

"It would. But the longer you deal, the higher your chances of being found out. If Cory or Paula had something to do with drugs, they'd go for hundreds of thousands, millions. Then it would be worth the risk."

"I guess."

"I thought about stealing expensive sperm from high-priced stallions. Now, could they do it? Neither one could handle a stallion and collect from the animal. They'd be injured or dead."

"True enough, but they could steal it from someone who had. Particularly if the straws were in liquid nitrogen and stored to be shipped the next day. The problem with that theory is that whoever was missing the straws of sperm would report them missing immediately."

"No such reports." Coop put her fingers together like a steeple. "And how would they even know the value of a stallion's semen? That's not the answer."

"No."

"Then I thought about shipping organs," Coop said. "But the cylinder isn't big enough. There is a huge black market for organs."

"I didn't know that."

"In our country—in other countries, too. Sometimes a single man is at a bar and a pretty woman baits him, so the stories go. Mr. Gullible goes to her hotel room, is knocked over the head, anesthetized, and operated on—usually, it's taking one kidney; they don't kill these people. Then they place them in the tub, ice pack on the incision. When the guy awakens, there's a note on the ice pack telling him what has happened and to call nine-one-one. It's big, big business, and still some horny men are dumb enough to walk off with a woman they don't know. Can you imagine a woman doing that?" Coop threw up her hands.

"Yes, but not to the numbers that men do it."

"Well, as far as I know, there is not one report of a woman being robbed of her kidney. Who knows? Now, there might be one today, but so far it's men. Imagine getting out of a tub, a fresh incision, one organ removed, no painkiller, and finding the phone in the hotel room."

Harry grimaced. "Awful."

They sat there thinking about these things. "I even thought there could be a scheme involving stealing drugs from the hospital—Percodan, OxyContin—packing them in the cylinders, and sending them out again. But there are much easier ways to distribute stolen prescription drugs."

"Figure out what goes in those cylinders, and I expect you'll find the killer."

Coop leaned forward. "You're so observant, and you're at the hospital every week for your support group. Keep your eyes open."

"I will."

"*That means we have to figure out how to get into the hospital,*" Mrs. Murphy worried.

"*Not so easy,*" Tucker said, stating the obvious.

"*If you were a teacup dog, you could hide in Harry's handbag. But with your bubble butt, you couldn't even hide in a potato sack.*" Pewter peered over the countertop to harass the dog.

"*Zat so? Well, they'd need a gurney just for you, Miss Tubby.*"

The gray cat launched off the counter, right onto the sturdy dog. The two rolled across the floor amid furious yowling and growling.

Harry stood up. "That's enough."

This had no effect, so she ran over to the sink, pulled out the sprayer,

and shot water at the animals. The dog and cat ran in opposite directions.

"I don't know what gets into those two," Harry said as she knelt
down to wipe up the floor.

Coop knelt down to help, but she couldn't stop laughing. She didn't
know which was funnier, the dog and cat or Harry with the sprayer.

33

*B*ack down and reverse arms," Noddy commanded. "You're going to do ten of these for each arm."

"Noddy, you can be hateful."

"That's right." Noddy crossed her arms over her chest as she carefully monitored Harry.

After ten, the end of a long workout, Harry sat on the gym's floor. "I am so glad that's over."

"You're doing good. I think these exercises and the one balancing on the large ball are especially difficult. You're forced to use a lot of muscles, whereas in the weight room, you isolate one muscle, like your quads, and you work it to exhaustion. These exercises strengthen your entire body, especially your core, and they create better balance. Mind you, down the road, once the effects of the treatments are vanishing, if you want to add bulk, I'm glad to help. The biggest mistake women make is not developing their upper body. From the waist down leg power." She paused. "Men, women, doesn't matter. It's the upper body where most women are afraid to look muscular. Obviously, that was never my problem."

"I never thought about it."

"You're fit and strong. Farmwork is its own kind of workout. But look in magazines, the photos of models. No muscle tone. No muscle. Why don't they paint a big red V on their head for victim?"

"Never thought about that, either."

"Think about it this way. You're a drug addict desperate for a fix. No money. You've blown everything you have, lost jobs, you get the picture. You need to steal. Grabbing a purse and running is safer than robbing a grocery store. Two women are walking down the street, and you know these streets, so you know you can get away. One woman is well dressed, wearing a bit of heel, very pretty and slender. The other woman isn't bad-looking, but you can see she has some muscles in her arms. Who are you going to push and grab their purse?"

"The weak one."

"I rest my case. All right, hit the bike."

Harry, having caught her breath while listening to Noddy, walked into the narrow room with the bikes and stationary walkers. A large TV, tilted down, was tuned to CNN.

Harry was not much for TV unless it was The Weather Channel. She put on her earphones, tucked the player into her shorts' waistband, and listened to *Wolf Hall* by Hilary Mantel on tape.

She never listened to music or books when she was outside working. The conversation of all living things fascinated her far more than the work of humans. But once out of the fields and forest, she liked to learn. Fair had had a CD player installed in the old Ford F-150, since it was built before that technology existed. She could ride around and listen to a book. She tried to read before bedtime but usually fell asleep, the book on her chest. Fair would come in, gently lift up the book, and tell her to go to bed. If she was in bed, he'd take the book, put it on the nightstand, and cut the reading light. While he wasn't a night owl, he could still last longer than she could. When twilight faded into night, Harry started to fade with it.

But here, at 6:30 A.M., her workout finished except for the part with the stationary bike, she was wide awake.

Twenty minutes later, finished, she clicked off the portable player, dismounted, snatched her towel off the seat. She couldn't ride that bike, or any bike, without a towel. The seats were so uncomfortable. How men did it, she couldn't imagine.

Just as she dismounted, so did the man next to her. He was in his mid-thirties and was unfamiliar to her. She didn't know as many city people as she did country people. His body was a work of art and discipline.

He, however, knew of her. He'd asked around, because he found her very attractive. As she was married, he didn't pursue her, but he kept his eye on her if she was around.

"Good workout?" he asked.

"Was. What about you?"

"Good. I'm Dawson English."

She held out her hand. "Harry Haristeen. Well, actually, my name is Mary Minor Haristeen, but everyone has called me Harry since I was little because my clothes were always covered in cat and dog hair. I hope you don't have allergies."

"No, ma'am." He shook her hand.

He smiled, releasing her hand, much as he enjoyed holding it. "You're in good shape."

"Well, thank you. You, too. You must have a lot of motivation to create a body like that."

"I sit a lot on the job. I get to walk the floor a little, but I was putting on weight. Hated it, so five years ago I made up my mind to really work for the best body I could have."

"Staring at a computer?"

"No. I work at Flow Automotive. Sales. I like it. Well, when you have a good product, the cars sell themselves." He grinned. "Don't suppose you need a VW or a Porsche? Now, you would look spectacular in a Nine-eleven C-four."

"Zero to fifty in four-point-four seconds, and the Turbo is even faster." Harry looked up at him. "But you know, the new Cadillac CTS-V hits zero to sixty in, I think, three-point-nine seconds, which is hard to believe for a sports car, much less a big car."

Surprised, he leaned forward. "You like cars?"

"I love cars. I love tractors. I love anything with a motor in it. I even like riding mowers."

He laughed. "That's great."

"I'm sure you know that Don and Robin King are sponsors of a polo team, Team Flow, and they are the backbone of the Pink Ribbon Polo Classic, along with King Family Vineyards. They raise money for a good cause, and everyone has a great time. It's the social event of the summer, and it's not expensive to get in."

"I do know of it and had planned on attending. I'll look for you this year."

She smiled up at him. "I'm not the only female gearhead in Albemarle County. BoomBoom Craycroft is as big a nut as I am, but with a bigger budget."

"One of my co-workers took out another lady for a test drive. She was a doctor, ummm—Anna, Anna something."

"Annalise Veronese. Was she going to buy a Porsche?" Harry felt a twinge of envy.

"No, she drove a Jetta. The gas mileage on the diesel interested her, and I think she liked the fit and finish of the car. She's called him back, but so far no sale."

"Gotta be tough, sales."

"I like it, though."

"Dawson, I have horses, and I can spot one that's been on steroids from one who hasn't in the racing world. I think I can spot it with people, too. Bodybuilders and athletes who use them get big, of course, and stronger, no doubt. I notice the muscle has a kind of smooth quality." She lightly touched his forearm. "You've done it the hard way."

"You don't miss much."

"I don't know about that."

The two of them walked together toward their separate locker rooms.

Stopping in front of the women's locker room, Harry, with an impish grin, asked, "Are you married?"

Really, she shouldn't have been so direct. Her mother and grandmother were turning in their graves. But often Harry could get away with things others could not, thanks to that impish quality.

"No. I know you are. Noddy told me. Wish you weren't." He grinned back.

"How flattering." She meant it. "I have some wonderful girlfriends. Most are married, but some aren't. And friends have friends. If you're going to be at the polo match out in Greenwood on Father's Day, I'll introduce you. Since it's a big event, it will be natural, know what I mean?"

"Thanks. I look forward to it."

On the drive home, Harry, buoyed by the attention, whistled to herself. She'd never dream of stepping out on Fair, but oh, how sweet when a handsome man pays attention to you.

• • •

Days later, the polo game proved close and exciting. The field was only seven miles from Harry's farm in Crozet. It was set in a vineyard. People loved the views, the acre upon acre of vines, the clean, non-fussy design of the farm buildings. She introduced Dawson to BoomBoom and Alicia, who introduced him to their girlfriends. She thought about the people buying tickets to the Pink Ribbon Polo Classic. Steroids weren't much help to riders in this game.

Watching from her director's chair, Harry heard the voice of Diana Farrell, the announcer, saying, "One out of eight women in America will be diagnosed with breast cancer in her lifetime."

Harry was now that woman.

After the game, she turned onto Route 250 and felt a wave crash over her. She thought of Tina Leiter, who spoke at halftime about her struggle with breast cancer. No self-pity, but helpful facts and truthful information came from Tina. Harry paid some attention, but mostly she had focused on the lady's lovely hat, wishing she'd had the style to wear one.

Then she thought of the horses, the players, the umpires, and all the sponsors, and suddenly Harry was sobbing, heaving. She drove into the parking lot of Western Albemarle High School and pulled over. She was one of those women. Those players and those beautiful ponies were playing for her. The Kings' generosity was for her, as was the Flows', and she felt a gratitude she could never express. She wanted to write everyone a thank-you. She wanted to kiss them, which would probably embarrass everybody but the horses.

She got hold of herself. Tears still flowing, she silently gave a prayer of thanks for all those people all across America working with the American Cancer Society, coming up with fund-raisers.

The cancer attacked her body, but she looked to be all right. She still had a way to go, but she had never reckoned with what the cancer would do to her heart. Where did these emotions come from? What happened to her reserve? Last year she was proud of everyone who ran the 5K and thrilled at the polo match, but now . . . now everything and everyone looked different.

It wasn't until the middle of the night when she got up just to see the first lightning bugs and to hear the night birds that she understood Dawson English had walked her one step closer to the killer.

34

"Why don't they hurry up?" Pewter paced on the kitchen counter, her food bowl depressingly empty.

"She's got a bee in her bonnet," Mrs. Murphy explained. "The poor man can't shave in peace. She's perched on the toilet seat, yakking away."

"I don't care if she's late for her breakfast. I want mine on time."

The brass pendulum with the large rounded bottom swung in the old railroad clock. Harry loved that clock because it was so easy to read and because it came from the old whistle-stop in Crozet. Her mother saved the clock from the pretty little brick station when it was phased out.

Tucker looked up at the rhythmic swing.

Harry, old large T-shirt serving as a nightshirt, padded into the kitchen in her elk-skin slippers. She could have snuck up on a human, but the three animals heard her.

"Where's my breakfast?" the gray cat demanded.

"Who said you were first?" Tucker grumbled from the floor.

"Pewter, shut up. I'm getting to it." Harry slapped down a can of food but did not yet open it. First, she washed out the cat bowls, followed by the dog bowl.

"I don't care if the bowl is clean."

"I do." Mrs. Murphy quietly waited.

"You're a priss." Pewter kept bumping Harry's elbow as she washed.

"Pewter, leave me alone. I have half a mind not to give you canned food."

"*Never! Never. I will exact a revenge more terrible than you can imagine,*" the gray threatened, but she did stop bumping.

Dressed for work, Fair came into the kitchen. "Thinking about what you said."

Harry walked over to the coffeepot, which she'd set up the night before, now pressing the on button.

"*Don't make coffee. Feed me!*" Pewter howled.

Finally, Harry took the manual can opener and opened the can, the aroma of chopped beef filling the room. She bypassed electric can openers because she thought they wasted electricity, but also she wanted to use the muscles between her thumb and forefinger. A manual can opener gives them a workout.

"*I'm feeling faint.*" Pewter wobbled.

"*Give this cat a scholarship to the American Academy of Dramatic Arts.*" Mrs. Murphy had had about enough.

Harry filled the two bowls. Pewter immediately shut up. Then Harry opened a can for Tucker and put the food in her ceramic bowl.

"*Thank you,*" the corgi politely responded.

"Peace and quiet." Harry poured her husband's coffee.

"You didn't want eggs, did you?"

"Honey, no," she said. "Cereal's good."

He'd put down two bowls before asking, so now he opened the fridge, took out milk, and poured some in a striped ceramic pitcher.

As they settled at the table, Fair returned to the conversation in the bathroom. "Steroids used by equines are usually in bottles about the size of a pint of milk. Glass. It would make no sense to put a glass bottle of steroids, whatever the type, in one of those cylinders. Plus, there wouldn't be enough money in shipping just one bottle at a time."

"That's what Coop said about cocaine and prescription drugs. The cylinders are too small, but Fair"—she put down her spoon, lightly smacking the table for emphasis—"the cylinders are not a coincidence. They mean something important."

"Honey, they might. But whatever it is, I have no idea. Those cylinders are perfect for shipping sperm. I don't know if they are perfect for anything else."

"Okay, back to steroids. Is there a lot of money to be made?" Harry asked.

"Not so much in the equine world. There are laws against using them in flat racing. Enforcement is another problem, but you can use them in other equine sports and—unless there is blood testing at the events— you can get away with it. Steroids, I mean."

"Fair, you look at a horse and you can tell."

"You can. I can. A person assigned by the government to draw blood, maybe not. They aren't always vets. I hate to say this about my own profession, but someone offers twenty-five thousand dollars to shut up at that event, someone else might just take it. Or you take a sample of blood that's clean and substitute that for the blood of the horse loaded up on steroids. Kind of on par with urine testing for humans. Before the authorities cracked down, you could use someone else's urine or someone else's blood. Now you pee on command."

They both laughed.

Then Fair continued, "But the thing about steroids is if you give them to a yearling, the animal develops a robust musculature. But the bones aren't completely set, especially at the joints. And I do not believe they are at two, but we race them at two, and you know how I feel about that, so I'll shut up."

"I feel the same way, but this has as much to do with a tax structure that mitigates against agricultural pursuits. The way things are now, a breeder, an owner, needs to put the horses on the track way too early. You just can't afford to keep them that extra year while they continue to mature."

"That's why I love sitting with my beautiful wife at the breakfast table. You're off and running."

"I know." She lowered her eyes for a moment.

"Trainers are so sophisticated these days about when to use steroids and when to drop off, even I have difficulty telling sometimes. But if I'm looking at a two-year-old that looks like a perfectly conditioned three-year-old? Steroids, no doubt. Beyond that, when they're older, if I don't draw blood, I don't know, because the musculature is consistent with age. And it's the same for humans. Steroids give any competitor an edge."

"Especially in strength sports or sports where you take a beating."

"And there is a fortune in selling them. But using cylinders to ship? No. I'm no help to you. I'm frustrated, too. I guess you could ship contraband diamonds or emeralds. But we haven't seen any jewelry around here."

"It's driving me crazy."

Fair savored his coffee, then set the heavy Bennington pottery mug down. "Let it be. You have more important things to focus on, like your recovery."

"I feel fine."

"Harry."

"Okay. I don't feel fine after radiation, but then I come back. I feel good right now."

"And you still have your hair."

"Haven't had enough radiation to lose it. Boy, when you see what happens to the people who get the one-two punch, chemo and radiation, it's amazing they can stand up."

"Speaking of steroids, doctors give steroids to help patients with the effect."

"Back to legal and illegal drugs. What would you do if I lost my hair?"

"Sweep it up." He smiled.

"I'd just shave it off, what was left. The hell with it. I'd wear a hat or something, but I'd make a preemptive strike."

He rubbed the top of his blond head. "If I were losing mine, think I'd do the same thing."

"It's funny, isn't it? People are sexually attracted to each other because of their looks, and then you lose them one way or the other: illness or age."

"You will always be that gorgeous girl I fell in love with when you were a junior in high school. Don't care if you're one hundred."

"Ha!" She loved it, though.

"*He's smart,*" Mrs. Murphy noted.

"Hey, he keeps her happy." Tucker adored Fair.

"If he doesn't keep her happy, some other man will," Pewter, finished, declared.

"You are such a sourpuss," Mrs. Murphy said.

"No, I'm not. I tell the truth. That's the way humans are. They need to pay constant attention to one another or else. One cat's observation"—she puffed out her chest—"but what a cat."

Mrs. Murphy made a gagging sound. "I'm going to throw up."

Harry stood up, grabbed a paper towel. "You eat too fast, too much, and then you drink water."

"It's Pewter. I'm fine." Mrs. Murphy jumped off the counter and exited through the cat door to the small screened-in porch off the back door.

Then she went out the pet door in the outside door and trotted to the barn.

"It can now be said that you can empty a room."

"Oh, shut up. She's acting like an old Virginia biddy." Pewter snarled at the dog.

• • •

Three hours later, the chores were done and the cats and dogs were returning to their normal good humor—or as good as Pewter could manage. Harry lifted the hatch on the Volvo, and the cats jumped in.

On her hind legs, Tucker put her front paws on the car's back end.

"Upsy-daisy." Harry lifted Tucker's hind end, and the dog was in.

First Harry stopped at her husband's clinic. He was in the lay-up barn, checking on a patient who had a twisted gut. Fair had operated in time: No portion of bowel had atrophied or become necrotic. He removed the knot, and the animal would make a full recovery. The trick was in keeping the horse calm while the incision healed. For a time, that meant administering a light sedative.

While he was in the barn, Harry plucked a yellow shipping cylinder from the storage room. She didn't tell Fair, and he didn't know she was there.

Her next stop was Heavy Metal Gym.

At 10:30 A.M., the place was much quieter than it was when she worked out. The lunch crowd—looking for a fast workout—would trickle in starting at 11:30 and fade out by 1:30 P.M. Then, at 5:30 P.M., people would come in and the gym would be full until about 8:00 or 9:00 P.M., depending on the day. The late-night crowd wrapped it up at 11:00 P.M.

Another perfect day at seventy-two degrees. Harry, following one of her odd hunches, put the windows down two inches for the animals and grabbed the cylinder. "I'll be right back."

The three said nothing, but as she left, Mrs. Murphy said, *"I wish she hadn't taken that cylinder."*

The other two nodded in agreement.

Out on the floor, Noddy was spotting for Annalise, flat on her back at the bench press.

Waiting until Annalise finished her exercise, Harry walked over. "Hey, what are you doing here at this hour?"

"My day off. It's nice and quiet now. I don't have to listen to that awful music the men play."

Noddy replied, "Yeah, it is awful, but they love it. Unfortunately, there are more of them than people with good musical taste. Cock rock, as I call it, does nothing to make you lift harder and better. But it's one of those myths that will die hard. They believe it, so therefore it helps them."

Annalise laughed. "True. Still, it might be hard to work out to Mozart." She noticed the cylinder. "What do you have in there?"

"Nothing. It's used to ship horse semen."

Annalise's hand fluttered to her breast. "Glad you said that. I'd be worried if you'd come in here for the guys."

Harry laughed. "They give it away for free. If it belongs to a horse, you pay and you pay a lot."

At this, the three cracked up.

Noddy asked, "Need something?"

"Oh, I dropped by to ask you if you think steroids could be shipped in this. Fair says they come in big bottles and you couldn't ship enough in this cylinder."

"Harry," Noddy said evenly, "if I tell you I know where to buy steroids, even what the stuff comes in, then I'm compromised. Every serious gym owner in America has to be extra-careful."

Chagrined, Harry apologized. "Noddy, I'm so sorry. It never occurred to me."

"Well, there's no one here but us, but Jesus, Harry, don't even ask me anything like that in public. Do I know about the stuff? Of course I do. Is it sold in my gym? I'm not selling it, and no one is selling it inside these walls. I'd lose everything I've worked for and my good name to boot."

"Again, I'm sorry, Noddy."

"Is it sold outside?" Noddy shrugged. "I have no doubt, but I don't pry. However, anyone can go to any serious gym, and I emphasize 'serious gym'—not the matching-leotard-and-top kind of gym—and find their way to better living through chemistry."

Annalise seconded this. "That's the truth." She looked at Harry. "You know what our drug laws do? Screw up everybody but those on the take. We can't stop drugs. I don't care if it's cocaine or steroids. So why don't we grow up and consider these substances something to be controlled, like tobacco and alcohol? For one thing, it would stop a lot of suffering. For another thing, it would devastate organized crime. And if you quote me, I will say you are making it up. Our drug laws have turned me and most doctors into hypocrites. Actually, they've turned most Americans into hypocrites."

"That and sex." Noddy now sat on the bench next to Annalise.

"If a fifteen-year-old kid playing linebacker on the JV football team was considering taking anabolic steroids and they were controlled but legal, he could talk openly to a sports doctor. And that doctor, if he or she was responsible, would inform the kid that yes, they will improve his performance, but at his age they could have terrible consequences for his health later. For one thing, they could really damage his liver, and for another thing, there can be unpleasant emotional side effects while one is taking them."

Noddy nodded vigorously. "She's right, Harry. As it now stands, that fifteen-year-old reads some studies, Googles information from body-building sites that show muscle growth through chemistry, and the kid learns to buy stuff on the black market. He then takes powerful drugs with no supervision. I see it more than most. A kid like that always takes too much."

Annalise jumped in again. "The other thing, Harry, is what if you have a bad reaction to an illegal substance—any illegal substance? You'd be afraid to tell your doctor. Instead, you'll wait and hope it passes. What if it doesn't, and you overdose? The policies we have now are cruel, flat-out cruel, and bloody stupid."

"Noddy, did you ever take them?"

"Harry, you go right for the throat." Noddy shook her head. "Yes. When I was young, I was very, very lucky to find a doctor—call him crooked if you like—but I followed instructions, never went over the line, and stopped when I'd achieved my goal. My competitive days are long gone, and I stopped shall we say 'chemical enhancement' years ago. There's nothing in my system."

"Wouldn't you be stripped of your bodybuilding titles like that Olympic sprinter?"

"Yes. More than one athlete has been stripped, but you're referring to Ben Johnson," Noddy said, naming the great Canadian athlete. "And the ones prancing about saying it was unfair competition, that when they ran they were clean. I don't believe one word."

"Come on, Noddy. Some athletes are clean," Harry argued.

Annalise said, "It's true. Not everyone takes those things, and not everyone is a liar, although I think most are. They have to be."

"If they didn't take the drugs, who would pay to watch baseball, football, or basketball?" said Noddy. "We've become accustomed to fantastic performance. Really fantastic, in all professional sports. We'd be bored. When you get right down to it, the reason all this goes on is because more people want it than don't."

"I opened a can of worms. I'm sorry." Harry looked at the cylinder, still no closer to her objective but full of information about other things. "I'm sorry."

"It's all right." Noddy meant it, too.

• • •

Later, about 3:30 P.M., way in the back with her sunflowers, Harry reached into her hip pocket for her cellphone. What was going on had hit her like a bolt of lightning. It was obvious, but before now she couldn't see it. Nor could anyone else. Well, something is obvious once you know.

The animals tagged after her as she headed for the barn, where she'd left her cell in the tack room.

In the distance, she heard the crackle of wheels on the dirt road. She ran for the tack room. Too late.

35

*S*hortro and Tomahawk watched in wonderment as the old Saab bumped over the open meadow behind the barn.

Harry turned back from the barn, running for all she was worth toward the creek. She knew Annalise couldn't get the Saab over the steep banks. If Annalise was going to kill Harry, she'd have to get out and run after her.

Tucker flew to the paddocks. *"Jump out! Jump out!"*

Shortro needed no further provocation. The Saddlebred took three trotting strides to gracefully arc over the three-board fence, which stood at three feet eight inches.

In the same paddock, Tomahawk soared over, too. The mares and youngsters remained in their paddocks.

"Follow me!" The corgi tore after the Saab, tiny bits of soil flying off her claws.

Mrs. Murphy and Pewter sped alongside Harry. Bouncing over the pasture, Annalise bore down on Harry—now zigzagging to present a tougher target to hit. Windows up, the doctor didn't hear the horses coming up behind her.

The steep creek, thirty yards off, might be Harry's salvation. Running evasively delayed her reaching the wooded high banks.

Tomahawk and Shortro thundered up on Annalise's left side. She could have cared less whether she killed the horses, but she knew if she turned into them they'd damage her car. She needed the car to get out of here once the deed was done.

No fool, Harry ran to the left at a diagonal, finally reaching the creek. She slid down the banks above the beaver dam, where the water was lower.

Annalise skidded to a stop, her car's nose in a pricker bush, and got out of the car, Colt MKIV .38 in hand. The gun, while well balanced, was heavy in her hand.

Tucker slammed into Annalise behind the knees. Down she went. Annalise rolled down the bank, the little dog right behind her, the horses peering over the bank. She never loosened her grip on the gun.

Pewter and Mrs. Murphy swam to the other side of the creek. Harry, who had been knee-deep, clambered up the steep side, slipping as she went. She grasped a protruding root, pulling herself up.

The beavers, out of their lodge now, began slapping the water with their broad, flat tails.

Annalise plunged in, holding her gun straight up over her head. Harry, already over the bank, proved a difficult target. Annalise needed to pull up over the bank.

Swimming behind her, Tucker called to the horses, "*Get in the water. Follow me!*"

Harry turned, saw Annalise climbing up, more difficult for her while carrying a pistol.

"*Go back to the creek bank! Use the trees!*" Mrs. Murphy hollered, heading to the creek bed to show Harry.

Whether she understood the cat or figured it out herself, Harry dodged behind a large old sycamore, large sheets of bark on the ground.

Pewter acted like a rear guard, slowing to watch Annalise, then telling Mrs. Murphy, "*She's taking aim.*"

A report, then a thud as a bullet hit the sycamore. Harry moved down into the creek bed, but she couldn't go fast, for she was now below the beaver dam, and the water was high, the creek bed soggy.

"*Won't work,*" Mrs. Murphy screamed. "*Get back up, use the trees. It's your only hope.*"

Fit, Annalise was fast. By the time she reached the sycamore, Harry had hauled herself back up on the creek's bank again. Senses razor-sharp, Harry dug in her toes, bent low like a runner coming out of the blocks on hearing the pistol shot. But unlike those on the track, the pistol shot was aimed at her.

Again, moving from tree to tree, Harry continued downstream, sprinting, bent over, when she could. The only plan she had was to get to Coop's house, if she made it that far down, or try to reach her own barn. She would be exposed when she ran across the back pastures to her sunflowers, which were not high enough to cover her. She'd also be a clear target in Coop's newly mown pasture. She still might make it again, zigging and zagging. She didn't know whether to again cross the creek into her farm or to keep on Coop's side. Sooner or later, Annalise would empty out her clip. She'd counted three shots—five would be left. Then she'd run for all she was worth for about fifteen paces, hit the dirt, roll, and run some more.

Compromised as Harry was due to radiation treatments, she was pumped with adrenaline and running for her life.

Tucker kept at Annalise's heels. Much as the physician wanted to plug the irritating dog, she'd been counting bullets, too. Harry's speed and evasive actions were proving to be a real problem.

Taking aim, she fired again. This time the bullet burrowed into the black ridged bark of a sweet gum tree. Harry backed away from the tree, pushing through Virginia thornbushes, trampling wild lilies, sown courtesy of birds. She dodged behind the trees near Coop's cutover lower pasture. The level ground there meant she could burn the wind, but fast as she was, a bullet was faster.

Annalise saw a flash of Harry's blue T-shirt. She missed the cats, running with her, darting in and out of low bush.

Harry's lungs seared. She needed to bend over and take a deep breath. If she did, she'd expose herself and allow her pursuer to draw closer. Behind an ancient Fiddle oak, Harry veered right to a hickory at the pasture's edge. Annalise, slower, was running in the mown pasture to catch up. As the ground was flatter and drier, she gained on Harry. Harry had little time in which to decide whether to try for Coop's house or to go back into the creek. The water was deeper down here. It might be difficult getting across before Annalise reached the bank.

Now aware of his master's fragile position, Tomahawk said to Shortro, "*Do what I do. Get behind me.*"

The seventeen-year-old Thoroughbred trotted twenty yards behind Annalise. She turned for the creek bed. The cats called out Harry's location to Tomahawk.

"*Get her before she makes it to the trees!*" Pewter shrieked as loud as she could, sank her claws into a tree, and climbed at warp speed. She hoped Annalise would walk under this tree, since it was at the best crossing. If she got this far, Pewter could drop onto her. Pewter devoutly hoped the doctor wouldn't get to that point.

Harry's face and hands bled from the thorns. Her T-shirt was ripped, her body looking like she'd run through barbed wire. Her mind remained clear. No panic. She felt she had a slim chance.

Annalise saw movement in the grasses. Birds flew out of the shrubs. She saw a flash of shoe as Harry slipped down toward the crossing. Taking aim, she fired, just missing Harry's boot heel.

In a gallop, Tomahawk rode right onto Annalise, knocking her down. She knew the horses were behind her, but it never occurred to her she'd be in danger from them. Flat on her face, Annalise struggled to rise, the gun knocked out of her hand. Before she could rise to her knees, Shortro plowed into her, full weight on her back. The massive weight on those iron-shod hooves broke her back.

Annalise couldn't move her legs. Her upper body worked. She pulled herself toward the gun, but Tucker grabbed her wrist, biting down for all she was worth. Then the dog grabbed the gun, running to give it to Harry.

Harry slid down to the water's edge. She caught her breath as the dog gave her the gun.

"*Tucker!*" Mrs. Murphy rubbed against the panting dog.

Speechless for once, Pewter backed down the tree.

Having neutralized Annalise, Tomahawk and Shortro noticed the alfalfa and orchard grass in Coop's back pasture. They walked away, put their heads down, and enjoyed it. Someone else's pasture always seemed better than one's own.

Harry wiped her forehead, smearing blood all over. She then noticed her hands were torn. Blood dripped down her cheeks, seeping through her torn T-shirt—an old favorite. Whatever was on the thorns began to sting.

Hearing Annalise's shriek of pain, Harry hugged her dog, blood now on Tucker's fur. Both cats sat at her feet.

Pewter, who'd had the best view, said, *"You wouldn't believe what Tomahawk and Shortro did to Annalise!"*

Harry looked down. "You all stayed right up with me." She choked up, cleared her throat, then warily walked out, using trees as cover, to see where Annalise was. Harry might have Annalise's gun, but she was keenly aware how powerful Annalise was. She was shocked when she saw her lying in the pasture.

The doctor had rolled on her back. "Can't move my legs."

"Hurt?" Harry asked.

"No. My hand hurts more," Annalise replied. "You look like hell."

"If you had your way, I'd be dead." Harry put the safety on the pistol. "This gun is heavy."

"Cost me a thousand dollars. And yes, you would be dead. I like you. I like you a lot, Harry, but you were going to ruin my project."

"Got a cellphone on you?"

"No." She asked, "Pull me to a tree and prop me up?"

"No. You're stronger than I am. I saw your bench press, remember? You'll try to choke me."

Annalise didn't deny it. "Then shoot me. I know you won't give me the gun to shoot myself. Just shoot me. Self-defense. Everyone will buy it."

"They might, but I won't."

"Harry, is it possible to be too principled?"

"How would you know? In your case, you haven't any."

Annalise's eyes flashed. "I was helping hundreds of people over the years. The stupidity of our government causes so much suffering, prevents millions—literally millions—from healthy lives. I cut through all the bullshit and helped them myself."

Harry sat a bit away from Annalise so the prone woman couldn't reach her. The animals listened, too. They remained vigilant.

"I don't know about that, but once I knew it was you, I figured you had to be making a lot of money."

Annalise began talking too fast. At first she made no sense. "He first

got wobbly when a piece of skull, the base, which is just above the pituitary gland, was on his desk. I swore it was Thadia, who was so obsessed with him, she had to have been spying. I have no doubt she got into the hospital morgue, not all that difficult, rolled out a harvested corpse, and checked it out. Our removals wouldn't be obvious, not like a missing arm. But Thadia, like most dedicated addicts, knew a great deal about the human body and body chemistry. Thadia knew where that small pituitary gland was located. She'd know if it was removed. She knew. It's amazing the woman lived as long as she did, and I think one of the reasons was she understood drugs' effect on her own body and on others'. Think of the good she could have done if she'd taken organic chemistry, gotten into med school."

Annalise stopped, then started anew. "That woman was a complete waste. Cory and I both made a lot of money, but that wasn't my primary purpose. After I killed Paula, he said he wanted out, once he figured it out—which took him ten days. Well, how long before wanting out meant chickening out, or even possibly turning me in to save himself if he thought our business might be discovered? Weak. Didn't want to kill him—or anyone else—but it really was them or me. My work must be protected."

"*How can you do good when you kill people?*" Pewter asked.

"*It's a human thing.*" Mrs. Murphy lifted the tip of her tail, then let it flutter down again. "*You can kill anyone, and as many as you want, if you justify it by religion or calling someone an enemy. I don't know. Doesn't matter if it makes sense to us. They kill us, too. We just kill to eat.*"

Harry sighed. "It's a long walk to the barn." She wiped her cheek, still dripping blood, with the back of her hand. "I liked you. I just don't get it."

"In some ways, we're alike. You figured out I removed Paula, Thadia, and Cory using some reasoning and your instincts. Maybe a better way to put it is you thought by synthesis instead of analysis. If it hadn't been for you, I think I could have gotten another job, say, on the West Coast, with excellent references, a big bank account, and continued my efforts out there."

"Maybe. You underestimate Sheriff Shaw and Coop. They aren't hick law enforcement people."

"Maybe not, but it would have taken them so much longer. If nothing else, the tangle of laws would have slowed them down. It would have been a while before they could arrest me. And you have to admit my program is ingenious." She shook her hand. "Tucker has strong jaws."

"Next time I'll bite your hand clean off," the dog threatened.

"Why did you kill Paula?"

"She was meticulous, observant. She made notes about things that weren't even her province, like the bodies coming in after car wrecks or whatever for organ harvests. She knew who was operating when. She knew who received an organ transplant. She knew when a liver was shipped out. Her interests exceeded the operating room. She noticed that Cory and sometimes Jennifer attended my autopsies and organ harvests. Cory almost always attended when I worked on a healthy, young person.

"Once we disagreed about an operating time—oh, from months back—and she showed me her notebook. She was right about the time. That's when I realized she could be dangerous. Another one of those rigidly moral people who lose the forest for the trees.

"My mistake wasn't so much in killing her. I would have easily gotten away with that except for you. It was miscalculating how much it would take to destroy her files. I overdid it at Pinnacle Records."

"You set that fire?"

"Of course not. I paid a professional. Once you know where to look and who to call, you can get many services performed. I'd taken her computer, saw what was in there, and knew I had to destroy any backup. The damned Vitebsks, another principled pair, would never have let me into her file cabinet. And the security there was so tight I couldn't get in. All I wanted was one lousy file cabinet."

"Liquid nitrogen." Harry lifted her eyebrows, which hurt, as the right one had been sliced by the thorns.

"We sent the harvested pituitary glands to an equine clinic in Lexington, Kentucky, where Cory had a friend who was a glamour vet, huge practice. Cylinders full of semen and liquid nitrogen come into the clinic every day. The vet knew how to harvest the human growth hormone from that. Vets can work on humans if they have to, and all he had to do was understand endocrinology, which he does. The lab there is fantastic. The HGH was distributed out of Lexington."

"Where did you get a liquid nitrogen cylinder?" Harry inquired.

"Cory had the Lexington vet ship me one. And I really knew I had to be extremely watchful when one went missing from my car trunk. I rarely lock my trunk, just throw junk in there. I never found it."

"Heavy Metal?"

Annalise shook her head. "Noddy didn't know. Her competitive days just overlapped the beginning of human growth hormone in sports. She's ignorant of anything I've done. I helped a few people there, but very quietly."

"She'll be devastated. A lot of people will."

"I'm sorry for the ones I trained with, but I'm not sorry for what I've done, and I'd do it again. With HGH, I have helped people recapture their youth, grow muscle if they need it, strengthen their ligaments, and I believe sharpen mental function. HGH is a miracle our bodies produce themselves. When it begins to wane at about age twenty-five, that's when the injuries pick up, aging truly begins."

"Thadia figured out HGH, right?"

"Given her background, Thadia could spot any kind of evasion, cover-up. She did ultimately realize we were removing pituitary glands. She'd thought Cory was covering up our affair. That's what started her snooping." Harry's eyes widened, and Annalise continued. "He was fun, but he had to go. Don't think I would spare him or anybody. My work had to continue. Anyway, Thadia shadowed him. It was a matter of time before she'd run her mouth and create big problems. If he'd slept with her, pretended to be attracted, she would have been mollified. Apart from being unstable, she was silly. No man is worth that much effort.

"Paula was much smarter. She once asked me, 'Why is Cory always there when you harvest organs and eyes?' And I said he needs to see healthy bodies. She believed it for a while, but eventually her suspicions were aroused, too."

"How did you kill her?"

"Injected her with potassium. Creates cardiac arrhythmia, quick death. Not a trace. Appears totally natural. Then all I had to do was, once she was dead, inject her with bee venom."

"But how could you inject her? Why didn't she fight you off?"

"I had a bottle of cyanocobalamin, B-twelve. When I stopped by to pick up brochures that other cancer benefits had printed. I'd asked to see them, to compare with ours. You all saw them at the meetings. I told Paula I'd give her a B-twelve shot, as she'd complained of being tired. She hated to give herself shots. I gave her a shot in her vein. It took her a second for reality to click in. She started to pull away, because B-twelve is put in the muscle, but I had half of the syringe in and quickly emptied the rest in her vein inside her elbow. Potassium works quickly. I'd made sure to really load her up. She was dead in fifteen seconds. She hadn't time to struggle. It's a swift death. The bee venom produced the bodily effects of anaphylactic shock. As she was literally only dead a second, it worked on her body. Then I put the dead hornet next to her."

"Why did she trust you to give her a shot?"

"Why not? She never thought I'd want to kill her. Even if she thought I was up to something, she wouldn't have considered herself in danger. Maybe a month or two later she would have."

"Did you know she had a cylinder under her counter in a cartridge box?"

"No." Annalise exhaled, hand throbbing now. "I was lucky, very lucky, she hadn't put two and two together just yet. But people don't think of pituitary glands."

"How'd you get the potassium?"

Annalise laughed. "Harry, don't be naïve. I'm a doctor. I can get anything, and potassium isn't considered dangerous."

"Oh, Annalise, how I wish you hadn't killed those people."

"You can't give a damn about Thadia."

"I didn't like her, but I would hardly wish her throat slit."

"Harry, she was a complete fool. One of those subjective people who sees everything through their emotional needs. An idiot. People ruled by their emotions always are."

"That's cruel."

"Life is cruel. Consider how people who impede progress are removed. The natives who lived here got in our way. We killed them. Now, a century and more from that time, the dominant party, you and I, feel guilty about it. If we were alive in 1835, we'd feel differently. You can only go forward if you remove whatever obstacles are in the way of progress, be they obstacles of time and travel, geography, or people. Unfortunately, Paula, Thadia, and Cory became obstacles."

"I don't feel that way. How did you trap Thadia?"

"She called and said she'd tell people about my affair with Cory if I didn't end it. I told her we should talk about it somewhere quiet and safe. Like I said, the woman was an idiot. I put a wrapped box of Oxy-Contin in the car, thought it might send law enforcement in the wrong direction, but it was never mentioned in the papers." Annalise took a deep breath. "I feel a little guilty about killing Paula. I really wish Paula and Cory hadn't presented problems."

"I don't need to know about Cory. I know how you did it, and now I know why. Annalise, you'll be here for maybe an hour or more, and I'm not going to move you."

"My spinal cord is snapped. I'm a doctor, I know my back is broken and I can't move my legs. End of story."

"Well, I can't drag you, so you'll have to lie there."

As Harry turned to go, Annalise propped herself up on one elbow. "Harry!"

"Yes." She turned, as did her animals.

"I didn't underestimate you. Your mind moves very fast, and like I said, you trust your instincts."

"An—" Harry didn't know what to say.

"And you'll beat the cancer. You will." She stayed propped up as she watched Harry recede.

• • •

When Coop, Rick, and Harry arrived at the scene, horses still grazing in the next meadow, Annalise was dead. She'd gotten her pocketknife, a three-and-a-half-inch sharp blade, out of her jeans and tore her throat. Given the state of her right hand, it was not a clean slice, and it must have taken her time.

"Jesus." Coop looked at the blood. "The willpower."

"The delusion," Harry sadly noted.

36

"unny how things work out." Harry sat under the walnut tree outside the house, the sun setting.

Fair, enjoying the Sunday evening, nodded. "Yes, it is. When Nita and Al won the BMW at the five-K ball, it seemed a kind of recompense." He turned to her. "You had your last treatment. My wife is her healthy, beautiful self."

Harry beamed. "You are such a flatterer." Then she hastily added, "Don't let me stop you."

He rose from his chair, bent over, and kissed her. "Beautiful."

"Fair, I've had a lot of time to think. You and I endured a rough patch way back in what I think of as our time of troubles, but we ironed it out. I don't think I would have gotten through all this as well as I have without you."

"*Hey, what about me!*" Pewter, sprawled on another outdoor chair, piped up.

"*Magic powers,*" Tucker, under the chair, teased her.

"It's been a wild ride." Harry held Fair's hand as he perched on the wide arm of the wooden chair. "And, you know, the biggest shock was Annalise. I still can't believe she did what she did."

"Me neither, but since B.C. people have justified killing in the millions by saying it's for the greater common good. The millions doing the killing believe it, but the dead always remain dead. I swear the spirits return for vengeance. It may take centuries, but more misery is created."

"Justice," Harry simply replied.

"Revenge."

She looked up at her husband. "Revenge. Justice. It's the same to me, anyway."

He smiled. "Many would argue differently, but I'm with you. The same. What we call justice is dressed-up revenge, and it's necessary. You can't have a society where wrongdoing isn't punished." He took a deep breath, beheld the mountains, then leaned over to kiss her again. "I thank God you're alive."

"*We saved her.*" Pewter puffed up.

"*Shortro and Tomahawk had a lot to do with it.*" Tucker watched the two buddies out in their paddock.

"*They sure did,*" Mrs. Murphy, in another chair, agreed.

"*I think it's fine that Fair thanks the Almighty*"—Pewter paused, then a beatific expression passed over her gray face—"*but he should remember that in ancient Egypt, cats were worshipped. Really, I think the practice should be reintroduced, along with daily heapings of catnip.*"

Quick on the draw, Mrs. Murphy said, "*Means you have to have your ears pierced and wear earrings.*"

"*No way!*" Pewter's ears swept back.

"*She's right, Pewts. All the statues and mummies wear gold earrings. My, you'd look so-o-o fetching.*" Tucker laughed.

Rising, Pewter peered over the seat of the chair. "*Name one place where dogs were worshipped.*"

"*None. We won't wear earrings.*"

Pewter's pupils enlarged as she puffed up even more.

Mrs. Murphy counseled, "*Pewter, will you calm down.*"

"*Well, we were worshipped. Who will worship this worthless, fat dog?*"

"*And how shall I address you? Your Eminence? Mother Pewter? I know, the Great Puss Bottom,*" Tucker sassed.

Off the chair, Pewter hit the dog with her considerable weight. The two rolled over each other. Wrenching free of Pewter's claws, Tucker took off like a shot, Pewter in hot pursuit. The corgi dodged, feinted, keeping Pewter running.

Mrs. Murphy joined in. Pewter made a big show of her anger, but by now it was all pure fun.

Shortro and Tomahawk watched the two cats and dog. So they chased each other.

Fair and Harry laughed, then Fair said, "I'll give you a head start. Bet I can catch you."

"Ha." Harry bolted out of the chair.

Everybody was chasing everybody else.

Life is good.

Afterword

Like you, reader, I have lost friends to cancer. We all have, and in the last year it seems, in my life, these numbers are increasing, particularly among young people.

Cancer is also cropping up in horses and hounds, and I have lost some animals to this horrible disease, in all its guises.

Is there more of it, or are we better at identifying it, or both? You can be the judge.

Given that medical terminology is cumbersome, I kept things as clear as possible while being as accurate as possible. The various forms of cancer treatment change rapidly. The treatment Harry undergoes in this book is different from that endured by one of my friends, who suffered breast cancer six years ago.

By the time you read this mystery, some of the information may be outdated or superseded.

As this mystery involves cancer, more than usual we feel the presence of the Angel of Death. There is a one hundred percent chance that I will perish, and so will you. Let me pass on the wisdom of my late mother, Julia Ellen Buckingham Brown:

"You're going to be dead a long time. Do it now."

She never identified what "it" is, leaving that up to me, as I leave it up to you.

2 August 2010

Author's Note

David and Ellen King hosted the Pink Ribbon Polo Classic on their polo field at the vineyards. Both teams were well matched in the 2010 contest; both played well and played clean. Mr. King, aggressive and smart, enlivened the game. I mention this because so often patrons, the sponsors of a team, aren't too good on the field. Rob Rinehart and Gary Leonard—the umpires, rarely celebrated—did a wonderful job.

Joan Hamilton endured endless questions about liquid nitrogen and shipping equine semen after which we would veer off, as usual, into a conversation about bloodlines. I couldn't live without Joan. For one thing, she's so much smarter than I am she can steer me back on course if needs be.

A. P. Indy, a stallion at Lane's End Farm, in 2011 has a stud fee of $150,000. Before the depression his fee was $300,000, maybe a bit more. The human variety of this magical substance is far less expensive, proving, perhaps, that horses are more valuable than humans.

Setting the Record Straight

All these years, my human and that Goody Two-shoes, Sneaky Pie, have been using me as the butt of their jokes. Finally, I've been able to sneak in the truth at the very last minute with the corrected galley proofs. They'll never know.

I am not fat. I am not old but am sort of middle-aged. I have lustrous green eyes and gray fur. I am supremely intelligent. There wouldn't be plots worth squat without me in them.

As to my real life, I will kill that blue jay. I am tired of my prior attempts at murder being put in the books as though I haven't a prayer.

I do have a prayer. "God helps those who help themselves." I will help myself to that cussed blue jay.

There. The truth at last.

Pewter

About the Authors

RITA MAE BROWN is the bestselling author of several books. An Emmy-nominated screenwriter and poet, she lives in Afton, Virginia. Her website is www.ritamaebrown.com. She does not own a computer. God willing, she never will. Sometimes the website manager sends your queries. The safest way to reach her is in care of Bantam Books.

SNEAKY PIE BROWN, a tiger cat born somewhere in Albemarle County, Virginia, was discovered by Rita Mae Brown at her local SPCA. They have collaborated on nineteen Mrs. Murphy mysteries: *Wish You Were Here*; *Rest in Pieces*; *Murder at Monticello*; *Pay Dirt*; *Murder, She Meowed*; *Murder on the Prowl*; *Cat on the Scent*; *Pawing Through the Past*; *Claws and Effect*; *Catch as Cat Can*; *The Tail of the Tip-Off*; *Whisker of Evil*; *Cat's Eyewitness*; *Sour Puss*; *Puss 'n Cahoots*; *The Purrfect Murder*; *Santa Clawed*; *Cat of the Century*; and *Hiss of Death*, in addition to *Sneaky Pie's Cookbook for Mystery Lovers*.